Thursday's Child

HELEN FORRESTER was born in Hoylake,
Cheshire, the eldest of seven children, and
Liverpool was her home for many years until
she married. For the past twenty-eight years
she and her husband and their son have made
their home in Canada, in Edmonton, Alberta.
Together they have travelled in Europe, India,
the United States and Mexico.

The three volumes of Helen Forrester's
autobiography are also published in Fontana,
as are her novels, *Liverpool Daisy* and *Three
Women of Liverpool*.

HELEN FORRESTER

Thursday's Child

FONTANA/Collins

First published in 1959 as *Alien There Is None*
by Hodder and Stoughton Ltd
First issued in Fontana Paperbacks 1985

Copyright © J. Rana 1959

Made and printed in Great Britain by
William Collins Sons & Co. Ltd, Glasgow

*This is a novel, and its situation and characters are
imaginary. Whatever similarity there may be of name,
no reference is made or intended to any person living
or dead.*

When one knows thee, then alien there is none,
then no door is shut.

Gitanjali-Rabindranath Tagore

CHAPTER ONE

'Dawn't be a fool,' shouted James as he slapped me hard across the face.

I stopped shrieking and began to weep, rocking myself backwards and forwards, my hands clutching at my nightgown as if to tear it.

James, with tears running down his face, was saying: 'Now, dawn't take on so, luv.'

His Lancashire accent, usually carefully suppressed, was homely and comforting, and gradually my weeping lessened and I lay back on the pillow. The medicine bottles on the mantelpiece changed from red blobs to definite shapes, and James's face, so like Barney's, ceased to be a blurred mirage and I saw how exhausted he looked.

That last winter of the war had seemed particularly long and cold. Although in Wetherport bombing raids had ceased some time before, most of its inhabitants were worn down by overwork and poor food, and Mother was not surprised, therefore, when at the end of March I caught influenza. On the morning that James called, I was feeling better, and, with the promise that on the following day I should get up, Mother had tucked me up in bed with two hot-water bottles, and had gone out to shop. She had been gone only five minutes when the doorbell rang.

I let it ring twice, in the hope that whoever was at the door would go away, but the third ring was such a prolonged one that in desperation I got out of bed, hastily wrapped myself in a blanket and pattered along the icy upper hall and down the equally icy Victorian staircase to answer it.

On the doorstep stood James, looking as white as if he had just seen the sticky result of a direct hit on an air-raid shelter. Mist had formed little globules of moisture on his red hair and on his muffler; his face was blue with cold.

'What's the matter?' I asked apprehensively, and

shivered in the draught from the open door.

'Get back into bed and ah'll tell thee,' said James.

In spite of ten days of illness, I ran up the stairs and scrambled into bed, my heart pounding with foreboding.

'It's Barney,' I muttered, my teeth chattering. 'Something has happened to Barney.'

James limped slowly up the stairs, drawing off his gloves as he came, entered my bedroom and sat down heavily on the bedside chair.

One of my hands lay on the coverlet and he took it in his.

'Peggie, dear, Barney was killed the day before yesterday. Mother got the news this morning.' The words came in the precise, clear tones he used when clarifying a point of law for one of his clients.

Although the news was something I had feared daily for months, I was stupefied by it and could not for a moment grasp the implication of his words. It was said that lightning did not strike twice in the same place, and it seemed impossible to me that in one war a woman could really lose two fiancés.

Jackie had gone down in the *Swallow* in 1939, a month before our wedding, and it broke my heart, but I was young then – and young hearts mend – so that when Barney proposed to me four years later life once more became worth living.

I had known Barney all my life. He was big, red-headed and impetuous, and I fell in love all over again. His only sorrow seemed to be that his twin brother, James, was lame and could not, therefore, join the Army with him. This had separated them for the first time in their lives – and now they were separated for ever.

'Kill me, Lord, kill me too,' I had shouted in my agony, as James's words bit into my heart and mind.

I must have had hysterics; otherwise James would never have struck me, but I remember only an enveloping, physical pain. Barney was dead, and the knowledge of it killed part of me.

I clung to James's hand: 'Why did he have to die?' I sobbed. 'Why not take a useless fool like me, not a good man like him? Why couldn't I die instead?'

James loosed his hand and put his arm around me. He smoothed the hair away from my eyes: 'The good God must have other work for you to do,' he said.

James was not the kind of man to talk about God, and his words stuck in my mind, but at that time I just lay in his arms with his face close to mine, and thought only of my own misery and not of his. He and Barney were identical twins, and he must have felt as if one of his limbs had been amputated without anaesthetic – yet he never mentioned his mother's or his own suffering.

James was still nursing me against his damp overcoat when Mother returned from shopping. She could never tell the brothers apart unless she saw James limp, and she thought it was Barney sitting beside me.

'Barney, how nice to see you. Leave at last!'

James said, 'I'm James,' and Mother understood.

'My poor darlings,' she said. 'Your poor mother.'

In her time, Mother had faced many crises, and she was wonderfully patient with James and me that day. It was she who remembered to telephone James's office – James was a solicitor, as was Barney – to ask his clerk to cancel his morning appointments, and it was she who later bundled him off to work, after letting him talk to her about Barney while she prepared lunch for him.

'Is someone with your mother?' she asked.

'My aunt is with her.'

'Then when you have eaten this, go away and work. Work is a good opiate.'

When he had gone, she came and sat on my bed and talked to me. She did not talk about Barney, but about James, of his brilliant brain, his sensitiveness and the sorrow he must be feeling. She said firmly that Angela, who is my younger sister, and I must help to comfort him and his widowed mother.

I listened dully. At that moment I did not care about anybody except Barney, and every time I thought of his lying, blown to pieces, in a German field, sobs shook me and I writhed in my bed, so that the pillows grew damp and the sheets became hopelessly twisted.

When Mother realised that it was too soon to divert my

9

thoughts to other people, she sat quietly by me until Father and Angela returned from work. Perhaps she knew what I had not realised, that James loved me more than Barney did; and maybe she hoped that when the pain had worn off, I would transfer my love of one brother to the other.

Father came in and stared down at me with pitying eyes.

'I am sorry, child,' he said.

He bent and kissed me: 'Have courage, little girl.'

He went away to eat his dinner, and I heard the quiet murmur of his and Mother's voices in the room below.

I heard also Angela's key in the lock of the front door, and the patter of Mother's slippers as she went to meet her in the hall. I heard Angela give a little cry of anguish; Mother must have told her the news immediately, so that she did not blunder when she came up to see me.

There was a pause and then Angela's dragging footsteps up the stairs. Enwrapped in my own misery as I was, even I thought how tired she must be to come so slowly.

Angela came into the room. She had taken off her hat and coat, but still wore the slacks and the overall she used in her work as a 'back-room girl'. She had studied electronics, but none of the family really knew exactly what she did in the closely guarded Government laboratory where much of her life was spent.

She shut the door behind her and leaned against it. Her face was an unearthly white and, despite the heat of the sickroom, she was shivering.

'Pegs.' Her voice was only a whisper.

She looked so stricken that I motioned her to come to me. I had not imagined that my elegant, sophisticated sister had so much feeling in her, and I was jolted out of my self-pity.

She came and sat down on the bed, her shoulders hunched and her hands dangling hopelessly between her trousered knees. This ugly posture was enough to tell me how deeply she had been affected by the news of Barney's death; usually she sat very gracefully, with straight back and ordered hands.

Suddenly she flung herself across me and wept, her breath coming in harsh gasps. I said nothing, feeling too full of grief myself to speak.

'Dinner's ready, Angela,' called Mother.

'Give me a handkerchief,' said Angela, looking up quickly, her sobs hastily stifled.

I gave her a very wet handkerchief and she wiped her eyes and blew her nose. She tried to smile at me, as she said: 'Woman must eat as well as weep.'

She went across to the dressing-table and powdered her nose with my puff, then came back to the bed, and in almost motherly fashion, straightened my top sheet and kissed me on the forehead. I could feel her lips trembling as they touched my skin, although she looked fairly composed as she walked to the door.

As she went out, she said: 'I'll come up after dinner and keep you company while you eat your supper.'

'I can't eat,' I said.

'My dear, you must. In times like this, one must keep strong – and you have a long way to go yet.'

'I wish I was dead,' I said.

After Angela had gone downstairs, I lay for a long time, thinking of Barney. I had always had a great affection for him, hot-tempered and ruthless as he often was; when we were younger, I had imagined that he preferred Angela to me as he had taken her out frequently, but it was to me that he proposed during the last Christmas he had spent at home. I had been so happy; it seemed as if the war could not possibly last much longer, and we planned to be married as soon as Barney was demobbed. He had survived the invasion of France safely and had enjoyed one more leave when his badly mauled regiment was brought home to be reformed. He had been tired and morose during that last leave, as if he had a premonition of what was to come, but after he was rested he became more cheerful and we spent two or three happy days together before he went back to his barracks.

I had begun to collect linen and china for the small flat we hoped to find. I wanted Barney to enjoy all the comforts I could scrounge for him in a tightly rationed country. I had bought sheets on the black-market, made pillowcases out of bleached flour bags, begged old curtains from Mother, and had bought from auction sales pieces of painted china and prewar silverware. Even now, on the bedside table, lay a half-finished tablecloth, which I was contriving by faggoting together tiny pieces of linen left over from the manufacture of aeroplane wings.

In a paroxysm of rage, I sat up and flung the tablecloth and the coloured embroidery silks across the room. Unfortunately, I flung the water glass as well; but the explosion it made when it crashed released the tension in me, and when Mother came running into the room, I was crying with steady, hopeless sobs.

Mother picked up the cloth and folded it carefully. It was to be a long time before I would spread it on a table, and if some, self-appointed prophet had told me where the table would be, he would not have been believed.

CHAPTER TWO

When I was seven, my father, Thomas Delaney, came to Wetherport to work in the Income Tax Offices. In order to be near his work, he bought a Victorian house not far from the middle of the city. It had a walled back garden, in which my father managed to grow the daffodils for which he was famous locally. In spite of the heavy fall of soot and the fact that the surrounding houses had long since deteriorated into apartments or boarding houses, the family was very fond of its home and we refused to be dislodged from it, even during the heaviest bombing; and when we surveyed it on Victory Day, five weeks after Barney's death, we were happy to find that it was in as good condition as when we first entered it.

From this house, I had gone out to school and later to the University; and now when my long day's work was done, it was the place to which I thankfully returned each night.

About half a mile from home there was a very old part of the city, which bordered upon the docks, and it was in this area that, after taking a degree, I took up social work amongst unwanted and neglected children. A scar on my lung kept me out of the Forces during the war, and I was left undisturbed by the Ministry of Labour and National Service to continue my work. Most of the prostitutes of Wetherport lived in my district, and the place swarmed with troops and sailors of every nationality. Many of the residents were coloured – part West African Negro, part Arab and part Chinese, with a few Indians scattered amongst them. Their poverty was great and was intensified by the bombing which they bravely endured. They knew me as 'the lady from the Welfare' and I was classed with 'the man from the parish', that is, the Relieving Officer, as someone to whom the front door could be opened without hesitation. The war brought work to those who were dock labourers and seamen, and the young men were called into the Army, so that their fighting cocks tended to languish in their backyards, but games of fan-tan and crown and anchor flourished, and betting and drinking carried away much that was earned; the poverty and filth of their homes remained.

As the war progressed, illegitimate children seemed to be born faster than I could cope with them and my work was always far behind. I therefore returned to the office a week after James's visit, still feeling shaky from the effects of the influenza.

The elderly voluntary workers, who were my staff, were horribly kind. They had seen Barney's name in the 'Killed in Action' column of the *Wetherport Telegram*, and they handled me as if I was a delicate ornament, liable to breakage. They tiptoed in and out of my room, brought me specially made cups of tea, and murmured that I was looking better or looking worse. I felt like screaming at them to stop, to be normal, to make some vulgar joke, so that the automaton that was me could try and laugh.

One day James rang me up and asked me to join his walking club – it was surprising how far his lame leg could carry him over rough country. By the end of the summer, I had become, at his instigation, an unprotesting member of a music club and an opera society. He kept me in

13

circulation firmly; every time I showed signs of slinking back to the family fireplace to weep he hauled me out again.

Very few of our friends came home from the war, and, in the topsy-turvy world in which we found ourselves, Angela also seemed glad of James's company, and she frequently came with us on our outings. She was witty and she often made James laugh; he had the same throaty chuckle as Barney – and it hurt me to hear him. I love to hear merriment, but a dead man's laugh is saddening, especially when you still love him.

Occasionally it was very like torture to have James striding along beside me, looking just as Barney always did, and then to catch his eye and see a different soul, a strange mind, peering out at me; but he was an old friend and I did not have to make a special effort to be pleasant in his company, so I clung to him, and for nearly three years saw him from time to time, either at the various clubs to which he had introduced me or at his mother's home, which I visited occasionally. His mother welcomed my visits and, presumably, hoped that I would marry him. This solution had not occurred to me and James gave no hint that it had occurred to him; he continued to behave in his usual silently courteous manner and asked nothing except my company. He had other women friends, with some of whom I was also acquainted, but he never showed any particular preference for one of them.

I gradually picked up the fragments of my life and stuck them together again as best I could. The sickening reaction from the effort entailed by the war had, however, set in, and like many others I felt low and dispirited. I had been the only young woman left in our organisation at a time when our work was increasing; the war itself had brought many problems which were not the concern of any particular authority and I often found myself doing work far removed from the care of children. Many were the days when there was no time to eat and many the nights I spent on an old sofa in the office rather than waste time by going home. Once the Japanese war had been brought to a horrifying finish by the atom bomb, however, new social workers were recruited and my hours of work became normal. I should have been grateful for a life once more returned to a peaceful routine, but I found myself intolerably bored and very tired of solving other people's problems.

In the autumn of 1948, however, James's love of chocolate caused a sharp change in my life. We were attending a first night at the Royal Theatre, and I had elected to wait in the foyer, while James carried on a delicate negotiation with the girl in the sweet shop next door, for the purchase of a box of rare, handmade chocolates, for which he had not enough ration coupons. I stood idly watching the people arriving for the show. Every tram that stopped outside unloaded a fresh mass of shabby humanity; a few small private cars added their quota of patrons. Dressed in old sweaters, tweeds and raincoats, the women hatless like myself, they poured into the theatre. They certainly did not care much about outward appearances, but I knew they would form an attentive and critical audience.

I had just seen a Duchess slip quietly into the auditorium, chivvied from behind by two students who were afraid of being late, when a voice behind me gushed: 'My deah, where have you been all these years?'

The voice was familiar, and I turned round quickly, to face a middle-aged woman who was extending a black-gloved hand to me.

'Bessie,' I cried, overjoyed at meeting someone I had known before the war. The last time I had seen Bessie she had been in khaki uniform – a sort of female brass hat – but there was nothing of that about her now. Her black suit and frilly, red hat made her completely feminine.

'My deah, you are just the woman for whom I've been looking. Can you dance?'

'Yes,' I said blankly.

James came up to us, triumphantly bearing his box of chocolates, and was introduced. The foyer bell rang, and Bessie said hastily: 'Come and see me, my deah, to-morrow evening at 42 Belfrey Street – the McShane Club. Come at seven.' She looked about anxiously.

'Please excuse me – I must find my party.'

She waved one plump hand vaguely in the direction of the front door and tripped across the hall, her high heels clicking merrily on the marble floor, and to my amazement, joined a party of Negroes. She greeted them gaily and vanished with them into the auditorium.

James's eyebrows lifted, as he asked: 'Who are they?'

'No idea,' I said.

'Have a chocolate,' said James, tearing off wrappings.

James had invited a young married couple to join us, and as soon as they arrived we went in to see the play. It was a good play about the escape of a prisoner of war from a German stalag – but my mind was on Bessie.

Bessie Forbes used to live in a flat near to us. Her husband had been a lieutenant in the Regular Army and had been at Wetherport Barracks for nearly a year before the war broke out. He had been sent to Norway and had been posted as Missing. Bessie waited for further news but none came, and, as she had no children, she enlisted in the Army Territorial Service. I knew she had done very well in the Service, but presumably she had now taken her discharge. I wondered if she had married again. And what was she doing in the company of Negroes? Negroes were an everyday part of my working life – but that was unusual. It was not reasonable to suppose that a woman of Bessie's station in society would be well acquainted with any – the colour bar still functioned in England quite effectively in respect of Negroes.

At the end of the second interval, as the audience was surging back to its seats, I was tossed against Bessie, and she smiled at me.

'Who are you with?' I whispered, nearly dead with curiosity.

'Nigerian chieftains,' she said. 'See you tomorrow,' and she was swept away from me.

The mystery was beyond me, so I ate James's chocolates and tried to concentrate on the play.

James and I walked leisurely home together. The night was clear and there was a sweet smell of rotting leaves in the park. We did not talk much on the way, knowing each other well enough not to have to make conversation. He lingered at our gate and I asked him in.

'No, I – I won't come in tonight,' he said.

He made no move to depart, however, and leaned awkwardly against the gate pillar, his fingers drumming on its dirty, granite sides.

He said abruptly: 'Peggie, will you marry me?'

My mind was on Nigerian chieftains, but the answer came without hesitation, and I surprised myself with the certainty of it.

'No, Jamie,' I said gently, 'I can't.'

James stopped drumming on the gate pillar and gripped it hard.

'Why not, Peggie? Ah love thee.'

'I know, dear, and I'm sorry.' I paused, and looked at him in the light of the street lamp. 'You are so like Barney, Jamie, that I would love you because of the likeness and not because you are you. It would not be fair to you.'

He stood there, silently biting his lower lip, just as Barney used to when puzzled.

'Ah might've guessed it,' he said at length. 'Are you sure, Pegs?' The light-blue eyes gleamed suddenly in the poor light and there was pain in them.

My resolve faltered; James would make a good husband, I knew. He had a depth of character which Barney had lacked. I looked up at him again. The light was playing tricks with him and it seemed as if Barney was standing there, instead of James; like a tormenting dream, I thought bitterly.

'I can't, Jamie. You're the finest man I know – but I can't marry you – I just can't.'

'Dawn't fret yourself, luv. Ah do understand.' He lifted my chin with one hand, so that the lamplight fell upon my face. His lips were curved with pity. 'Just remember, that ah'm always around if you want me,' he said softly. His arm dropped to his side and he turned to go. 'Good night, Peggie, luv.'

'Good night, Jamie – I'm truly sorry.'

He looked back at me as I stood by the gate: 'Ah told

thee – dawn't fret,' he called as he limped into the darkness.

I knew I had hurt badly someone who loved me very much, and as I climbed the front steps I reproached myself mercilessly for being so foolish as to see so much of him when I had no intention of marrying him.

I let myself in. Everybody was in bed, and only the tick of the grandfather clock broke the quietness. On the bottom step of the staircase lay Tomkins, our cat, and I sat down by him and scratched his ears. He stood up, stretched, and leaped up on to my shoulder, to rub himself against my neck. The house seemed so peaceful, so normal, just as it had been since I was a little girl. Only the little girl had grown and changed into a disheartened woman.

I burst into tears, and Tomkins fled up the stairs.

A door opened and Angela leaned over the banisters.

'What's the matter, Peg?'

'Nothing much,' I whispered, 'I am all right,' and I picked up my handbag and went slowly up the stairs.

Angela was standing in a shaft of light from her bedroom, fairylike in a nylon nightgown, her fair hair tumbling about her shoulders. She looked tired, however, as if she had not slept well for a long time.

I smiled wanly at her and she followed me into my bedroom.

'You look tired,' I said.

'Me? Oh, I am blooming. I never did sleep much.'

'Go to bed now – there's nothing the matter with me – I'm just grizzling – it was nice of you to come, though.' I caught her by the shoulders and kissed her impulsively. 'You're a darling, Angela,' I said.

'Am I?' Her lips were tight across her teeth in a wry smile.

'Of course you are. Now go to bed and don't worry about me.'

A look of weariness crossed her face. She seemed suddenly much older.

'Sure you're all right? No more tears?'

'No.'

'I'll go then. Nighty-night.' And she trailed across the passage to her own room and quietly shut the door.

18

I switched on the electric fire, undressed in front of it and then went to the dressing-table to take the pins from my hair. Although I was shivering a little from the clammy coldness of the big room, I paused to look at the shadowy reflection in the mirror.

My hair fell thick and brown to my waist. I lacked the courage to bleach it golden as Angela did. Large hazel eyes peered anxiously between the tousled locks.

'You are abominably average,' I addressed myself. 'Stock size figure and long legs included.' I peered closer. 'What on earth can a man see in that?'

Tomkins meowed at my feet and I bent to stroke him.

'Tomkins,' I said, 'if I was half as beautiful as Angela, I would have married a king – and he would not have had to be killed,' I added sharply.

Why, I wondered idly, as I got into bed, had Angela not married? She must meet many scientists in the course of her work – but science is not a lucrative profession, I reminded myself, and Angela is distinctively expensive-looking.

Tomkins heaved himself on to the bed and settled down in the curve of my knees.

'Tomkins,' I said, 'you'd better have some kittens to keep Angela and me company when we grow old – because it doesn't look as if either of us is destined for matrimony.'

I turned over and Tomkins meowed protestingly, as if to say that he would if he could.

'Well, find yourself a pretty lady pussy,' I said drowsily, and fell asleep.

CHAPTER THREE

I was still puzzling about Bessie and the Negroes as I walked swiftly through the badly-lit streets, to keep my appointment at 42 Belfrey Street. I felt a subdued excitement at the thought of seeing her again – after all, Bessie belonged to that part of my life which had been

sunlit and full of hope, when the war was still a long wa
off in places like Poland and Norway.

I had been unable to remember what kind of a club th
McShane was, but the moment I walked through its swin
doors and a gust of conversation swept round me,
wondered how I could have forgotten.

Angus McShane, a native of Wetherport and a grea
believer in the excellence of British culture, had at hi
death asked that his considerable fortune be used to buil
a club for the purpose of propagating British ideas among:
foreign visitors to Britain.

The City Council, faced with all the difficulties inherer
in ruling a port full of foreigners of every nationality, ha
supported the idea, and the result was a suite of pleasantl
furnished rooms in the middle of the city, where foreig
visitors and students could entertain their friends and als
make friends with English people. Dances were helc
English was taught; a canteen dispensed English food – an
confirmed the opinion of its customers, that the Britis
were the world's worst cooks; a library held an assortmer
of donated books ranging from classics to the latest Erne:
Hemingway and the newest magazines; and the lounge int
which I walked that autumn evening seemed to contain
representative from every country in the world – and the
were nearly all men.

Shyness swept over me and I hesitated, while the doo
behind me made a steady plopping sound as they swun
back and forth. Four men in American-cut suits stood nea
me. They were coffee-skinned, and I could feel their ey
looking me over. Their gaze was not insolent and the
seemed to approve of me, for they sighed softly as I passed
Two Negroes sitting near bowed their heads sel
consciously over a magazine as my skirt brushed the sma
table in front of them. They made me feel thorough
womanly, and I enjoyed the change from being Mi
Margaret Delaney, the lady from the Welfare.

A white-haired lady was sitting by one of the two fir
that blazed in the room, and she was playing chess with
young Chinese. As I looked round, she crie
'Checkmate,' triumphantly, and her opponent's ey

20

vanished into slits as he laughed.

'Excellent play, most excellent,' he said.

The lady looked up and saw me and I went to her, and asked where Mrs Forbes could be found.

'She is probably in her office on the floor above.' The voice was quiet and cultured.

The Chinese bowed slightly: 'Permit me to take the lady up,' he said.

His opponent smiled graciously and said that Dr Wu would be pleased to direct me.

Dr Wu rose and bowed to me: 'Come this way,' he said.

He led me out of the lounge and up a flight of stairs to a series of offices.

'This is your first visit here?' he inquired, his eyes twinkling behind rimless spectacles and his hands making neat, small gestures to guide me along the passage.

'Yes, it is.'

'I trust that we may have the pleasure of seeing you here again,' he said, as he knocked at the door. He bowed again and left me, as Bessie called, 'Come in.'

'My deah,' said Bessie, 'I'm delighted to see you. Sit down and have a cigarette.'

Bessie, out of uniform, had more charm than most women. That evening she was wearing a pink cardigan that gave colour to her naturally pale complexion. Her dark hair was brushed up in a Pompadour style. As she lit my cigarette I tried to imagine her drilling on a parade ground, but failed hopelessly. The determination and discipline which had lain under her uniform was still with her, however, as I was soon to find out.

'Bessie, what are you doing here?'

'I'm the Entertainment Secretary – it's my job to see that visitors here enjoy themselves.'

I nodded. That explained the Nigerian chieftains at the theatre.

'Do you like it?'

'Rather. I meet anybody who is anybody – and no two days are alike.'

'What have you in mind for me to do?'

'I'm starting a dancing class – very good teacher, but not

enough partners. If you are free, I wondered if you would volunteer to come along on Thursday evenings and act as a partner. I can assure you that there are less amusing ways of spending an evening.'

'But women are two a penny in this town, Bessie. Why pick on a rather dull person like me?'

'Two-a-penny women are not required in this establishment,' said Bessie. 'Every woman crossing the threshold of this club has to be vouched for personally by a member of the staff or by some other responsible person. Each member has a pass which she must show to the commissionaire at the door.'

'No commissionaire was there when I came in.'

'Oh,' said Bessie, and seized the telephone. Her conversation was brief and frigid. The commissionaire never again left his post without being relieved by his colleague. After Bessie had dealt with him, I think he would have stuck there like the guard at the gate of Pompeii, even to being engulfed by boiling lava.

Bessie turned back to me.

'You always struck me as someone whose head was well screwed on, and I badly need helpers like that. I noticed at the theatre that you are still single. Any ideas of matrimony?'

'No,' I said, my throat tight.

Bessie looked at my plainly combed, long hair, my tailored suit and my far too sensible, flat-heeled shoes: 'No, I suppose not,' she said in a specially kind tone of voice.

I felt angry. I am not beautiful and my work demanded that I should dress very plainly, but Barney, James and Jackie had loved me, so I could not be entirely lacking in charm. Still, the dancing class promised to be a new experience, so I asked her to explain exactly what was entailed by acting as a partner.

Bessie explained about times and lessons, and I agreed to come the following evening. Then a little silence came between us.

Hesitatingly, I asked if she had ever heard what happened to Lieutenant Forbes.

She gave a fluttering sigh: 'No,' she said. 'He was presumed killed.'

'I'm sorry, Bessie.'

She sighed again and fiddled with the fountain pen on her desk: 'It's quite all right, deah,' she said, 'I was lucky to have him for as long as I did.'

I saw that it was time to go and I rose. She got up and walked with me downstairs and as far as the swing doors, which the commissionaire opened. She told him that I would be coming on the following day and that I was to be brought straight up to her. Then she shook my hand.

'You will enjoy it here – meet some new people – have some fun,' she said.

I murmured that the nicest thing was seeing her again – and I meant it.

When I got home, Father was sitting by the fire reading Gibbon's *Decline and Fall*. He rose and kissed me. Our house always smells of polish and flowers, and the outside door is invariably open and welcoming; his warm greeting and the habit he has of pushing forward the most comfortable chair for you, make the shyest visitor feel that his arrival is a pleasure. He has long since lived down the fact that he is 'in the Income Tax', and everybody knows him as Mr Delaney who has such a lovely show of daffodils.

'Where's Mother?' I asked, taking off my dark jacket and eyeing it disgustedly.

'She's in the kitchen, making chili con carne for your supper.'

'How good she is,' I said. I love hot dishes, but as no one else in the family liked them, I did not eat them often, so I kissed Father on his bald patch and wandered hopefully kitchenwards.

The house may be Victorian, but the kitchen is not. Father had the old kitchen ripped out, just before the war began, and Mother worked in an atmosphere reminiscent of the advertisements in American magazines.

Mother was really cooking chili con carne.

'The butcher gave me some extra meat,' she explained, 'and I've had the beans for years.'

I sniffed appreciatively and sat on the primrose-coloured

table, while I told her about the McShane Club. I also told her ruefully about Bessie's tone of voice when marriage was mentioned.

Mother looked at me shrewdly from the corners of her eyes. She said: 'The war lasted too long. Now it is finished, it is time to wear pretty clothes again. You should buy a "new look" dress.'

'Good heavens, Mother, they are too ultra-fashionable. I've never seen anyone in Wetherport wearing one yet.'

'Don't be silly,' said Mother, 'they are in the shops – I've seen them – and you have just the figure for one. You've plenty of money – you saved all through the war for – ' she stopped.

'For my marriage,' I finished off.

'Yes, dear,' said Mother sadly.

It was true. I had three hundred pounds in the bank. I sighed; but when on the following day I had finished a round of visits to foster-parents, I slipped into a dress shop and spent an hour buying a dress and coat, followed by another hour in hat and shoe shops. I wondered if I would ever have the courage to wear my purchases, but it did not take much bullying from Mother to make me put them all on, and, when I arrived at the club, Bessie was full of admiration for my appearance. She ushered me into the room in which the dancing class was being held, with the advice that many of the pupils were Muslims, who had not mixed much with women before, and that I should be careful.

Fifteen male pairs of eyes took in every detail of me. Seven female pairs of eyes smiled with relief.

'Welcome to the battleground,' said one young lady.

'How do you do,' said the teacher. 'Will you kindly partner Mr Popolopogas. We shall just go over the basic steps of the waltz again.'

We went over them – Mr Popolopogas went over my feet as well. He was a willow of a man, topped with outsize horn-rimmed spectacles, and upon inquiry he informed me in slow, correct English that he was a Greek and was studying medicine.

I graduated from Mr Popolopogas to Mr Ramid Ali, Egyptian cotton merchant's son, sent to Lancashire to see our methods of spinning. Then I did a quickstep with an officer in the French Air Force, who was about a foot shorter than me. Finally, the dancing teacher picked out one or two advanced pupils to teach them another step of the tango. I was asked to partner a Negro. Although many Negroes lived in the district in which I worked and I knew some of them quite well, I had never been touched by a Negro, and I was nervous – not nervous because he was as black as I was white, but because I knew the shy reserve of black people and I wanted him to feel that I liked dancing with him.

We did the exercise while he held me very stiffly and at a distance, but to dance a good tango the partners must be close and the woman must be held snugly against the man. I, therefore, stopped dancing and explained the proper stance. He immediately held me correctly and it was obvious that he knew the proper hold, but had been too afraid of me to use it. I could feel him trembling slightly against me as we moved off again to the throbbing notes of 'Jealousy'. We were to dance the whole record through, and after a minute I realised that the man guiding me was far more expert than I was.

I concentrated on the steps and followed carefully. He did not dance with the polite diffidence of an Englishman, but with the full ardour that the South American rhythm demanded. My heart beat faster and I began to enjoy myself. Soon there was nothing in the world except the piercing wail of violins backed by the steady beat of drums, and a compelling body which gently but insistently persuaded me into figures I had never danced before. I did not even notice the slight gap between two records. A wild, sensuous happiness enveloped me. The dark cheek above me rested very close to mine. A separate me appreciated the beauty of the line from chin to ear, finely chiselled out of ebony. Sweat was pouring from him but he smelled clean and sweet, and he danced as nature intended us to dance, to the complete relaxation of mind and body.

Suddenly a burst of applause hit me. My partner let go of me and pulled out a pocket handkerchief to mop the perspiration off his face. He was laughing joyously. I was embarrassed to find that we were the only couple on the floor and had indeed danced alone through the last record, while the rest of the pupils formed an interested audience. I blushed hotly as everyone began to laugh, but it was all so good-natured that I had to laugh too.

The dancing teacher came to us and explained to my partner that he should now lead me back to my seat and say 'thank you very much', which he did, still laughing exuberantly.

The class then broke up, and I went with the other girls, who were all younger than me, to powder my nose. They were ordinary, middle-class girls, some of them students, with pleasant, accentless speech. They were full of little jokes about the dancing class and teased me about the tango I had danced. They told me I had danced beautifully and said they hoped to see me the following week. I felt very cheerful and I was glad that Bessie had found such nice young women for our foreign visitors to meet. From my work, I knew very well how difficult it was for strangers to know English families, more especially so if the stranger's skin was not white.

On the bus going home, I realised guiltily that for a whole day I had not thought of Barney, and I wondered if he would mind. Then I thought of how he would have laughed at my discomfiture after the tango and I giggled behind my gloved hand. Looking out through the rain-lashed window I seemed to see him laughing with me, and I thought that perhaps he would be happy that I was feeling happier.

CHAPTER FOUR

I soon became acquainted with all the staff and most of the members of the McShane. Bessie introduced me to the Director, Dr Gantry, a short, wiry man of uncertain temper and many accomplishments. He spoke seven languages well and managed to make himself understood in several more. He was almost womanly in his insistence that the club must have a homely atmosphere; it must look like a well-cared-for house, not too fashionable or too shabby; there must be flowers and it must be warm and airy. He went through the premises daily, inspecting every corner like the Chief Steward of a liner; he met diplomats when their ships docked at Wetherport, and found digs for vegetarian students; he kept up a lively correspondence with ex-members of the club, who had returned to their own countries; he encouraged every kind of Anglo-Other Country society to meet at the club, provided they steered clear of political pitfalls; he led panting young men up and down mountains in the Lake District and in and out of the best country pubs – he would say: 'You haven't seen England if you haven't been in a pub'; he took great care of the women who helped him with their voluntary work in the club, and any man about whom they complained was summoned to his office and if he did not mend his ways his pass was taken from him. This last was a delicate problem, but Dr Gantry had a fair idea of when a man had made a genuine mistake or when a woman's behaviour might be at fault. He used to say, however, that he sometimes thought he was running a marriage bureau, not a club. So many visitors were men, still young and single. They outnumbered their sisters by four to one, and as a result of the Committee's care in the choice of ladies allowed inside the club, these men met very marriageable young women. Almost every week Dr Gantry gave his blessing to a new couple about to marry, and he always said that Britain's best export was wives.

At the end of two months of helping with the dancing class and sometimes helping Bessie with a particularly large influx of visitors, Dr Gantry offered me a position on the staff of the club.

'The Government has made so much use of our services that we have been able to obtain a grant from them to extend our work,' Dr Gantry said one day, as he chatted to me in the lounge, where I was waiting for the dancing class to begin, 'and it has long been my opinion that lady visitors to this country have many problems peculiar to women. I put this point to the Committee the other day and it was agreed that we should ask you to join our staff and look after our lady members.'

His offer was very unexpected but I was most interested and murmured that I was flattered by it.

'Mrs Forbes tells me that much of your present work is in connection with women and children. She said also that you have a degree in Economics – is that so? and that you can speak French and German?'

'Yes, it is so.' My face must have shown my interest, because he went on to tell me about the salary and the working hours. The staff worked in shifts, and sometimes I would have to be on duty during week-ends and in the evening; this did not trouble me as I had often worked irregular hours; and as he went on to describe the work to be done, I felt a great desire to leave my present employment, in which I saw only the more sordid and degraded side of women, and do work of a pleasant nature.

'I can be free in two months' time,' I said, my mind made up. 'Will that be all right?'

'Just in time for the rush of summer visitors,' said Dr Gantry, wringing my hand, and then, before I could take breath, he shot across the room to talk to an Indian in a pink turban.

So I became part of the life of the McShane. It was for me a new and exciting life after the many years I had spent amongst the less fortunate inhabitants of the city. I helped Indian ladies with their shopping, shepherded American ladies round castles and museums, introduced wan German girls, imported as nurses, to the delights of having enough to eat, arranged tours for Gold Coast ladies whose knowledge of Shakespeare was frightening and who always wanted to see Anne Hathaway's cottage. I led hikes into the Welsh mountains, into the Lake District and into the Peak District, arranged tours round biscuit factories, cotton mills, docks, power stations and new housing estates; and I enjoyed every minute of it.

I encouraged my often-shy bunches of ladies to talk to everyone they met, with the result that many a factory hand heard of Somaliland for the first time, and many a farmer saw India as a cluster of multicoloured saris fluttering round his cow-shed.

I rediscovered England myself, and the beauty of it was intensified for me by the many years spent working in an industrial town. When nowadays I sometimes feel a little homesick, I think of Tarn Hows in a rainstorm or the green pools of Snowdonia glittering in the sun, and my mind is diverted and the mood passes.

So the summer and autumn passed in a holocaust of work. Father was amused at what he called my Wogs, but he was pleased to see my enthusiasm, and Mother was delighted about my improved health – plenty of fresh air was putting pink into my cheeks and improving my appetite. I no longer wept. The pain that was Barney was with me still, although I tried not to disturb the wrappings with which time was insulating it.

James sometimes invited Angela and me to the theatre or to a concert, but he was careful not to be alone with me, and marriage was not mentioned by either of us again.

I never forgot the tango which I danced with the Negro, Paul Stacey, and neither did he. Whenever I attended one of the dances given at the McShane, he always danced a tango with me, and I always felt slightly drunk after it. He had a girl friend, a Polish refugee, and they clung to each other through many social difficulties. She could not tango, however, and she used to stand and watch us dance and clap her hands to the rhythm of the music. She had been in a concentration camp and her eyes were full of the horrors she had seen, and yet when she was with Paul she was completely at peace. He knew exactly how to chase the ghosts from her mind and bring quiet to her restless body, and he never deserted her except to dance the tango.

The tango undid the good which many months of quiet discipline had done. When I knew that Barney would never come back to me, physical desire had raged within me. I knew, however, that to live I must find peace of body as well as of mind, and I therefore worked long hours and concentrated painstakingly on the problems of my clients. Gradually some respite came until, consciously or unconsciously, in the space of five minutes Paul made

29

naught of all my efforts. At first I felt humiliated and ashamed that, without encouragement, I could feel such desires – but comon sense told me that I was still young and must expect such feelings, so again I did my best to channel my energies into my work.

One day Bessie came and told me that a party of Egyptians was expected that evening. They were a rich and influential group of young men, who were touring Britain. It was Sunday and they were stranded in Wetherport until morning. Their guide, a harassed Government official, had telephoned to ask if we could entertain them for the evening, and, since a dance was held every Sunday evening, Dr Gantry had said that we could.

'They're Muslims,' said Bessie in disgust. She was normally extremely tolerant, but for some reason she had taken a dislike to all followers of the Prophet, and it took her all her self-control to be pleasant to them. Like everything else about the staff, this was well known in the club. Probably she did not like them because, on their arrival in Britain, she was often the first Englishwoman – sometimes the first woman outside their family – to whom they had ever addressed themselves; and she suffered from their lack of knowledge of Western conventions.

Anyway, Bessie galvanised the canteen into baking in their honour, rounded up by telephone some girls with whom they could dance and begged me to help in the ballroom as well, although I protested laughingly that I was tired, after tramping round the cathedral with a party of American ladies.

When the Egyptians arrived, I was having a cheerful argument with Dr Wu, who believed ardently in the Chinese Communists' cause and wished to convert me to his views, so I did not see them enter the room.

A silence stole over the lounge and I turned to see about a dozen exquisitely tailored young men surveying the room languidly, while a very indifferently tailored Englishman with a decidedly hunted look was dithering in front of them.

'Excuse me,' I said to Dr Wu, and went to the rescue.

The Englishman clutched my hand, said he was

delighted to meet me and introduced me to his charges as Mrs Forbes. All the Egyptians immediately voiced their delight too, so it seemed pointless to explain that I was not Mrs Forbes.

I took their coats from them, found them easy chairs near the fire and asked the steward to find out what they would like to drink. The party was split evenly between whiskies and sodas and cups of tea. Since Bessie had not appeared, I asked Dr Wu, in a whisper, if he would kindly find her for me. Then I sat down amongst the new arrivals and chatted to them about their tour. Their English was a pleasure to hear, every word being clearly enunciated.

Dr Gantry arrived, followed by Bessie, so I moved away from the circle and went to speak to the group of American ladies, who had congregated in one corner. They were curious to know who the new visitors were, and when I told them that they had come to dance, the ladies promptly announced that they wanted to dance too and charged off to the cloakroom to 'pretty up', as they called it.

It looked as if the evening would be lively, so I sat down in a corner to rest for a few minutes. I had hardly seated myself when Dr Wu came up and silently handed me a cup of coffee – he must have seen my fatigue and gone specially to the buffet to get it. I was touched.

'Please don't mention it,' he said when I thanked him, 'it is a pleasure to me.'

I looked at Wu with new interest. Up to then he had just been another Chinese with Communist ideals, but when he expressed his pleasure he became suddenly a real person to me for the first time.

'You are very kind, Dr Wu,' I said, as I sipped the coffee appreciatively.

Wu smiled. 'You are very kind to us,' he said. 'Madame Li has told me of your many kindnesses to her and to the other ladies in your charge.'

'It is nothing,' I said, the old shyness creeping over me. 'I just do my work.'

'You do much more than your work,' said Wu. 'We all know that,' and he waved one hand as if to associate with his remarks the many faces in the background.

This was the first indication I had had that anyone other than the ladies I escorted appreciated the amount of work which I put into the club, and I was pleased. Through Wu's polite remarks I glimpsed also how much foreigners like himself depended on the club for its friendly atmosphere.

'I must desert you and go to the dance,' I said, hastily finishing my coffee. 'I have promised to help Mrs Forbes.'

Wu rose, bowed and smiled so that his eyes nearly vanished.

'Alas,' he said, 'dancing is beyond me. My stupid feet fail to understand what the music tells them to do.' His hands fluttered hopelessly.

I laughed.

'Soon my friend will arrive and we will both come to the ballroom to watch you dance. Mr Stacey says that you dance most excellently.'

'Mr Stacey is too kind. Do I know your friend?'

'I think not. May I have the pleasure of introducing him to you later in the evening?'

'I should be delighted to meet him,' I said, and went away to dance with the Egyptians.

CHAPTER FIVE

The usual mixed crowd was gyrating slowly round the ballroom floor to the strains of a waltz. The room was already overhot and the Englishman in charge of the radiogram was perspiring. The lights had been lowered for the waltz and the whole room looked dreamy and unreal. I felt very tired.

Bessie ushered in most of the Egyptians – one or two older ones had stayed with their English guide and Dr Gantry in the lounge, preferring the cosy fire and Dr Gantry's lively conversation to dancing.

I went to Bessie. She was wearing a pink dress and her best hostess manner; and I noted that she had already enchanted a rather portly, but extremely aristocratic-looking, member of the party. She promptly pushed him on to me and we finished the waltz together.

The club had long since found that to encourage new members to dance, it was advisable in the first instance for one of the staff to ask them to dance, after which they usually had enough courage to ask someone else to dance. I therefore went to each Egyptian in turn and took him on to the floor, after which I let him loose amongst the other women present. Most of them danced very well and their conversation was polite.

The lights had again been lowered for a waltz, and I swam out with my fifth Egyptian. This one hugged me tightly to him, and we had hardly circulated once round the room before he asked me to accompany him to Manchester the following day and spend the evening with him.

I regretted that I was not free as I worked at the club. He said calmly that he would arrange it with Dr Gantry, who was a friend of his father's. He wanted, he said soulfully, to take me to a ball and dance the whole evening with me. Retreating, I said that it was impossible and that I had no suitable clothes.

He said he would buy me all the clothes I could desire.

I was in real difficulty. Dr Gantry had expressly asked that we be careful in handling these young men, whose fathers were either high-ranking Government officials or well-to-do aristocrats. All his life this young man had probably had everything he wanted, and it would not be easy to gainsay him.

The record player seemed to be playing for an interminable time, and the Egyptian's lips were brushing my ear as he murmured: 'We are agreed that there are many more beautiful women in England, but you – you are the most seductive woman we have seen.'

I wanted to giggle. Miss Delaney, until lately helper of girls in distress, to be called seductive and to be so tempted! I had to get out of my predicament somehow – and get out of it gracefully. I looked round for a staff member or some English helper to whom I might have introduced my partner and thus created a diversion and made my escape; but almost everyone was dancing and the record-playing

Englishman seemed to have vanished.

My partner was saying: 'You should wear pearls in your ears – you must let me buy you some.'

I resisted a temptation to slap his face. Then over his shoulder I saw Dr Wu enter with a brown-skinned man – presumably the friend he had mentioned earlier. Dr Wu would do very nicely – but by the time we had danced round to the door where he had been standing, he had gone and there was only his friend, leaning against the doorpost and puffing at a pipe. I did not know this man and so continued to dance. The Egyptian had taken my silence for acquiescence and was breathing sweet nothings down my neck. Once more we came near to the door. I looked up and straight into the eyes of the brown-faced stranger. They were the most honest eyes imaginable, and when I looked they had such an unexpectedly gentle expression that I felt I had inadvertently peeped into his private life, and I dropped my own eyes. The music stopped and I guided the Egyptian firmly towards his friends. He was saying: 'Please say where I shall meet you tomorrow.'

'I am sorry I cannot come,' I said, and turned round and fled.

Just at the door I looked back. The Egyptian was fighting his way through the swarm of dancers. Whatever should I do? 'Come with me,' said a voice.

I looked up. The stranger was laughing down at me. A thousand times better than twenty Egyptians, I thought. He opened the door opposite the ballroom door. The library, of course. So simple a means of escape – across the floor and down the tiny back staircase to the canteen on the floor below.

'Thank you very much,' I said, as we descended the staircase. 'How did you guess?'

The stranger looked embarrassed and said shyly: 'I was looking at your face.' He stood uncertainly before me, pipe in one hand, the other making nervous gestures. I smiled, and he gained enough courage to say: 'I come here every Saturday and Sunday to see you.'

I was surprised. 'But I have never seen you before,' I exclaimed.

'You have to take care of all the ladies. How is it that you will see me?'

'But – but . . .' Words would not come. The evening was getting to the stage of fantasy, and I was so tired.

'Is your work ended?' asked the stranger, seeing my embarrassment and trying to change the subject. He drew out of his pocket an old-fashioned gold watch. 'The time is ten o'clock.'

'Oh, yes, Mrs Forbes asked me to stay only until 9.30.'

'May I obtain for you a cup of tea before you go? We could – we could sit and drink tea safely in this corner, where you cannot be seen from the door by the Muslim.'

My legs were feeling unaccountably wobbly, my head ached and the canteen was quiet, except for two German girls talking with their English escorts. I sat down where he had indicated.

Mrs Barnes, the Canteen Manageress, evidently knew the stranger who liked to look at me every Saturday and Sunday, because she drew from under the counter and gave to him some cheese straws and some chocolate biscuits, which were in short supply at the time. Armed with these and some tea he came and sat down by me. My head was clearing and when I thanked him I took a good look at him. He was dressed in an old tweed jacket and baggy, grey trousers; his white shirt made his skin look very dark but his features were clear cut and delicate; both in expression and outline his face reminded me of a Saint in an old Italian painting; his hands also, as they invited me to eat and drink, used the gestures portrayed in the same paintings.

'From which country do you come?' I asked, 'and may I ask your name?'

'I am from India and I am called Ajit Singh. You are Miss Margaret Delaney and you live in this city, yes?'

'Yes,' I said, and inquired if he was at the University.

'I am writing my thesis – I spend much time, however, at the Berkeley Street power station – for experience.'

'Oh,' I said blankly, wondering what kind of experience a power station offered.

'Instruments,' said Ajit, as if divining my thoughts.

The tea was reviving me. My eyes twinkled with the

35

mischief I felt, as I asked suddenly: 'Why do you come to see me on Saturdays and Sundays?'

'I have to work very much from Monday to Friday,' was the calm rejoinder.

I laughed outright: 'But I have never met you.'

'There was no one to introduce us.'

'That does not seem to deter the others.'

'My father has said that in England an introduction is necessary before a gentleman speaks to a lady. Tonight I see the Egyptian frighten you – and I know Father is right.'

'The Egyptian was introduced to me – he was not, however, acquainted with our customs. It must have been difficult for him to understand the subtle relationship between men and women in the West.'

'It was difficult for me – but I have not frightened you, have I?'

'No,' I smiled.

He looked as if he was about to say something that was important to him, but changed his mind and said merely: 'This evening my friend, Dr Wu, had promised to introduce us, but we have managed very well by ourselves, have we not?' He flashed a little grin at me, as he took out his tobacco pouch and filled his pipe: 'May I smoke?' he asked.

This then was Dr Wu's friend. Presumably they had met at the University.

'Please do smoke,' I said. 'I must go – otherwise I shall miss the last bus home.'

He rose as I did, and opened the door for me.

'Thank you again for rescuing me,' I said, pausing by the door.

'It is nothing,' he said, his face inexplicably sad.

'I hope to see you next Saturday,' I said, desiring to clear the melancholy shadow away.

The sun shone immediately. 'I wish that I will see you,' he said, and I went to fetch my coat and hat.

As I hurried through the swing doors on my way out, I met Dr Wu looking harassed.

'Are you looking for Mr Singh?' I asked.

'Yes, Miss Delaney, I am.'

'You will find him in the canteen,' I said, and ran down the stairs. As I went through the glass outer door, I turned. Wu was standing at the top of the stairs grinning down at me, as if I were the subject of some private joke.

CHAPTER SIX

My term of duty on the following day did not start until two o'clock, so I missed the fun when Bessie received a telephone call. As a result of the Egyptian invasion, poor Bessie had worked until late on Sunday evening but had returned to work at her usual hour on the Monday morning, in order to act as Chairman at a meeting of an Anglo-Polish organisation. She was at the meeting when the club telephonist called her out of the room and said that someone who would not give his name wished to speak to her urgently.

She lifted the receiver and a reproachful voice immediately upbraided her. Could she not recognise love when she saw it – his heart was broken – one day was all he asked.

'Who are you and what do you think you are talking about?' asked an outraged Bessie.

When he gave his name she became more polite – the stony politeness reserved for Muslims.

'I think a mistake has been made,' she said guardedly.

'You are the Mrs Forbes, the beautiful Mrs Forbes with whom I danced last night?'

'Well, I am Mrs Forbes, but I did not dance with anyone last night – I was too busy.'

'Yes, I remember – I remember – there were two Mrs Forbes – you are the lady of the blue dress?'

'No,' said Bessie. 'I'm the lady of the pink dress.' Then she thought of my blue dress. All Bessie's latent motherly instincts came to the fore. Deliver me to this lunatic? No. She dealt summarily with the Egyptian and returned, full of apologies, to her Committee.

'Bessie, dear, what did you say to him?' I asked, after I explained the confusion over the initial introductions the previous evening.

Bessie looked at me sideways. 'I told him that your reluctance to accompany him was natural, because you had an Italian husband six feet tall and expert with a knife.'

'Bessie,' I gasped, 'you're a dreadful scallywag.'

'It was effective,' said Bessie dryly.

During the afternoon I took two Americans round the docks, after which they were to take dinner with an English family. I left them at their hotel and walked through the crowded streets towards the club, meaning to do a couple of hours of work at my desk before taking dinner in the canteen. One way of avoiding the more crowded pavements was to take a short cut through a store which had its front and back entrances on adjoining streets, and this I did, only to collide with Mother.

'Hello, dear,' said Mother, clutching her parcels to her.

'Hello, Mum. What are you doing here?'

'Christmas shopping.'

Mother was looking worn, so I asked her to come and have some tea. We turned back into the store, and were fighting our way through the Cosmetics Department, towards the lift which would carry us up to the restaurant, when I suddenly saw a familiar face bent over an array of perfume bottles, while a bored shop assistant stood behind the counter and dealt with other customers between addressing the perfume buyer. I heard her say: 'Passion of Paris is considered most alluring.'

'Mr Singh,' I said.

'Who?' asked Mother, peering through her eye veil.

'Mr Singh. Come and meet him – he is quite amusing.'

Mother loves meeting new people, so we walked across to the perfume counter and I asked if I could help him, and then introduced him to Mother.

'Please do help me,' implored Mr Singh. 'My friends at my digs say that dragons like scent for Christmas – they do not tell me which perfume to buy – it is most confusing.'

'Dragons?' I queried.

'Landladies,' said Mr Singh unsmilingly.

I heard Mother stifle a laugh behind her parcels, and I hastily straightened my own face and looked gravely through the collection of bottles. I was very conscious of Mr Singh standing by me. He did not look at my face, but he watched my hands as I sought for the best bargain for him. He took out a finely tooled leather pocket book and paid for the present, and then looked hesitatingly at Mother and me.

'Will you join me to drink tea in the restaurant before continuing your shoppings?' he asked.

Before I could open my mouth, Mother said that we would be delighted. She had never met an Indian before and was evidently excited at the prospect of examining further the specimen before her. Her neat, grey curls danced as she talked vivaciously to Mr Singh, and it was obvious that she enjoyed the tea party that followed. Mr Singh held open the doors for her and helped her with her parcels, pulled out chairs, and insisted on ordering masses of buttered toast, since the restaurant had sold out of cake. Mother was conquered by him before the meal was ended.

At the end of an hour I remembered guiltily my piled-up desk and said that I must return to work. We collected the parcels and Mr Singh paid the bill.

As we were waiting for the lift to take us down again, Mr Singh asked: 'We are – that is – the Indian community is giving a Christmas party – I wonder – Mrs Delaney – Miss Delaney – would you like to come?'

This was a rare honour. The small Indian community tended to mix amongst themselves and rarely asked outsiders to their entertainments. In any case, no opportunity to refuse was given me. Mother accepted with alacrity for both of us.

'We are mostly students,' said Mr Singh. 'It will be held in the club canteen.'

The canteen was decorated for the occasion with the Indian national flag and a picture of Gandhiji framed with flowers. It was a good party, although everything went wrong. The lights fused, the hot food, cooked by the students themselves, arrived cold, and the ice cream melted, but nobody was upset. Leisurely our hosts lit matches while the Canteen Manageress mended the fuse, somehow the Indian food tasted good, though strange to Western taste – and Mother felt like an empress.

As the eldest lady there she was specially looked after, and she was enchanted by the respect shown to her. She was soon surrounded by an assortment of men in Indian costumes; and three girls were almost tearing off their saris in an effort to show her how they were put on. As soon as their first shyness had worn off, they all talked at once, and I could hear her clear English voice rising above theirs, as she asked questions about their studies, their costumes and their homes.

Mr Singh looked after me and brought his special friends to meet me. He was very nervous and seemed fearful that I would criticise the arrangements for the party.

'This food is not typical of India. The ladies who cooked it are not used to cooking – in India each family employs a cook.'

I assured him that the food was excellent.

'We should have put up more decorations – the room looks bare.'

I reassured him on that point too.

Gradually he relaxed and soon he was laughing and joking with the little circle who had gathered round us. I sat quietly and listened, occasionally adding some small remark to the conversation. He was very popular amongst his own people, of that there was no doubt. Occasionally he broke into his own language and after these interludes there was always a roar of laughter.

'Singh knows more jokes and riddles than anyone here,' confided a small, handsome woman in an orange sari.

'He should tell me some in English,' I said, 'I'm sure they must be good.'

Singh looked at me, full of contrition. 'I forgot,' he said.

'Afterwards you shall tell them all over again in English,' I teased.

He salaamed. 'It will be my pleasure,' he said.

I could see some of the girls present giving each other knowing looks at this promise of a private conversation; it meant nothing to me at the time, but it meant everything to them, and speculation as to Singh's intentions ran high.

Mother asked Ajit – for Ajit he had become by the end of the party – to Christmas dinner at our house, and although I was pleased at her offering hospitality to a visitor, I wondered with some trepidation what Father would say about an Indian coming into the house.

Father did not make any special comment. He just looked very shrewdly at the man before him, the same careful look with which I am sure he scrutinises income tax returns, and then made him sit down and drink sherry, while Angela, Mother and I arranged the dinner table.

Although I had lived the whole of my life with my parents, I learned something new about Father that evening. It was apparent that he did not feel at all awkward about his foreign guest; there was none of that strained manner which is often apparent when even the most courteous man of one colour meets a man of another colour. It was as if Father had never heard of a colour bar – and I was proud of him. Strangely, too, I felt proud of Ajit. Father yarned happily about how he had fought with the Japanese in Russia and how well they had endured the cold winter, and Ajit told him how the Madrasi soldiers had successfully fought in a Kashmiri winter. Then they went on to the adaptability of mankind in general, from there to religions, and, by the time the port was served, they were old friends.

Angela sat down at the piano and played carols as we sat round the fire; and I watched the face of this stranger, who had tumbled into the middle of our family. The flickering firelight sometimes silhouetted the almost Greek profile and sometimes lit up the full face, so that its calm gentleness was fully revealed.

Father must have been looking too, as he smoked his after-dinner pipe and plied his guest with tobacco. He asked to which caste he belonged.

'I am kshatriya – warrior caste,' answered Ajit. 'That is the second caste.'

'A very gentle warrior,' I thought.

When our guest took his leave and Father was bolting the

front door for the night, he said to me as I started to mount the staircase: 'The first young man I have met for a long time who has both brains and manners. Got any more like him at your club?' And he grinned a little wickedly.

'Plenty,' I said, blowing him a kiss, 'of all shades.'

Upstairs Angela was hanging up her frock in the big wardrobe in my room. She said, without preamble: 'He's rather a pet, isn't he?'

'Who?'

'Ajit Singh.'

I started to pull the hairpins out of my bun. 'Yes,' I said almost reluctantly, 'I suppose he is.'

On the evening of Boxing Day I was on duty at the club to make sure that the few ladies who had no private invitations had something or someone to entertain them. As I went from one easy chair to another in the lounge, I found myself looking for Ajit Singh. The room was lit with coloured lights half hidden in evergreens. A German architect had amused himself by decorating the room and the result was a soft glow with an occasional sparkle of tinsel or silver balls. It would be easy to miss someone in such dim light, and I had just decided that he had not come, when a voice from a particularly dark corner said: 'Hello.'

I jumped, the cushion I had been shaking up still held in one hand.

'It is Singh.'

He was sitting cross-legged in a deep settee and was smoking his pipe.

I said: 'Good evening. How are you?'

'Very well. Can you sit with me – today everybody is out, and I think your work is not great.'

'I haven't much to do.' I sat down beside him. He continued to smoke, saying nothing and looking reflectively at me.

'Will you come to the University Ball with me on New Year's Eve?' he asked.

Before I could stop myself I had answered in the affirmative, and when I saw his face soften, I was glad I had said yes. I foresaw all kinds of complications arising from that simple 'yes', but his pleasure was unbounded and I did not regret it. He thanked me effusively and also added thanks for the previous day's invitation.

I said we were glad to have him and then asked him about Indian Festivals, which subject kept up the conversation until Dr Wu came in with Madame Li and the conversation became general.

Ajit Singh did not dance well, but the University Ball was fun. I knew several people present and was amused to see their eyebrows shoot up as they noted my Indian escort.

I did not care. I was enjoying being made a fuss of by a man who liked to come and look at me on Saturdays and Sundays.

We were eating ice cream when a very tall Indian, with a very short redhead on his arm, came up to us and roared: 'Ajit, old chap, introduce me.'

'Miss Delaney, may I introduce to you Mr Chundabhai Patel – my friend.'

My hand was enveloped in an enormous brown one. Chundabhai was the biggest ugliest Indian I had ever seen, but I could not help liking him. Six feet six inches was topped by a bullet head, blessed with small, twinkling eyes. His hair was cut to within an inch of his head, like a dog's coat. His suit was of a quality rarely available in England at that time, and his shirt was silk.

He pulled forward his lady friend. Her name was Sheila Ferguson and she was doing chemistry under the same Professor as Chundabhai. Her freckled nose wrinkled and she tossed her red hair, as she described the Professor's despair over the work of both of them.

When they went away to dance, I asked Ajit who Chundabhai was.

'He is a Banya, the son of a rich chemical manufacturer. Soon he will go home to Shahpur to work with his father.'

So I heard the name of Shahpur for the first time; but it was just the name of an Indian town, a name more easily pronounceable than many. I asked where it was and whether it was a big city.

'It is one of the richest of Indian cities. It has many industries – cotton, metalware, chemicals – but it has little water as it lies at the juncture of three deserts.'

'Is the Government trying to improve the water supply?'

'Certainly it is. Further north there is a river which is being dammed. From it they will obtain power for Shahpur and with the power water will be pumped from new deep wells. One day perhaps there will be a better way of bringing water to Shahpur, but Government has much work to do – it cannot do it all at once.' He grinned at me, and added: 'The British did not expect to harvest much tax from the district round Shahpur, so they did not care about providing water for it.'

It was the first time I had heard him criticise the British régime in India. His usual attitude was to ignore the past and speak only of the future of his country. Other Indians sometimes said that the Germans or the French would have been worse taskmasters and would have made their struggle for freedom both longer and bloodier.

'Don't be too hard on my fellow countrymen,' I said.

He thought he had hurt me and to comfort me he said immediately that India had much that was good to learn from England, and that India was indebted to many fine English administrators.

Chundabhai came back to the table. Sheila followed with two English friends of Ajit and Chundabhai, and the party became hilarious.

This was the first of many occasions that Ajit and I enjoyed together, sometimes with a group from the club, sometimes just the two of us. It was a peculiar relationship. Ajit never asked anything of me – he seemed just content to be with me; and I was grateful for his peaceful presence. Part of me cried out to be loved, but I could not imagine being loved by anyone but Barney – and Barney was dead.

Very occasionally Ajit came to our house for an hour or so on Sunday evening, when I was not on duty. Mother always made him stay to supper and he basked in the comfortable, domestic atmosphere. After one of these visits, as we walked down the path to the gate, he said to me rather wistfully: 'You have a splendid home.'

'I think you must have a nice one too,' I said.

'I have,' he said absently, 'but I cannot hope to provide

for my wife what Father provided for Mother. Middle-class people in India do not have so much money in our days.'

'It is the same in England,' I said. 'If Angela or I got married, we would probably start in a two-roomed flat.'

'Would you?' he asked eagerly.

'Of course.'

He shook my hand and went through the gate. I leaned over it and watched him out of sight. I was troubled because I saw myself hurting yet another man by refusing his proposal.

But I flattered myself. No proposal came.

CHAPTER SEVEN

A year went by, a year full of contented work for me. I began to have friends all over the world. After our visitors had gone, they often wrote to members of the staff, inviting them to spend holidays in cities as far apart as Delhi and Santiago. The feeling that I could go to almost any large town in the world and find a friend there to make me welcome, gave me a confidence that I had not enjoyed before.

I met also many English people, who took an interest in the club's activities, and I learned how hospitable they could be, rationed and servantless as they were. I sometimes accepted an invitation to tea myself, and Mother helped me to entertain in return. By this means the number of her acquaintances was enlarged, and she found new interests to replace the slackening demands made on her by her daughters.

It was after one of these tea parties, when we were washing up, that Mother said: 'Are we going to have a marriage in the family, darling?'

My hands froze amongst the soapsuds of the washing-up water. Had she misunderstood Ajit's and my relationship, and if she had, how could I explain its special quality?

'I don't know, Mummy,' I said guardedly.

'I think so, dear – Angela and Jamie.'

I sighed with relief. Mother knew nothing of James's proposal to me; all she knew was that he used to pay equal attention to both her daughters, but recently he had taken Angela out alone on one or two occasions.

'I hope you are right, Mother,' I said, as I shook more soap flakes into the water.

Mother looked troubled.

'I sometimes worry about Angela,' she said. 'I can never get close to her as I can to you – even when she was a small child she seemed remote and independent.'

'Don't worry, Mother. Angela is a very capable young woman and well able to take care of herself.'

Mother sighed.

'I expect you are right, darling – it would be so nice if she married James – he's so dependable.'

So Mother felt the same as I did about Angela. As far as her personal affairs were concerned, she was bafflingly unapproachable – and yet we both loved her. Whenever I thought of Angela I thought of kindness. We had shared our toys, lent each other clothes for special occasions, rarely quarrelled. When we were at Grammar School we had confided in each other about our boy friends and small triumphs and disappointments; but when I preceded her to University that closeness seemed to vanish, probably just because we saw less of each other.

What did I know of Angela, the grown-up, sophisticated Angela, who, now that the war was over, was beginning to publish modest papers on her work?

She was a shadowy figure who had rejoiced with me over my engagement to Jackie; held me tightly while I got over his death and had been glad when I became engaged to Barney – or had she been glad? She had seemed surprised, almost shocked at first.

As I carefully laid the plates on the draining-board for Mother to dry, I thought again of that terrible last year of the war and of the events that led up to my engagement to Barney.

The twins had lived down the road from us since they were small boys and we had often played together. Barney,

James, Angela and me, and as we grew older we had occasionally paired off – my heart missed a beat – not Barney and Peggie, and James and Angela, but Barney and Angela, with James and me left to our own devices.

I dropped a cup and smashed it.

'My love, I hope you are not upset about James and Angela,' said Mother, helping me to pick up the bits.

'Oh, no, Mummy,' I said truthfully, 'I am very pleased.'

I put the bits of broken china into the sink basket and apologised for my clumsiness.

Barney's actual wooing of me, apart from odd kisses at children's parties, had been short and sweet. It had been compressed into fourteen days' leave during which we had become engaged, and one subsequent leave. In between there had been letters every two or three days – love letters.

I had been very flattered by the sudden special attention from a man who had stood high in my affection from childhood. His hot, almost desperate passion had awakened an equal passion in me, and the idea of spending the rest of my life with him made me glow with happiness.

Mechanically I emptied the teapot as I thought back to the days before Barney had volunteered for military service – and I was afraid. A fine sweat trickled down my back and I clutched the teapot firmly in case its fate should be the same as the broken teacup. I began to remember odd times when the four of us had gone out together, when we were all students – and I saw sudden little pictures of Barney hauling Angela up Scafell, Barney and Angela picking gooseberries in our garden and quarrelling at the same time, only to fall silent when I approached, Angela kissing someone good night under the laburnum – I had thought it was James she kissed, but it could have been Barney – Angela making a point of meeting the postman on her way out to work during the war and taking her letters from him.

I tried, as I scrubbed the kitchen sink, to remember Angela's other men friends. There were one or two vague figures escorting her during her teens, but I realised with a growing feeling of nausea that, if I excepted a fellow scientist who had written a paper with her, I knew of no man with whom she had gone out alone either during or since the war, except Gaylord, an American officer, towards the end of the war.

I tried to crush down my fears. I did not really know who were her admirers – she could have been in love with the entire British Army – and we should not have known at home.

I was afraid to pursue the subject further and yet a morbid fascination led me on from one damning consideration to another. Try and be sensible, I told myself. He is dead anyway. Maybe he did admire Angela, loving her like a sister and you like a wife-to-be. But the kiss under the laburnum tree was not a sisterly kiss, said my memory.

I dried my hands. 'Mother, I think I will lie down for a while before going to work.'

I felt like lying down to die, like the laddie in the Scottish song.

The winter twilight had already closed in, as I lay down on my bed. Why had I never thought of this before? Probably because I had never thought of being in competition with Angela. I was nearer the age of the twin brothers, being three years older than she was – and I had always imagined that her sweethearts would be younger men. Three years' difference in age is nothing between adults – but it is between children, and I was still carrying on the same childish attitude that I had when she was four and I was seven. She had always been my little sister – too young to really feel what I was feeling. Too young to suffer what I was suffering.

Too young to suffer what I was suffering? My heart leaped with pity for Angela. If she and Barney had been sweethearts, what must she have suffered when he was killed? I remembered her tears on the day the news came and I mentally kicked myself for being so stupid. What must she have felt when he became engaged to me? How did it come about that he proposed to me instead of her? I buried my head in the pillow as if to shut out further thought.

The light was switched on – Angela walked to the clothes

cupboard, singing under her breath. She hesitated when she unexpectedly discovered that I was resting on the bed.

'Sorry to disturb you, Pegs,' she said. 'I wanted a dress from the wardrobe.'

'It is all right,' I said, 'I have to go to work soon.'

She took out the dress and came and sat on the bed by me. She was in her petticoat, and I looked at her coldly. She was beautiful, I thought regretfully, in comparison with my English prettiness.

'At this minute you look just like Father,' she said, and then broke off. She must have seen my eyes glistening with unshed tears.

'Don't cry, Pegs,' she said, her voice full of sympathy.

My eyes examined her face critically. It was lined quite heavily under her powder, and there was a maturity about it that spoke of acquaintance with pain. Something had taken away her springy youthfulness.

I tried to behave like my normal self, and smiled at her.

'That's better,' she said.

'Angela, is it true about you and James?'

'James and me?'

'Yes, Mother was saying she thought you might be getting married.'

'Well – er, no – he's never asked me. We went to the Law Society Ball together – and to a popular lecture on nuclear physics, that's all.' She laughed. 'Mother is romancing.'

'Would you marry him if he asked you?'

She opened and closed the zip fastener on the back of the dress she was holding, before she answered thoughtfully: 'I suppose I would – I'd be stupid not to – he's a good catch.' She looked at me mischievously. 'Would you mind if I did?'

'No, no, I'd be delighted.' I did not say anything about his proposal to me. I looked at her through my lashes and imagined Barney kissing her shoulder. It hurt.

'Angela – ' I faltered, and yet I felt if I did not know I should die. 'Angela, will you tell me something – I won't be angry, whatever you reply.'

She looked mystified and although she answered 'certainly' her voice had a defensive note.

I raised myself on my elbow until I was looking closely into her eyes.

'Angela, were you in love with Barney?'

A flush crept over her face and neck and perspiration started on her forehead, but she answered me steadily: 'Yes.'

I took a long breath.

'Was he in love with you?'

'Yes.' She half rose, to leave me, but I restrained her by catching her wrist, and looking at her imploringly.

'Angela, why in the name of Mercy did he become engaged to me?'

'It was the best revenge he could think of.'

'Revenge? On whom?'

'On me.' She stood up, and there was anger in her voice as she spoke: 'Our heroic Barney was nothing but a handsome jealous cat.'

'Tell me,' I said, a chill creeping over me, 'were you his mistress?'

'We were always lovers – ever since my seventeenth birthday party.'

I shivered. That party was in 1939. I remembered it well – everybody had got a little drunk and Mother had been upset about it – but the first months of the war had upset all of us.

'Why did you not get married?'

'At first he was studying and had no money. When he and James took over his father's practice, he said that before either of them married they must re-establish the firm. Then he volunteered.' Her voice trembled. 'When he came home on leave he expected to make love, though he never mentioned getting married. Once I asked him – but he laughed it off – said the end of the war would be time enough. A man never wants to marry his mistress,' she finished up bitterly.

'Well, what did you do?'

'Gaylord came along. He was really sweet to me, so I thought I would marry a man who loved me rather than one whom I loved. After about twelve months, he told me he was going home to his wife – it was the first indication he had given me that he was married.' She shrugged her shoulders, and continued: 'I suppose he was no different from most men away from their homes.'

There seemed to be more to come – Angela's lips were quivering, so I said: 'Go on.'

'Barney came home on leave unexpectedly and caught us one night at the gate. He glared at the pair of us as if we were scum, and marched on into the house. He never spoke to me again, except when I was amongst the family. He wanted everything without responsibility, and, when he saw that he was going to lose me to someone else, he tried to punish me – perhaps he thought when he became engaged to you I would crawl at his feet rather than see you marry him.'

'And how soon after that did he become engaged to me?'

'During his next leave.'

I felt sick, horribly sick. Barney making love to me to revenge himself on my sister, whose only fault it seemed to me was that she had trusted a lifelong friend too well.

Angela crouched on the bed and hid her face in her hands. I felt a great anger against Barney – such disregard of the damage he had been doing was unforgivable. I sat up and put my arms around Angela.

'Angela,' I said softly, 'he's dead. One day you will marry a more worthwhile man – perhaps James – he is a good man.'

'Pegs,' she wailed, clinging to me, 'it was awful.'

Now it was my turn to comfort her. I stroked her head and thought how many times she had comforted me.

'My love,' I said, 'why didn't you tell me? I would have boxed his ears and told him to stop acting like a child. I would have sent him back to you.'

'I have some pride – and you were so happy.'

'Of course.'

Dazed with misery, I sat for a while, automatically stroking the blonde head. In those minutes I realised how little I knew about men. Most of my knowledge of them had come at second-hand through the cases I had handled and through books. Jackie, my first fiancé, had been the brother of a girl friend of mine and had been at sea for months at a time. The club had been my first opportunity to meet many strangers – previously I had gone to balls and dances as one of a party. How blind I had been, not to realise what Barney was doing. How blind and how full of false pride. Hatred surged through me – hatred of a man who had humiliated me in my own sight.

The alarm clock whirred and brought my sanity back sharply. Time to go to work.

Angela and I got up together and dressed silently, Angela to keep some mysterious appointment, and I to make out a list of cultural centres in which South African schoolteachers visiting the north might be interested.

Before we went downstairs, I kissed Angela and the kiss was warmly returned. I felt humbly grateful for the comfort of the forgiveness it conveyed.

CHAPTER EIGHT

I worked until midnight, when the club closed. The thought of going home to bed made me feel sleepless, and, as the last bus had just left, I decided that, rather than take a taxi, I would walk home. I walked slowly through the night mist and, when at last I reached our gate, I thought irritably that I would never sleep if I went in, so I walked round the block. The policeman on the beat knew me, and said: 'Good night, Miss.'

I returned the salutation. I came again to our gate but continued past it, walking the same route. The constable met me again and asked if I had lost anything.

Wearily, I said: 'No, thank you. I am just taking a stroll before going to bed.'

'It's not too safe round here late at night, Miss.'

I agreed, and walked back to our gate with him. It appeared that I would have to go to bed, but my nerves were jangled and I felt that to scream would be a great relief.

At home I made myself some cocoa and at three o'clock

I got into bed. Every time I closed my eyes I saw Barney laughing at me, until I could have shrieked at him to go away and never haunt me again.

I switched on the bedside lamp and took from the side table the studio portrait which he had given me just before leaving on his last journey back to barracks. I sat up in bed and for a long time examined the face portrayed. The lips smiled at me, but when I covered them up and looked at the eyes alone, they were cold and staring.

At five o'clock I got up. It was Sunday morning, and the church bells soon began to ring for the first service of the day. Mother heard me washing in the bathroom and called to ask if I was poorly. I said I was quite all right and was preparing to go to church. I heard her bed creak as, satisfied, she turned over to sleep again.

I had no intention of going to church, but it was the simplest explanation to save Mother getting up to see what she could do to help me. Garbed in slacks and woollen sweaters, I went out into the garden. Lighted only by the shaft of light from the front door, it was as bleak and shrivelled as my heart. I went inside, boiled some water and washed up the supper dishes for Mother, after which I laid the table for breakfast.

I had just refilled the sugar basin when, to my astonishment, the telephone bell rang. I answered it quickly, to avoid its waking the entire household.

'I wish to speak to Miss Delaney,' said Ajit.

'Speaking,' I said. 'Hello.'

Ajit's cool tone melted into a warm hello.

'I am reminding you that you must be ready at ten o'clock,' he said.

'Oh, Lord!' I ejaculated.

'Is there trouble?'

'No, no,' I said. I had forgotten that I had promised to walk along the coast with him to a village inn which specialised in bacon and egg teas. He had taken great trouble to pick a Sunday when I would be free and when the tide would be high and at its wintry best. The thought of being bright and entertaining throughout the day was too much for me. I opened my mouth to make an excuse.

'I hope I do not telephone too early. We Indians rise rather early.'

'No, I was already up.'

'Then we will meet at ten o'clock.'

It seemed unkind to disappoint him, so I said that I would be ready and would bring some sandwiches for lunch.

The happiness of his response when I said this could hardly be construed as enthusiasm for sandwiches, so I was glad I had not refused to go.

Ajit had not been at the club the night before. He was working very hard, trying to cram in as much experience and study as he could before going home. He had just finished an arduous round of visits to the factories of electrical instrument makers, and had determined to make this Sunday a holiday.

He met me at the corner of the road in which my home stood. I was early and shivering in the north wind which whined through the leafless trees. The sun peeped only intermittently through the clouds, and the deserted streets looked dismal. I turned up the collar of my leather windjammer.

Ajit was apologetic about my having to wait for him. He glanced at my face, which I knew looked drawn in spite of careful make-up.

'Are you well?' he asked. 'We need not go if you do not wish it.'

I assured him, with a brisk smile, that I was quite well. He looked doubting, but the bus came and we boarded it.

The sea was a heaving mass of grey, except where far out the waves were hitting a sandbank and breaking into white spray. As we started along the top of the sea wall, only the slapping of the water against the base of it and the cries of gulls broke the silence. We walked steadily, the wind behind us, and gradually my body warmed with the exercise and the fresh air cleared my head.

In the coarse grass covering the sand at the back of the wall, I saw a rabbit peeping up at us and, laughingly, I pointed it out to Ajit.

He had been looking at me from time to time rather anxiously, but he was apparently satisfied when I laughed, because he laughed too. He told me about the squirrels that lived in the neem trees in the garden of his home in Delhi, and of the lizards that always made a home in the window curtains, no matter how frequently they were shaken out. I shivered at the idea of lizards in the house, but he said they were harmless creatures with yellow bodies and sparkling eyes, and they kept the room free from insects. He told me also about the mongoose that lived in the inner courtyard to guard it from snakes.

'Snakes are sacred, are they not?'

'Village people sometimes worship cobras as a manifestation of God – but it is the cow which is really sacred – she gives us milk, clarified butter and curd, and in return she must be fed and protected and on no account slaughtered.

'It would be merciful to kill some of the cows which are sick and old,' he added ruefully.

'I read once that one of the Hindu Gods is a destroyer. Is that true?'

'Yes, Shiva destroys – without thought or mercy,' he said, bitterness in his voice.

I thought of the famines, the floods, the earthquakes, the riots of India. It was not surprising that they believed in a God who destroyed.

'Well, who creates?'

'Brahma creates. From the holocaust which Shiva makes, he recreates. So life is born anew and nothing is wasted.'

Nothing is wasted. From the devastation which emotions leave, does Brahma spin again the threads of life? I wondered. It was a new idea to me – a harsh idea – that destruction was a necessary preliminary to the creation of fresh life.

'Do you believe in such Gods?'

'No, these Gods are for simple people. I must seek the truths behind them.' He glanced at me and saw that I was not bored, so he continued: 'There is a part of an Indian's life which is given to the study of religion. When his sons are grown up and he can rest from his work, he spends many hours of his day in contemplation and in the study of Sacred Books, such as the Gita and the Upanishads, and he prays for enlightenment. A few renounce their wealth and their families and become beggars, asking only for food from the householders and cotton cloth to cover their bodies.'

'By ridding himself of worldly ties, he expects to give all his thoughts to God?'

'The same idea exists in the Christian religion,' he said, nodding his head in assent to my question. 'It is, however, in one particular different. In Christianity blind faith is required. In Hinduism faith is not asked. A man must by earnest contemplation discover what he feels to be true, and in that only he must believe.'

'It is a hard religion.'

'On the contrary. It provides for every man. It asks only belief to the best of a man's ability – no more.'

Mother and Father had brought up their daughters to go to church on Sundays and babble the Lord's Prayer every night. They had also taught us the accepted rules of conduct in society. Good children, they said, did not lie or cheat. Good young women lay only with their husbands; they were not too vain; they did not gossip unkindly, and so on. I had often questioned these teachings, but it was clear that they contributed to the peace of the community, so I accepted them. But when the war came to our city with all its savagery of persistent air raids, when most of the boys with whom I had grown up were dead in an apparently futile war, my mind sought for a reason for all the suffering I saw – and found none. And subsequently had not found any.

I had dug amid rubble with nothing but a coal shovel and bare hands to free a mother and children from the cellar of their ruined home, and had prayed at the same time that God would not let the tottering walls around me fall and crush me too. They had not fallen – but I had not then believed in God. With a crushed child in one's arms it is hard to believe in any kind of Divine Mercy. My confused mind seemed symbolic of a whole world which faced the same issues.

Rather than continue a discussion which threatened to

resurrect old worries, I suggested that we have lunch, and we sought shelter from the wind in a deep hollow ringed with rough grasses. It was a pleasant place, and the sun which had strengthened as we walked warmed us as we munched the sandwiches that I had brought. Afterwards we sat and smoked in silence.

Ajit took my hand and opened it. Very lightly he traced the lines upon it with his finger.

'Your hand is full of good,' he said finally.

'I suppose I am really a fortunate woman,' I said, 'but I do not feel so.'

He puffed at his pipe, and looked again at the hand.

'The early life is broken, full of small illnesses and disappointments – later on it greatly improves.'

'Does it?' I asked hopefully, leaning closer to him to have a better look.

He caught his breath as I moved nearer, but went on: 'Yes, there is a husband – and three children.' He broke off and then asked: 'Have you been married? Forgive me for asking.'

It was my turn to catch my breath. 'Not quite,' I said, 'I have been engaged twice and both my fiancés were killed.'

'Forgive me,' he repeated. 'I should not have asked, although it is written in your hand.' He closed the hand but kept it in his own firm grasp. His head was bent as he stared at our clasped hands; his hair was glossy, like the back of a cat.

He looked up, straight into my eyes: 'Why are you so unhappy today?' he asked.

Although I was totally unprepared for such a question, I tried to evade it lightly, as I said with forced gaiety: 'Do I look unhappy? It must be old age creeping up on me.'

'Age – you?' he exclaimed. 'No, some shock has come to you – and I wondered if I could be of comfort.' He stroked my hand absentmindedly.

At his words, my mind was flooded with the pain and humiliation of yesterday. The quivering of my lips became a general trembling, which he felt in the hand he stroked.

'Say to me,' he said very gently.

'I – er – it is rather a personal matter.'

'Naturally it is personal – that much I realise. It is good when in trouble to speak to another of one's personal matters – it makes better.'

His voice was full of sympathy and, after a hesitating start, the whole story poured from me in short, bitter sentences, and, just as he had said, it made me feel better.

Finally I said: 'Unknowingly I hurt Angela, who loved me enough not to let me see the jealousy she must have felt.'

During the recital he had continued to hold my hand as he sat stiffly cross-legged, but as I finished he let go of it and lay down on his back and relit his pipe. The smoke rose in cloudlets, as he thought. Then he looked at me and grinned mischievously. Feeling very self-conscious at having confided in a stranger and a man, I smiled rather tremulously back at him.

'You are lovely when you smile,' he said, as if he had not heard the story at all.

The incongruity of the remark struck me and I laughed a little harshly.

'That is not a good laugh,' he said, raising himself on his elbow, so that he was quite close to me, and taking my hand again. 'I have some advice to give you.'

'Yes?'

'Let me marry you. Let me show you what life and love can really be.'

I started up as if to run away, but he would not let go of my hand.

'Don't go away. Hear me to the end.'

I looked down at him and was astonished at the beauty which flooded his face; it was transfigured. There was love in it such as I had previously seen only upon the face of a new mother – no lust – just a glow of affection. I knew I was seeing something rare, and I sat down again, hardly knowing what I did but fascinated by a loveliness I did not know a man's face could show.

'I have loved you from the first day I saw you – you must know it.'

I did know it although I had not acknowledged it to myself. I nodded.

'We would have to fight many difficulties together, as we are of different races – yet those difficulties could also make us cling together and know each other.' His eyes were imploring. 'I would love you so that sadness and weariness left your face, and contentment filled your life.'

'You do not ask me if I love you.'

'I do not ask your love now – only the chance to win it – and the privilege of giving you happiness.'

I felt curiously humble before him, very uncertain of myself, but the desire to run away had gone. It was as if unimagined treasures had been laid before me; and it seemed to me that I had done nothing to merit such a gift.

I tried to think clearly, to imagine what living with a man who was brown would be like. My mind refused to grasp anything, however, except that a delicate, brown finger was stroking my wrist and that a man of known integrity and ability was looking at me with adoration, and had just offered me all that he had and an entirely new life.

'Ajit – I am not worth all the sacrifice it would mean.'

'My Rani – my Queen, you are worth everything to me.' He slipped his arm round me and drew me closer. Suddenly I turned my face to his shoulder and wept wearily. I wept the last tears I had for Barney, who had been such a scallywag in life and was so pitiful in death. And for the first time for years I desired to make someone else happy instead of hugging my own miseries to myself.

The Chinese say that the time to court the widow is immediately after the funeral, and there had certainly been a funeral the day before, a funeral during which love had been replaced by hate and then by pity – pity for Barney, pity for Angela, pity for myself.

He let me cry until the sobs became less. Then a brown hand turned my face to his. Very carefully he pushed back the loose hairs from my face which must have been ugly from crying. He bent his head and softly caressed my cheek with his nose. A butterfly kiss went across my lips, and I lay still, too tired to protest.

Infinitely patient, he courted me as if I was a girl bride who had never seen him before and was afraid of being alone with him. He did not attempt to kiss me as Barney had kissed me. Just light kisses, softly across my mouth, until I began to desire more. His breath was sweet in my nostrils, and my arms almost of their own accord went up and round his neck.

When he felt my whole body stir uneasily, he said: 'Marry me?'

'Yes,' I said, and he released me slowly. He was beaming.

'You will be the Lakshmi of my house,' he said, 'the Goddess and Giver of all Good Things.'

The winter sun grew sharply stronger, as the clouds rolled away. I smiled at him very shyly although my pulses were pounding. I had just accepted a very difficult set of ties and yet I felt released from bondage. I sat back on my heels and surveyed my future husband.

Because I was for the first time imagining him as a partner, it was as if I had never seen him before. He lay and puffed his pipe contentedly and hummed under his breath, as if nothing had happened, his eyes shadowed by their dark lids and enormous lashes. A patient man, I thought. Anyone else would have followed up the advantage which my acceptance had given him. Some inner perception must have warned him to go slowly – or was it an infinitely subtle skill in the making of love?

At the thought of his really making love to me, a hot flush rose to my face and I scrambled to my feet. He got up too. He was shivering, whether with cold or desire I did not know, but I arranged his scarf for him and made him button his raincoat to the top.

'Hot tea and bacon and eggs,' I said as I pulled on my woollen gloves.

'These English women,' he said. 'So practical – and also so impractical,' and he swung me towards him and kissed me hard until my body slackened against his. I pulled myself away hastily.

'Bacon and eggs,' I said firmly, and ran up the sea wall to the top. The wind hit me as it blew straight off the sea.

'It's really cold,' I said as he joined me.

'Let us then run.'

So, laughing, we ran along the sea wall to get warm. As

I raced Ajit, the wind tearing at my hair and the waves roaring at my feet, some youth came back to me, and I was filled with young hope for the future.

CHAPTER NINE

There was a log fire in the parlour of the pub where we had out tea, and as we were the only customers, we afterwards sat hand in hand on an old wooden settle and watched the sparks fly up the chimney.

The landlady who served us looked upon us with disdain, but when she heard our voices, she confided audibly to her daughter behind the bar that: 'She isn't a common sort,' and she unbent enough to ask Ajit if he was a student from India. She also asked me if I was a student. I said vaguely that I was a social worker, not wishing to invite further questioning. The landlady was nonplussed by my answer and said to her daughter, as she took our dirty dishes to the sink behind the counter, that: 'It was a right rum combination – an Indian and a social aid worker.'

Both Ajit and I giggled when we heard this remark; but it reminded Ajit of another problem.

'What will your father say about your marriage to me?'

I was secretly worried about my parents' reaction to the marriage, although I did not want to communicate this worry to Ajit.

'Father likes you very much,' I said cautiously, 'although he will be very upset at my going to live so far away as in India.'

'We shall see – I do not wish that he should grieve.' He let go of my hand, picked up the poker and poked at the fire, while his fine eyebrows knitted and a frown broke the smoothness of his forehead.

'Peggie, in one month's time I have to return to India.'

'So soon?' I asked in astonishment.

'Yes, my Queen, I have obtained a post at the new power station at Pandipura, near Shahpur – where Chundabhai lives – and I must start work in two months' time.'

'But, darling . . .' I expostulated. I got no further, the rest of what I was about to say being smothered in a kiss. It was the first time I had used an endearment when speaking to him, and he was delighted. I had to laugh. He had picked just the right second in which to kiss me – the barmaid had bent down beneath her counter to put away a glass.

'Darling,' I protested, fighting my way free, 'not in public.' I relieved him of the poker which he had been brandishing in the air.

He immediately let go of me. 'I am sorry,' he said, looking very crestfallen.

I slipped my hand into his and said: 'You are sweet – and don't be sorry – the kiss meant a great deal to me – ' I stammered and could feel the colour mounting to my cheeks.

'I understand,' he said. 'It was naughty of me – in Bombay I would have been liable to a fine for such behaviour.'

'It was a little naughty – but very nice,' I said. 'Now, tell me about your return home.'

He did not immediately reply to my prompting about his journey home. After a moment or two, he said slowly: 'I have not yet told my father about my marriage to you.'

'How could you? You have only today asked me.'

'I have had the intention for twelve months,' he said calmly.

I grinned. I could imagine it. Although his ideas erupted suddenly into words, it was obvious that much preparatory thought had been given to them. I was glad that he, at least, had given thought to our marriage; I was still bewildered at the change he had brought into my life and at my temerity in accepting his proposal.

'Are you going to write to your father now?'

He did not answer the question directly, but said:

'My father will not wish us to marry. He will wish me to have a bride of his own choice from our own caste. It is possible that he will be most angry.'

I knew that the old customs were dying out in India and I queried his remarks.

'They are dying,' he said, 'but still they linger in families. I love my parents and I do not wish their anger – but I love you more and am determined to marry you.' His face darkened as he said this and he put his arm round my waist. 'Peggie,' he went on, his voice full of urgency, 'marry me now, quickly. What has been done cannot be undone.'

I had heard of the power of Indian parents, and I asked him what his father was likely to do if he defied him, as he suggested.

'I am fortunate,' said Ajit. 'I have a post and do not have to depend on my family. I do not think Father will use his influence to have me dismissed – he will not wish to ruin me. We shall, therefore, be assured of our income.' He stirred uneasily and went on, 'It must be hard for you to understand the tight bonds of an Indian family – here you leave your parents as a matter of course, but in India it is not so. It is the unity of our families which makes life bearable in a country where there is no other protection against catastrophe except the family.'

I thought this over. Then I asked: 'Why don't you get a job in this country, where life is easier and a quarrel with your father would not affect you so much?'

'Peggie, you have often told me of the difficulty of getting employment for coloured people in this city. You know the difficulties.'

I did know the difficulties. Although before the law all citizens had the same rights, when a man came before a prospective employer he had to balance his brown skin by being twice as good as the white man applying with him, even if they had been born and bred in the same district. It would be even more difficult for a foreigner. He might be lucky and obtain a post, but I writhed at the thought of the petty insults he might well have to endure from the men who served under him.

'I do know,' I said, my mind made up. 'We shall go to India, and we shall hope to win your parents' goodwill. You shall teach me carefully the customs of your caste, so that after a while people will half forget that I am English, and then perhaps your father will not be so angry and you can make peace with him.'

'You are good,' he said. 'You would not have to alter completely your way of life – you need only conform in public – perhaps wear a sari.'

His face cleared, and I said: 'You are right about being married soon. We will put up the banns immediately and we can then be married a week before you go.'

'What are banns?' he asked.

I explained about a registry office marriage. He was full of excitement. 'I will go to the Registrar tomorrow,' he said. He squeezed me hard against him, and then got up abruptly, fumbling in his pocket for money to pay our bill.

We decided to go back to town by bus, and as we waited in the darkness at the bus stop near the inn, he came close to me and held me to him, and talked quietly about our future life together.

Our children could be Christians, he said, if I wished it, but he would prefer to bring them up as Hindus as they would have to live in India. This question had already occurred to me, and I said that they should be Hindus. I knew from previous conversations with Ajit that the rules of conduct laid down for Hindus were wise, and all I asked of Ajit was that what we taught our children should be free from corruption or bigotry.

He chuckled. 'Don't be afraid,' he said, 'and put out of your mind most missionary writings about us. You will find purity of thought in India as well as here.'

'I shall be happy if our children are like you,' I said.

He trembled. 'I am not good,' he said. 'I . . . I want that we do not wait three weeks for our marriage.'

'The time will go quickly,' I said, unclasping myself from him, as the lights of the bus swept us.

As the bus jogged back to town, I puzzled over the best way to break the news of my engagement at home. My head was heavy from lack of sleep and I could not think very well, so I decided to leave the question until the following day.

Knowing that Ajit's dragon did not provide supper, I insisted that he should come home for a meal.

As our shoes were dirty, we went in through the back

door. My heart was pattering and I think Ajit's must have been too, but Mother was too busy to notice any difference in us. She was just taking a pie out of the oven.

'Come in, children,' she said. 'I hoped you would come soon. I have made a pie for supper. Peggie, pass me that cloth. Ajit, I am glad you have come. Perhaps you would like a wash. Hang the rucksack on the door.' She flew round the kitchen like a plump robin.

Ajit smiled at her, his slow, sweet smile, and my heart leaped. I gave her the oven cloth and took the rucksack from Ajit and hung it on the hook which she had indicated.

Father came out of the living-room, the Sunday paper in his hand, his old leather slippers on his feet.

'Hello,' he said. 'Have a good day?'

Ajit assented. I looked at Father with new eyes while I said: 'Yes, thank you, Daddy.' Father was getting on. Why, his hair was quite white; I had never noticed it before. It is going to hurt me to leave him, I thought, and a little pain nagged inside me when I realised that if I went to India it was possible that I would not see him again.

Mother did not give me much time to brood. 'Wash your hands, Peggie,' she said, as she filled the kettle at the tap, 'and lay the table for me.' To her, I was still a small girl, and I found myself thinking that I had been too long at home. It would be good for me to go away.

Ajit wiped his feet carefully on the mat by the kitchen door and went up the heavily carpeted staircase to the bathroom to wash, and then came down again to the living-room, where he sat down to chat with Father.

Father knew from experience that he would have to tell him to smoke before he would do so in front of an older man, so Father unscrewed his tobacco jar and passed it to Ajit. Ajit took out his old pipe and lovingly packed it with tobacco, while I laid the table and Father talked about the news in the paper.

'I see Nehru has had another try at getting the Hindu Code Bill through parliament,' he said. 'There is an article on how it would improve the status of women. What is the real status of a woman in India today?' he asked.

Ajit lit his pipe before answering.

'It depends,' he said, 'on the community to which they belong. They have equal rights with men before the law, they can vote and they can hold public office.' He leaned back in his easy chair and looked at the moulding on the ceiling. 'The Code Bill would give them rights of divorce and inheritance – it will clarify their position generally.'

He went on slowly: 'In our community, we are proud that our womenfolk are said to be the best taken care of in India. We do our best to see that they are nicely dressed and properly fed. We listen to them with respect, and in the home, of course, their rule is absolute.'

Father chuckled.

'I am in the same boat,' he said, 'ruled with a rod of iron by three women – they eat me out of house and home – and take all my clothing coupons into the bargain.'

I leaned over the back of his chair and pulled his hair, then fled to the kitchen as he rose in mock anger, brandishing his newspaper at me.

Ajit laughed, as I scuttled down the passage. I relieved Mother of our best silver teapot and carried it back into the living-room; Angela came in from church, looking wan and bored, and we all sat down to supper.

Afterwards, as we sat by the fire, I looked round the shabby comfortable room. Much of my life had been spent in it. I had done my homework on the oak table, cut out my first evening frock on the Axminster carpet, written up case histories as I sat by the fire while the guns outside roared and the shutters rattled, sewn two trousseaux under the light of the reading lamp; and now, in the same room, sat the man who was to take me away from it. What would he give me in its place? Would I, through days of heat, long for the steady warmth of our living-room fire, for the welcoming easy chair, for Father reading his endless history books and Mother doing her equally endless knitting? I must be mad, I thought, to want to leave such peace. But I did want to leave it – I felt stifled, penned in. I wanted to go out and know adventure, suffer hardship, be myself – not Mr and Mrs Delaney's elder daughter.

Angela had been talking about a conference she was to

attend in Manchester, and then we fell silent. I was feeling sleepy.

Suddenly I was roused to paralysed attention, when Ajit said: 'Mr Delaney, Sir – Mrs Delaney, I want to ask you something of special importance.'

Mother looked up from her knitting pattern. 'What is it, Ajit?' she asked.

Ajit took a long breath. 'Today I asked Peggie to marry me and she accepted. I ask your blessing.'

'Good heavens,' said Father, dropping his newspaper and clutching the arms of his chair. 'Good heavens, boy.'

Mother and Angela turned to me and said in chorus: 'Darling, how lovely.' Angela's face was lighted up with pleasure, and Mother took my hand and patted it: 'I am so pleased.'

She beamed pointedly at Father, fearing that he would make a fuss.

Father looked at Mother furiously. There was a great fear in his expression. I am sure all the missionaries' appeals for funds, the whole text of 'Mother India' and the contents of half a dozen books by British Army Colonels must have rushed into his mind at once, and he saw me facing all sorts of horrors, ranging from cholera epidemics to a sutti on Ajit's funeral pyre.

'Singh, do you realise what you are saying? Peggie, is this true?'

'It is true, Father,' I said, 'and I am very happy about it.'

I went over to him, sat on the arm of his chair and put my arm round his neck. He looked up at me. His eyes were moist and he was shaking. He was not angry, I realised, but only shocked.

'I want you to be happy about it, too,' I said.

Ajit saw that he had wounded my father deeply, and his voice was concerned as he said: 'Sir, do not fear for Peggie's life with me. It will not be the same as in your beautiful home here, but it will be a fairly comfortable life.' He continued, his voice very gentle, as Father held my hand tightly: 'I cannot promise to send her home for a holiday during the first year, but probably during the second year she could come, and, as my earning increases, she shall come as often as possible.'

Mother's featherweight brain had not taken in the full implications of Ajit's announcement: she was just pleased that I was to marry a nice man after all, even if he was brown. She saw, however, that Father was upset and she said comfortingly: 'Now don't get upset, Tom. Ajit's a nice boy – he will make Peggie happy,' and she beamed on Ajit and me. Turning again to Father, she patted his knee: 'There, there, my dear, Peggie will be all right, I am sure.'

Father was recovering his composure, but he held on to my hand, as he said: 'Singh, I cannot hide from you that this is a great shock to me – a very great shock – although I should, of course, have foreseen it.' He looked anxiously at me. 'Peggie is old enough to know what she wants, but I had hoped – hoped that she would marry someone in our own circle. She has had a lot of sorrow and I don't want her to have any more.'

'I understand, Sir – perfectly,' said Ajit in a polite, small voice.

Father turned to Mother. 'I would like to talk to these young people alone, Margaret, if you would not mind.'

It looked as if Mother minded very much, but she got up and said: 'Come, Angela,' and they both left the room.

There was silence for a moment. I had not imagined that Ajit would take the responsibility of telling my parents of our plans. I had been prepared to face alone the denouncements, upbraidings and tears, and had dreaded them.

Father said in a controlled kind of voice: 'Singh, I appreciate your coming to tell me yourself about this matter, especially as both Peggie and you are of an age to make decisions without advice from your parents.' He hesitated while he thoughtfully smoothed my fingers between his. 'You know that mixed marriages can cause a lot of sorrow, and they bring problems that do not arise in ordinary marriages.'

'Yes, Sir. I have given thought to this for two years – two years is a long time, Sir, to think about marriage – and I have asked Peggie to marry me because I believe that the problems of which you are thinking can be overcome.' He leaned forward, his voice earnest. 'India is changing rapidly, and I feel that Peggie would be able to adapt herself to the life of my people.'

'Have you got a job? What will you do about your children?'

Ajit told him about the Shahpur post and about the prospects of better posts later on, and then said: 'I have to speak further with Peggie about our children. I can say to you, however, that they will be considered to be of my caste and we shall save to educate them for professions. It would be easier for them if they were brought up as Hindus – if Peggie objects to this, I should not, of course, forbid a Christian upbringing.'

'You feel that their mixed blood would not stand against them in India?'

'No, Sir, as long as they are trained from the beginning to think of themselves as Indians, and not as people superior to or apart from Indians, there is no reason why they should not be happy. There is not much prejudice about whom one marries – as long as one's family has given its approval.'

'Does your father approve?'

'I have not yet told him – he will be distressed. Naturally he will wish that I marry into our own caste – but he has much wisdom and he is also benevolent – he knows that India is changing and the caste system is breaking down.'

Father told me afterwards that when Ajit said this, he immediately pictured a father in flowing robes and a turban, reading a holy book and counselling his son in a sing-song voice, using his hands in strange oriental gestures to emphasise his words. Somewhat different, he remarked ruefully, from a dry as dust civil servant like himself who lived in a Victorian house and had a garden full of daffodil bulbs.

'What is your father like?' asked my father, his voice becoming more natural, as fear gave way to curiosity. 'Have you a picture of your home?'

'Why, yes, pictures of home and of Father and Mother are here in my pocket.'

He rummaged in his wallet and handed a bunch of photographs to Father. I had not seen them, so I leaned over his shoulder to look. I had not said one word during the discussion, feeling it was better for the two men to talk without interruption.

After scrutinising them carefully, Father handed me two studio portraits, one of a plump lady whose grave expression was belied by laughter lines at the corners of the eyes. Her head was draped with a veil, and in the middle of her forehead was painted a round dot. Her carefully posed hands were small and the fingers were covered with numerous rings. On either wrist hung several bracelets. She wore also an elaborate necklace and ear-rings.

'Your mother looks very pretty,' I said, 'and her jewellery is exquisite.'

'Do you like the jewellery?' asked Ajit, anxious to make a point. 'You will have the same as soon as I am able to buy the gold and stones. Some also my parents will give you, and at Father's death he will give you gold and silver for ornaments.'

I must have looked a little incredulous and Father looked most surprised, for Ajit added: 'Truly it will be so.' He turned to Father. 'All jewellery given to a wife is her property – and can be her standby in time of need.'

'Hmm,' said Father non-committally. 'What is the dot in the middle of Mrs Singh's forehead?'

'It shows that she is a Hindu. She paints it each day with vermilion – now it is worn mostly for fashion – I have even seen Muslim ladies wear it.'

The second portrait was that of a man of great dignity, heavily moustached and black browed. He did not wear a turban. He had on instead a round, black cap, and he was buttoned into a high-necked black jacket.

I covered the lower half of the face with my hand and looked at the eyes alone. Without the moustache to distract attention, the eyes and forehead were surprisingly benign.

There were several snaps of relations and friends, all looking untidy in an assortment of draperies, and finally there was a photograph of a large, white building, reminiscent of a tiered wedding cake.

'What is this building?' asked Father.

'It is my father's house.'

'Really?' said Father. I echoed his surprise. The building had two floors and at each corner there was a tower like a minaret. There was a pillared entrance, and carved veranda rails ran the width of the house at both ground and first-floor levels. A fine sweep of steps led from a well-laid-out garden up to the front door. In a corner of the picture I could see the outline of a gardener at work.

'What is your father, Ajit?'

'He is a retired District Magistrate.'

Father asked many more questions, to which Ajit replied patiently. Both of them were doing well, considering their differing backgrounds.

In his youth Father had been taught, as indeed I had been at school, that Indians were natives who existed to serve the long-suffering British in return for our 'protection'. Englishmen went to India to rule or to make money and, in either case, they returned to England, to retire in comfort to a house in Harrogate or Bath. Probably the only history of India Father had learned at school was of Clive, the relief of Cawnpore, the Black Hole of Calcutta and, possibly, of the indictment of Hastings. Fortunately he had compensated for his public school education by much reading on every conceivable subject. During the First World War, he had fought in Russia in a polyglot army sent to fight the Bolsheviks. He always said he learned more about people during that period of his life than at any other time. I knew that he had learned Japanese and Russian from his fellow soldiers. It was upon these experiences that I think he drew in trying to understand Ajit, and because he had worked, fought, lived and eaten with men from the East that he regarded them as real people, who desired, loved, quarrelled and struggled through life just as he did – only their struggle was harder. He had always taken an interest in my work amongst coloured people in the city, and he was, therefore, prepared for the possible advent of coloured friends – but it had never occurred to him that I might take a brown husband.

Gradually the conversation petered out and he was left with an uneasy feeling that although he could find no concrete arguments against it, such an unconventional marriage should not take place. He said, with a sigh: 'Well, think this conversation over, Singh – and you too, Peggie – before you do anything rash.'

We assented and Ajit rose, shook Father's rather limp hand, and I saw him to the door. His face had the tightly shut-off look that I had seen before when he was thinking deeply. He knew he had not really convinced Father, and I was suddenly afraid that Father might have implanted in him doubts that would make him retreat. As this fear rose in me, I knew with certainty that I did not want to lose him at any cost – not at any cost.

He kissed me gently on the lips, said he would see me the following day at the club, and walked with the flat-footed gait of a man used to loose sandals down the path, out of the gate and along the road. I stood on the steps as long as I could hear his footfalls on the pavement, and then, feeling intensely lonely, I went slowly up to bed.

I lay sleepless for a long time, remembering how each time I had imagined I was to be happily married, the man concerned had been taken from me. Would Ajit, not wishing to harm me, voluntarily leave me?

When I slept I saw in my dreams Shiva dancing his dance of death; and he was laughing at my puny efforts to escape him.

CHAPTER TEN

On Monday, my hours of duty at the club were from ten in the morning until six in the evening, and when they had dragged to an end, I sat by the fire in the lounge, which was empty, and waited for Ajit. I had told Mother that I would take my dinner at the club, but the thought of food nauseated me; apprehension about the future filled me. Supposing Ajit backed out of his proposal, feeling that Father was right and I should marry amongst my own people. Supposing we did marry and it was not a success. What should I do?

A hand came over the back of my chair and lifted my chin. Ajit leaned over and kissed me. My fears left me; just by the assured touch of his fingers, I knew we would be married, and the rest would be what we made of it.

We announced our engagement, and Mother had a fine time preparing for a wedding. Father was sadly silent; he barely spoke to me, although he expressed his pleasure at my joy over the first presents which Ajit gave me – a red silk sari embroidered in gold, and a thick, gold bracelet. With the exception of the two engagement rings which lay in cotton wool in my dressing-table drawer, they were the most beautiful gifts I had ever received, and it was with some pride that I exhibited them to my friends.

The engagement announcement caused a fuss amongst Ajit's Indian fellow students, and arguments for and against the union raged in many cheap digs, but Ajit went steadily on with his arrangements, despite the dismal prophecies of his friends. All he hoped was that no one would write and tell his father, before he could get home and tell him himself. It was not possible for me to fly with him to India as passages were hard to obtain and, furthermore, I wished to give the McShane Club a month's notice of my intention to leave. It was, therefore, arranged that I should travel by sea, arriving in India about the middle of May.

'It will be very hot at that time,' said Ajit.

'Never mind, the sea voyage will give me plenty of rest, so that I shall be better able to cope with the heat,' I said cheerfully. 'Besides, to come by plane with you would be so expensive.'

'Miser,' he said, but he was pleased. Long afterwards he told me that he would not have dared to marry me, if it had not been apparent that I was careful with money. In India, he would not earn so much that he could risk having an extravagant wife.

The question of guests at our wedding was a difficult one. Grandma – my mother's mother – who was a product of a strict Victorian upbringing, thought it was a tremendous

73

lark, she said she only wished she was young enough to kick over the traces too, and promptly spent hours putting fine stiches into petticoats for me. Her single daughters, Mother's elder sisters, were horrified, and refused to associate themselves with the marriage at all, regarding Grandma as someone who had suddenly lost her senses. Father had one younger brother, living in London with his numerous family, and in reply to the invitation sent him, he wrote that he was sorry he could not come but he could not approve of such a union, to which his wife, Louise, had added a postscript that I should not take any notice of him – he just could not afford to come – but if things went wrong in India their home would always be open to me, and she and the children sent their good wishes with the enclosed. The enclosed proved to be two Benares brass vases made in Sheffield.

My friends' attitude generally was that sorrow had turned my brain, but that it was not their responsibility to interfere; and those I asked to the wedding accepted and were cordial to Ajit. A few, bless them, saw the calibre of the man I was to marry and congratulated me with enthusiasm.

Ajit asked a peculiar assortment of people, all sharply different from each other, but all with one interest in common – Ajit.

There was his Professor, who afterwards became a close friend of Father's; there was the riproaring Chundabhai and his Sheila Ferguson; there was a precise, quietly spoken English physicist with a plump, untidy wife, and an Indian physician with his English wife who impressed my parents greatly by her serene manner. There was also a large, important-looking business man with an equally large, important-looking wife, and although petrol was rationed, they arrived in a car which matched them – big and sleek. This man was the Production Director of a firm with whom Ajit had at various times done some practical work on instruments. Both he and his wife did much to make the reception a success – they moved amongst the other guests, talking politely all the time and being most helpful to my hard-pressed parents. They met Dr Gantry and Bessie and eventually became Committee members of the McShane.

Lastly, there was Dr Wu, who, encased in a new, dark suit for the occasion, was the best man. Although his hair had been carefully combed, it hung down over his forehead like a shaggy dog's, nearly touching the narrow eyes which crinkled up in laughter every few minutes. That same laughter softened his thin face, giving a kindly curve to the wide mouth and exposing unusually small, perfect teeth.

He greeted Angela as if she were an old friend although he had not met her before. He was acquainted with her work through the papers which she had published since the war, and she in turn knew about his work, so they had plenty to talk about in between discharging their respective duties at the wedding.

We were married before the law with a garble of words intoned over us by a disapproving Registrar; and with a flow of tender understanding between us we were married before the Creator.

The reception, which I had expected to be cold and stiff, was, on the contrary, a merry affair. Mother had opened up our big dining-room and lounge, and had asked a firm of caterers to supply the wedding breakfast. With prewar opulence, fires roared in both rooms, and the last of Grandfather's wine cellar flowed in our honour. Angela worked like a honey bee to make the party a success.

Father was much relieved when Ajit's Professor, warmed by several glasses of port, confided to him that his sister had married a Bengali Brahmin some twenty years before, that it had caused a near scandal but it had proved a great success – she was most happy – had come home on a visit only the previous year bringing two shy, adolescent sons – the elder boy was going to attend his lectures next year. He went on: 'Fine young man – this Singh – will make a name for himself one day.'

Father expanded, and when it was time for us to go, he came over to Ajit and wrung his hand.

'Take care of her,' he said.

'I will, Sir.'

A taxi was waiting and Ajit was calling. I was kissed by

everybody. James whispered: 'Good luck, old girl,' and then I was really alone with my husband for the first time since he had proposed to me – the taxi driver being kind enough not to turn round during the whole eight miles of the drive to the small inn where we were to spend three precious days together.

During the war, Angela and I had sometimes come out to this inn in order to get a night's sleep free of air raids, so I knew its clean, cold bedrooms well, and they did not inspire romance. I was astounded, therefore, when the Polish maid opened the door of our bedroom.

The brass bedstead had been pushed back, and a wood fire blazed in the hearth. In front of it was a table laid for a meal. A bottle of wine glowed warmly on a side table, which held also a basket of fruit and a bowl of flowers which looked as if it had been arranged by an artist. A box of chocolates, its lid alluringly half off, sat on the dressing-table. Some parcels tied with coloured ribbon lay on the bed.

'Ajit,' I cried, 'what have you been doing?'

Ajit grinned shyly.

'Chinese gentleman – he come this morning and see all is right – he make flowers in bowl,' the Polish girl said.

'I asked Wu to arrange for me, as Mother is not here to make ready for you,' said Ajit.

I looked with gratitude at the room and went and lovingly touched the flower arrangement. Two men had done all this! How could they have guessed at the shyness, the innermost fears of a not very young woman, and know how to divert her?

'You like dinner now?' asked the girl.

'In about three-quarters of an hour,' said Ajit, taking off his overcoat.

He helped me to remove my outdoor clothes and I kissed him. I had never done so before – he had always kissed me. He led me to an easy chair by the fire and sat down with me on his knee. I laid my head on his shoulder. I could feel his heart pattering furiously. He stroked my cheek with one finger. 'Rani,' he said.

There was a knock on the door. I sprang up. Mrs Samson, the innkeeper's wife, had come herself to serve our dinner. She pottered about the room, congratulating Ajit and at the same time serving us with roast chicken. She was fat and full of jokes, pressing us to eat more and telling anecdotes of her own youthful days in service. Finally, she added some logs to the fire and, taking the dishes with her, she left us to our port and ourselves.

Ajit took his port and climbed on to the bed and seated himself cross-legged as if he was on a divan. I curled up by him. While I sipped my port, he made me open the parcels. There was a pearl necklace, some nylon stockings, some embroidered handkerchiefs and some perfume. He watched me intently while I exclaimed over the various gifts, but gradually silence fell between us. He put down his glass on the side table and took mine and placed it beside his own. He lay down close to me and the slender fingers caressed my throat.

As we sipped our early morning tea and gossiped lazily, Ajit asked me if I did not find his brown skin ugly in comparison with my exquisite whiteness.

I stopped drinking tea. In the three days that we had been together it had never occurred to me that he was a different colour. All I could remember was a feeling of admiration that a man could look so handsome. I told him this, and his teeth sparkled in a grin and the eyes with their incredibly long lashes crinkled up wickedly.

CHAPTER ELEVEN

As I saw the London plane take off and circle round the airport, I could feel my legs giving way under me. No matter how many times I told myself that Ajit was going on an ordinary journey done every day by hundreds of people, I could not eradicate the feeling that this was a final farewell and I would never see him again; it was a feeling left over from the sad goodbyes of wartime, tied to the fact that his family might exert unbearable pressure upon him to desert me. It happened often enough, and, knowing that everybody had a breaking point, I did not think I would blame him if he failed to send for me. He loved me – but distance does not always make the heart grow fonder, said a cynical voice within me. I tried to think dispassionately of being left alone again, but I could not. I loved him. I ached with love.

Angela was waiting at the entrance to the airport. She had insisted on waiting outside for me, so that I could have a last few words with Ajit. We went home together, but I did no more than have a word with Mother and then took the bus down to the club. My honeymoon was over.

People came forward to shake my hand. Dr Wu had told all the club members about the wedding and they were very courteous about it. The attitude of the Indians towards me changed markedly. Whereas they normally tucked themselves away in corners, forming a tight clique, today they came and asked politely after my health and that of Ajit. They did not shake hands with me but raised their hands, palms together, in their own form of salute. I was one of them now and they were showing that they accepted me. They were charmed when I returned their salute in the same fashion and said: 'Namaste,' as Ajit had taught me. They would have kept me with them to talk, but I had work to do and had to leave them.

'Come soon and visit me,' said one of the girl students, pulling her sari round her.

'I will.'

I went to see Bessie. She told me I looked wonderful and, indeed, I knew I was glowing like a lamp newly lit.

'I didn't see Dr Wu in the lounge,' I said idly, as I pulled off my gloves and took off my coat. I saw that there was a pile of correspondence waiting for me on my desk.

'Haven't you heard?' asked Bessie in surprise. 'He had news yesterday that his father had been executed – his brothers have fled to Hongkong.'

'My God!' I said. 'How terrible!'

I sat down at my desk and stared unseeingly at the letters on it. 'I thought he was a member of the Communist Party – he fought with them – he's got a bullet wound in one leg,

I'm told. I always imagined that his family were very happy under the Communist régime – that it was the fulfilment of all their hopes.'

'He's not a party member, according to his application form,' said Bessie. 'I took the trouble of having a look, because it seemed queer to me too – he believed wholeheartedly in their cause – he was always talking about it.'

'Poor Wu,' I said. 'He is bereaved in more ways than one then – and he is such a kind soul. I wonder what he will do now.'

'Can't imagine,' said Bessie, picking up the telephone.

I started to go through the accumulation of letters. I wrote a letter to Wu expressing Ajit's and my sympathy and assuring him of our lasting friendship. Then I sent for a stenographer. Among the pile of letters I dictated was one to a London bookseller asking for a Gujerati grammar, dictionary and reader. Ajit and I had agreed that I should learn first the language of Shahpur district, and later on learn Hindi, which was his mother tongue.

The books arrived three days later. They were dilapidated second-hand copies – the only ones the dealer could obtain – but they answered the purpose. They became my constant companions. I read them on the bus going to and from work, and propped them in front of me while washing dishes or doing my hair. At the end of the week I had mastered the alphabet and the rest came more easily. The Indian girl who had invited me to visit her had a friend who was a Gujerati. The Gujerati girl, on the promise of reciprocal English lessons, was persuaded to come to the club four times a week to hear me read and, after a while, converse. At one time I had congratulated myself on acquiring a working knowledge of German in six months; now I wanted to learn an oriental language in six weeks at an age when languages do not come easily to the tongue. Spurred by necessity, however, I learned at least to understand simple conversation.

On the same day that the books arrived, Mother telephoned to say that a cable had come from Bombay telling of Ajit's safe arrival. A load slid off my back and I could admit how afraid I had been for his safety. As I put the telephone back on to the rest, I saw again the room at the inn, lit only by the falling logs in the fireplace, and I sighed wistfully.

'What did you say?' asked Bessie.

'Nothing,' I said hastily.

Ajit wrote to me every day and I to him. At his request, I sent my letters direct to Shahpur, in care of the Company for whom he was to work. He wanted to choose his own time for breaking his news to his parents, and frequent letters from England would have shown that he had some attachment there. A part of me which was cold and cynical wondered sometimes if he would tell his parents and if I would ever get to India. I went on with my preparations for the voyage, however, and booked a passage in a slow, Indian ship, as P. & O. liners were booked up for months to come.

One evening on the way to the club, I had paused to look at a window full of spring suits when a voice behind me said: 'Good evening, Mrs Singh.'

It was a second before it penetrated that I was Mrs Singh. The only time I had seen my married name used was on letters addressed to me – in the club I was still Miss Delaney, and my friends used my Christian name.

I whirled about.

Dr Wu bowed to me and asked how I was. I said I was very well. He looked heavy-eyed, but his teeth gleamed in a cheerful smile.

He thanked me for my letter. I said I was truly sorry to hear of his bad news.

He dismissed it with a little wave of one hand. 'It is life,' he said, the sadness of his voice belying the airy gesture of his hand. 'If you are going to the club, may I accompany you?'

I nodded agreement and we walked slowly along the busy pavement. I told him that I was off duty and had decided to spend an hour in the lounge and have some coffee.

'Have you had dinner yet, Mrs Singh?'

'No, I haven't.'

'Let us dine together. I know a good restaurant.'

I accepted. I longed for sympathetic companionship to ease the worries which consumed me about Ajit.

He took me to a small, clean, Chinese restaurant. I asked him to order, and, after speaking in Chinese to the proprietor, he gave the order. It was early for dining and the bare room was quiet, the lighting subdued. Two Chinese in a far corner were the only customers.

We chatted desultorily and then became silent. I was wondering what Wu was going to do, in view of the persecution of his family in Communist China and the probability that he would not be looked upon with favour if he returned home. I decided to ask him.

'Dr Wu,' I said. 'As an old friend and as the wife of an old friend, may I ask what plans you have, in view of the sorrows – difficulties . . .' I ran out of words.

His smile was wry. 'I expect to stay here. Today I spoke with my Professor, and it is likely that when I have my doctorate from Wetherport University – I have already, of course, a Chinese degree – I shall take a post in industry.'

Sympathy must have been apparent in my expression, because he went on in a burst of confidence: 'I hoped that the revolution at home would be followed by less bloodshed than was the Russian revolution; I still believe that there will be fewer excesses – the new régime must make itself secure, however, and it is my misfortune that my family must suffer. I do not have as yet any details of what brought the Government's wrath down upon my family, but we owned land and have in the past produced many Government officials – and our interests may well have clashed, although we fought in the army of the Communists against the Japanese.' He fiddled nervously with the spoons which the waiter had laid upon the table in front of him. 'It is likely that I could go home to China and work for the new China – I have not offended personally – but if my family is scattered, for what reason shall I work? How shall I ever feel confident or safe in such a situation?' His voice died to a whisper.

'China's loss will be our gain,' I said. 'You are one of the foremost young men in your field, I am told, and you will be welcome here.' I could not think of anything else to say. Here was a man whose family was scattered, whose beliefs had suffered a fearful blow. He had been so proud of his country's resurgence and it had struck at him through his parents. As he sat and plucked at the tablecloth, he seemed to be the quintessence of the suffering of our generation. Looking at him, I saw the hosts of the homeless, brotherless, dispossessed and disillusioned, and I was wrung with pity.

'Is your wife safely in Hongkong, Dr Wu?'

'I am a widower. My wife was killed in an air raid a few months after our marriage.'

'My God,' I said involuntarily.

My ejaculation brought him back to the realisation that he was supposed to be entertaining me.

'I am a bad host,' he said, 'boring you with my story. So bad of me. Are Mr and Mrs Delaney well?'

I tried to help him by launching into other subjects. Food came – Won Ton soup and chicken with almonds. Both of us felt better after eating; we leaned back and smoked and drank China tea out of handleless cups.

'I will take a few days' holiday,' said Wu. 'I am tired of my good landlady's cooking. I will go into your beautiful countryside and walk – and think about my thesis.'

His courageous acceptance of his loss of beliefs, country and family was at first shocking to me. I looked for rebellion against the forces that had stripped him, and resented the fact that I found none. He bowed his head like an aspen in the wind, and said: 'It is life.'

Then, as he talked quietly of the lovely places in England which we both knew, I realised that to rebel against the inevitable is to waste strength; and Wu, by his acceptance, was saving his strength for the long, tiring battles that lay ahead of him in this England which he loved so much. He needed a little time, however, in which to get his breath, and I encouraged the idea of a spring holiday.

'My sister has gone for ten days to Pentecost Bay,' I said. 'A break is always a good idea after a long winter's work.'

He poured himself another cup of tea, tasted it and

found it cold; so he signalled to the waiter to bring another pot.

'I have visited Pentecost Bay,' he said. 'The country there is hilly, is it not?'

'It is,' I said. 'Angela is staying at a farmhouse which takes summer visitors, about a mile out of the town. I hope she is giving herself a good rest – she works far too hard, and she was marvellous about helping with my wedding when she had so much else on her plate at the time.'

The conversation moved to Ajit. More tea arrived and Wu refilled my cup.

'It is so kind of you,' he said, 'to be patient with my long discourses.'

'It has been a most pleasant evening,' I assured him, when I said finally that I must go home.

At the door of the restaurant I paused to examine a showcase full of Chinese porcelain, and, as we walked down the narrow, dirty staircase, I asked him to tell me about the dragons depicted on the vases. He beamed, and told me about Imperial dragons, fairytale dragons and ordinary dragons, as we strolled leisurely to the bus stop, where he insisted upon waiting for the bus with me.

Tomkins was the only member of the family at home when I arrived there, so I scooped him up into my lap, as I sat down by the embers of the living-room fire. He purred softly as I stroked him while I leaned back in Father's easy chair and thought about Wu's patient acceptance of his sorrows.

'Tomkins,' I said severely, 'I am worrying about Ajit before there is any need to worry and I am ashamed of myself. Tonight a very brave man showed me how to face real troubles courageously.'

Tomkins grunted sleepily and submitted to being carried up to my bedroom to keep me company. Propped up on my dressing-table was a letter from Ajit which must have been delivered during the afternoon. I tore open the envelope eagerly.

CHAPTER TWELVE

In his letters Ajit told me in great detail all that passed after his return home. Later on I learned much more and gradually pieced together the whole story – not only Ajit's story, but also the story of Bhim, Nulini and Khan, whose tragedy was played within the compound walls of my father-in-law's house; and helped me indirectly.

The antiquated aeroplane, in which Ajit had flown from London, chose to land at Bombay instead of going on to Delhi. Repairs might take as long as forty-eight hours, he was told, and as no alternative plane reservation was available, he decided to travel the remainder of his journey by train.

As the train strained its way northwards, it felt strange to him to hear his own tongue spoken with increasing frequency. He found that Hindi no longer came naturally to him and he spoke it stiffly, like a foreigner. He felt foreign in his hot tweed jacket and worsted trousers amongst white cotton shirts and dhotis; and the food that he bought along the route seemed overspiced after years of English cooking.

Still it, was good to be home; to see the Western Ghats in the moonlight, and the barren hills of Rajastan glowering hotly over small villages; to be packed closely in a carriage with a multitude of well-behaved children and stacks of homely-looking luggage. It was comforting to see whole families travelling together, strong in their unity. No need to feel lonely here – these were his own people, whom he understood and who understood him and did not regard him as a curiosity. He took his shoes off and sat cross-legged on the carriage seat. A holy man, who was travelling without a ticket, had climbed through the window when the train paused to take water. He settled himself on an unencumbered part of the floor and arranged his orange robes round him; then he mopped his bald head, noticed

Ajit's shoes lying on the floor and asked if he had been abroad. Ajit said he had just returned. Glad to speak in his own language, Ajit talked with him for most of the journey. The man was going on a pilgrimage, and so that the pilgrimage should not be interrupted by irate ticket collectors, he made his namaste and departed through the window again just before the train entered Delhi.

Ajit put on his shoes, collected his unread detective novels and tightened the straps of his bedding roll. There was a general upheaval in the carriage, and the flash of a porter's turban as he leaped on to the step and clung to the outside of the door. The train tore past his brother, Bhim, towering out of the crush of people on the platform, and his father standing close to the train.

'Bhim,' yelled Ajit.

The coolie opened the door as the train came to a sudden halt. Ajit noted the coolie's number on the brass plate on his arm, pointed out his luggage and told him to put it on to the platform. The luggage attended to and one or two children hastily lifted down, Ajit jumped from the train and pushed his way towards the spot where he had seen Bhim.

Bhim saw him and came to him, smiles of greeting obliterating his usual absent-minded expression. His little sister, Shushila, nearly bursting with excitement, ran to him and slipped a garland of flowers round his neck, as he bent down to hug her. Her short plaits waggled as she burrowed her face into his neck. Her frock and white shoes and socks made her look uncannily like the little girls he knew in England; but he was amused to see that she wore a diamond in her pierced nose, and golden ear-rings.

He went to his father and bent to take dust from his feet, but the elder man caught his hands and raised him up.

'My son,' he said huskily, as he ran his eyes over Ajit.

'Father, it's good to be home,' he said.

He had forgotten how absurdly small, but how dignified, the old District Magistrate was. Although his handlebar moustache was flecked with white, he still had the same erect bearing and imperious manner that Ajit remembered.

Bhim attended to the luggage, and then the father, escorted by both his sons, trotted out of the station, receiving with the condescension of a ruling Raja the polite 'Namaste' of the station-master, who happened to be passing.

And so home through the moonlit evening, everyone talking at the top of his voice, and even the new chauffeur venturing an occasional remark.

Bhim had been married during Ajit's absence and accepted with a shy grin Ajit's jokes about it. Shushila, who might have been expected to talk about her new sister, was silent on the subject except to say that she was very pretty. Ajit knew, from Bhim's letters to him, that his father had chosen the bride, just as he had decided that Bhim should be a lawyer, and like a dutiful son, Bhim had accepted her. Bhim had just begun his law practice when he married, and whether it had been the crushing amount of study and new work which he had undertaken at the same time, or whether he did not like his wife, Ajit could not judge, but there had been a singular lack of enthusiasm in his letters mentioning his marriage. He had just said that his father had found a suitable, educated wife for him and that her dowry was reasonable, though not large.

Ajit knew Bhim's ability to shut himself up with his books and some obscure problem of inheritance or of evidence, and he wondered if a young wife had been able to tempt him away from his work. Bhim was an immensely kind person, provided his attention was drawn to a specific need of being kind, but otherwise flood and famine could come and go without his noticing it.

Ajit was sure that his own marriage would come as a dreadful blow to the family, and as the car bumped along the rutted road outside the city, he prayed that they would not be too angry and upset. Would Bhim understand, he wondered? How would Shushila accept a white sister?

While they were passing through the sweetsellers' bazaar, he was full of defiance; a man should be free to choose his own wife. But by the time they had hooted their way through collections of refugees' huts, he was sure he must have been mad to take such a step; even his elders, with a lifetime of experience behind them, arranged a marriage only after every factor affecting the whole family had been considered.

It was with a feeling of helplessness that he descended at last from the car when it drew up in his father's compound. Still, it was marvellous to be home, to see the same neem trees rustling in the corner, with a mongoose playing beneath them, and his mother standing at the top of the veranda steps, waiting to perform the Welcoming Ceremony. Behind her stood Ayah, holding the tray; the oil lamp on it flickered in the wind, casting unearthly shadows on to the two women and the small crowd of servants and nephews and nieces behind them. As he approached, the lamp flared up and showed the scarlet of his mother's sari and a glitter of bracelets. Then it died down to a flicker, making her look like a ghost from an India long dead.

Ajit paused at the foot of the steps; he wanted suddenly to run away, but his father was standing beside him expectantly, his white dhoti gleaming in the moonlight, and Shushila was pushing him impatiently from behind. Bhim seemed to sense what he was feeling, because he touched his elbow lightly, to propel him forward.

He saw his mother's sweet, plump face peeping out of her sari, and he wondered what I would find in common with her. He prayed as he ascended the steps: 'Ramji, Ramji, help me.'

He put his hands together in salutation, bowed low and took dust from her feet. Smiling through her tears, she took vermilion from the tray and imprinted upon his forehead the mark of a Hindu. When he felt her gentle fingers, he knew that the shackles of the family were again upon him. He, Ajit Singh, descendant of a thousand warriors, wearer of the sacred thread, electrical instrument engineer, was back in his father's house, a younger son who must submit to his father, his uncles and his elder brother.

The sweetmeat which his mother then put into his mouth was hard to swallow, but he loved her, and when he raised his face to her he smiled.

Thakkur, the bearer, and Pratap, the gardener, ran

forward to help with the luggage and to greet the man they had loved as a child. Thakkur's face, which was normally doleful, was today full of joy. Ajit remembered how he used to spend hours reciting the Gita for the benefit of a sleepy little boy.

'Have you any more grandchildren, Thakkur? And do you recite the Gita to them as you did to me?'

'Ji, hun, ji, hun, no less than three. They recite the Gita to me instead.'

'Pratap, have you grown any lady's fingers for me to eat? I hunger for your lady's fingers; I have not eaten them for so long.'

'Ji, hun, Sahib, plenty of lady's fingers are.'

After washing himself, Ajit went into the big stone kitchen, to take food. He sat on a straw mat and his mother insisted on serving him herself. Her slow, graceful movements seemed restful after the jerkiness of English women. In the background fluttered Ayah, her thin face wreathed in smiles of welcome for the man she had suckled as a baby. In the shadows, away from him, sat his new sister-in-law, Nulini. She was not introduced, nor did they address each other. It was just as if she had been there always, and Ajit had merely returned from a visit to the bazaar instead of from a three-year sojourn abroad. He noticed that her black sari was silk and richly embroidered in gold; he was embarrassed that she stared at him almost insolently. He thought irritably that she should veil her face and sit more modestly.

When the last pakaurhi was eaten and the last drop of tea drained, he sent Thakkur for one of his suitcases, and took from it three silk saris, purchased in Bombay as a wedding gift, and handed these to Nulini. Coyly, she smiled for the first time, and took them from him, taking care that in the movement she showed her hands and rounded arms to the best advantage.

He had an English china doll which he presented to an enchanted Shushila, a gold pendant and a handbag for his mother, a leather wallet from Port Said for Bhim and a leather-cased travelling clock for his father. Ayah had not been forgotten; there was a soft, white woollen shawl for her, and muslin dhotis for Cook Maharaj, Thakkur and Pratap. The kitchen resounded with cries of appreciation – what a good young master, what a good son.

Ajit felt like a traitor.

After chatting for a while with his mother, he picked up the clock and he and Bhim walked slowly across the inner courtyard to the room which his father used as a study. Walking in the half light of the moon the brothers tried to re-establish their old comradeship, but they were shy with each other and spoke only of Bhim's law practice.

Ajit heard his father talking to his clerk and, therefore, he knocked tentatively, but Ram Singh immediately bade him enter, and the clerk salaamed and withdrew.

Their father was sitting cross-legged on a wooden divan; beside him on the divan was a small desk littered with papers. Although Ram Singh had retired, his knowledge of Hindu law, particularly that of land tenure, was so great that he was frequently consulted both by Government officials and lawyer friends; and some hours of every day were still spent at his desk.

He motioned Ajit to a chair which stood by an old, English rolltop desk. The elder brother hovered in the background until his father told him to come and sit down too.

They waited respectfully for the elder man to speak, and he began asking Ajit about his air trip and about the University. They discussed these safe topics and news of his uncles' families for an hour.

Diffidently Ajit proffered the clock as a humble gift.

The old man was touched. He took the clock, opened it, wound it, listened to its subdued tick, and finally closed it, rubbing the leather case lovingly with his thin, knotted fingers. He was pleased that Ajit had not forgotten him in these years. I think he realised that Ajit must have saved carefully to bring back such a good present, and that he imagined the many small sacrifices that Ajit must have made in order to buy it.

'It is a very fine clock,' he said at last in a very husky voice.

Ram Singh's personal servant brought in his dinner to him, and the brothers rose and left him to eat in peace.

Hand in hand, they recrossed the courtyard and went to the dining-room, where the rest of the family was gathered for dinner.

There was general merriment in the big, cool room next to the kitchen. The family sat in a circle on low, carved stools, their brass eating trays before them, while Thakkur rushed back and forth to the kitchen, serving them with the bread that Cook Maharaj made as they ate.

As the light of the brass paraffin lamp glowed over the contented family with its contented servants, Ajit was torn by apprehension that his marriage might well disrupt all its peacefulness.

To marry without his father's permission, without even informing his family, was like spitting into their faces. Above all, to marry an English girl, who knew nothing of their way of life, was inflicting something upon them which was possibly more than they could bear.

In that instant he wished passionately that he had never been sent to England, had never met me, had never stirred from the age-old path of an Indian's life, mapped out by sages long ago and followed by his people ever since.

But then he thought of me, he said, as his lamp in darkness, his Lakshmi. He knew I trusted him, and he felt weak with love.

'Do you feel quite well?' asked his mother anxiously, having observed a spasm cross his face.

He looked at her, and she saw to her concern that something was indeed wrong, but he answered gently: 'I am quite well.'

'It is my imagination,' she said. 'I thought you were troubled.'

CHAPTER THIRTEEN

When writing to his father from England, Ajit had, of course, told him that he had obtained the post of instrument engineer at the new power house being built at

Pandipura, near Shahpur. The old man, in reply, had said frankly that he had expected to have to pull a number of political strings before getting his younger son settled in life; even in a country short of technicians, competition for the better-paid posts was formidable, and Ajit's qualifications must, therefore, have been considered exceptionally good. Ram Singh had spent thousands of rupees to send Ajit to England to continue his studies, and he now felt that his appointment to Shahpur had more than justified this expenditure.

Ram Singh was, therefore, in an extremely good temper on the morning following his son's return home. Before calling the boy to him, he bathed and dressed and went through his usual routine. He sat cross-legged on a stool in the small, pillared prayer room in a tower at the corner of his house, and said his morning prayers; when the light of the dawn became stronger, he took up his Gita and read some of the Lord Krishna's injunctions to Arjuna, and then meditated on them, after which he went for a short walk.

Ram Singh's life had been a difficult one, a life of constant compromise between the British rulers of India, whom he served, and his revolutionary countrymen, with whom his sympathies lay. As a District Magistrate, his livelihood depended upon the goodwill of the British, and when Gandhiji started to lead India towards independence, he had been faced with the choice of throwing up his career, as did many of his friends, and joining the passive resistance movement, with its inevitable prison sentences and, sometimes, death; or staying where he was and tempering the wind to the shorn lambs of revolution, as they came before him in the courts. Lacking the courage of his convictions he had done the latter, and many a Congressman had been relieved to receive from him the minimum of sentences.

When the day came for the British to leave India and the Congress Party came to power, they had remembered his clemency and his secret contributions to their funds, and he had served them until his recent retirement.

Now, as instructed by the scriptures, he was trying to turn his mind towards God, and to that end he had retired to his house outside Delhi and built himself a prayer room, in which he could pray, meditate and study holy books.

Knowing that he was getting old and that before he died it was his duty to find a wife for his son, he had recently consulted various friends of his own caste, who had families of the same age, and had found one with a daughter a few years younger than Ajit – a girl whose horoscope, cast at her birth, proclaimed her to be a suitable match.

Ram Singh knew the girl well. She was a friend of Nulini, his elder son's wife, and often visited his house, and presumably she would fit in happily if she became a member of the family. She was noted for her hot temper, but she was fair-skinned and healthy, and he had no doubt that marriage would tame her. Being a Punjabi, she was bigger built than many, and that would suit Ajit, who, by Indian standards, was not a small man. He found upon inquiry that she was a talented embroideress and could play the vina well. Furthermore, her father was offering a good dowry; this dowry could in turn be used to dower Ajit's younger sister, and so save her father parting with the dowry he had obtained for Bhim. This latter dowry he would keep in reserve, for use if he should be faced with the dowering of a niece or other relation left unexpectedly fatherless.

There is no doubt that Ram Singh felt very satisfied that his son's future was neatly taken care of; and as soon as he had eaten his morning meal and spent a few minutes gossiping with his wife, he sent for Ajit to acquaint him with his plans.

Although tired out by his long journey, Ajit had not been able to sleep during the night. He had lain and tossed on his hard wooden bed, wondering how to explain his unfilial behaviour to his father. For months he had pushed this gnawing worry into the background. Now it could no longer be pushed away; it had to be brought out, be examined, be tossed about from tongue to tongue through the family, until it would sound as if he had committed a major crime.

He sweated when he thought of how his uncles, who

lived in the house next door, would counsel his father to coerce him into breaking the marriage, even to the point of making him marry someone else. They would suggest that his father obtain his dismissal from his new post, that he be confined to his room until his ardour cooled, that he be cast out from his caste and family. He knew them – they would enjoy his disgrace, since it would show to good advantage the virtues of their own sons.

Ajit loved his proud parent, and he desired to love and serve him in his old age as a good son should. He knew that his marriage would come as a great shock, and he winced as he thought of the family humiliation it might well involve, the loss of caste and the domestic calamity.

His father was noted for his toleration of the unorthodox behaviour of others, and, in fact, his own household was by no means orthodox. Many Western innovations had crept in. He had, however, insisted upon the observance of certain customs. No meat or eggs ever entered his house, although he had been discreetly deaf when busybodies told him that his sons ate both of these in restaurants. Prayers were said, fasts and festivals were kept, food was prepared in accordance with caste rules, and his charity was unfailing. He accepted his sons' Western mode of dress, since it had long been adopted by civil servants and he himself wore it on official occasions; but when he was at home he wore the village-woven shirts and dhotis of his own people. When his father, Ajit's grandfather, died, Ram Singh abolished purdah throughout the family, much to his mother's disgust. He expected, however, that his womenfolk would not go out alone and would behave with modesty.

A few modifications to the old ways of life had sufficed up to now to keep his family happy. He still received the veneration of his younger brothers and their families, as well as that of his own family; his word was law in the old family mansion next door, which they shared – and which Ram Singh had deserted, when on the neighbouring plot he built his present house, which was more suited to his position as a senior civil servant.

Ram Singh ruled with justice what was still really a communal family, banded together for safety in troubled times and for the protection of their weak and helpless ones. He considered every action and every question raised from the viewpoint of what was best for the family as a whole, and this frequently meant the sublimation of the desires of one member for the good of the many. For generations this sublimation had been taken for granted; it often stifled the initiative and ability of one individual, causing him much suffering, but it ensured the survival of the family. The family's coffers filled as many toiled together, and their widows, orphans and cripples were fed. The amount of gold worn by their women increased generation after generation; there was gold for necessary bribes and there were plenty of young men to defend the walls of the old house when need arose.

As the family were not Brahmins, there was no taboo about their crossing the sea, and the family had early sent some of their men to study in the West and thus fit themselves for Government posts under the British. One of those chosen had been Ajit, and by their standards Ajit had played the traitor – and Ajit knew it.

So he tossed and turned all night, longing for me to be there, he said, to soothe and advise, and yet cursing his selfishness that put his own pleasure before the family's well-being. The independence of outlook which he had acquired in England slipped from him and he was again a younger son, to be pushed hither and thither at the behest of his elders.

And yet, in his heart, he was sure, he said, that I could be fitted into his family without undue upset, if he could only persuade his father that it could be done. He believed in my discretion and adaptability; I had seen so much in my life that was strange. His family was a normal, kindly one, so that I ought not to find it too difficult to bow a little to their customs and they to mine.

When Thakkur came to ask him to go to his father, he rose reluctantly and his feet dragged as he traversed the verandas. He had put on a dhoti and homespun shirt, and they flapped against his body, reminding him that he was an Indian at home, not a student enjoying the social whirl of the West, dividing his time between study, long technical arguments and dates with girl friends.

In the lounge, off which his father's study led, he hesitated. The chairs and tables, specially carved to his father's order, the green upholstered settees and the brocade curtains all spoke of Western influence, but Ajit knew the room was rarely used by the family, and had been intended for the many European visitors who came to Ram Singh's house before the British left India.

Ram Singh had heard his son's slippers flip-flapping across the drawing-room, and called: 'Come in, my son.'

His clerk, laden with papers, came out of the study, salaamed as best he could under his burden and scuttled away. Ram Singh's personal servant and chauffeur was squatting outside the office door and he quickly got to his feet and salaamed as Ajit approached. He was a new servant engaged during Ajit's absence, and Ajit stopped to ask his name and from where he came.

'I am called Khan. My home is near Dava – near the river Sutlej.' His Hindi was faltering.

'A hill man,' thought Ajit, his interest for the moment obliterating his own troubles, 'from Tibet, presumably.'

He looked at the man with some admiration. He was small but perfectly made, and the muscles rippled under his thin shirt. There was, however, no time to ask more. His father called again: 'Come in, my son.'

There was no escape, so Ajit went in, bowed and touched his father's feet. He stood and waited for Ram Singh to speak.

Ram Singh greeted Ajit jovially, pushed to one side the mahogany desk on which he had been working, and bade him sit down beside him. Ajit removed a pile of files, put them on a dusty side table, and climbed up beside his father. They sat cross-legged, nearly facing each other; and Ajit seemed to be again a little boy about to learn from his father a few more lines from the Ramayana.

'Ah, a dhoti,' said his father with approval and leaned forward to pat his son's muslin-covered knee.

He was in a high good humour. He often said that there was nothing he liked better than a good wedding, with the house swarming with relations, a kitchen stuffed with cooks and storerooms stuffed with food; and probably something of this was in his mind as he sat with his son. Certainly Kasher Chand Rana would spare no expense over his daughter's wedding – his wife would see to that.

'I am sad,' he said to Ajit, 'that you can stay only a short time with us. I had hoped that you would be able to live at home on your return from England – and that I might soon have a grandson to play with, eh?' His eyes twinkled.

Ajit stirred and hoped that his discomfiture was not apparent. Ram Singh might easily have a grandson quicker than he expected. The thought of my having a son made him feel better, he said, and strengthened him.

'Sir?' he queried, feeling that Ram Singh had something special to say to him.

Ram Singh smoothed his whiskers and knitted the heavy brows that had frightened many a malefactor in the courts. It signalled that he was about to deliver a pronouncement of importance. Then he sniffed and seemed to think better of what he was about to say.

'Describe to me, my son,' he said, obviously changing his tactics, 'the work which you will do in Shahpur.'

Thankful for a subject on which he could talk freely, Ajit explained the irrigation scheme, of which the power house was a small part, and how landless refugees from Pakistan would be settled in the district as soon as deep wells could be bored and electricity was available to pump up the water. In his enthusiasm he foretold an era of prosperity for the whole province. He loved India and longed to see the peasants freed from famine. His work would be to him a crusade against hunger.

Ram Singh had, of course, heard of the scheme, but he was interested to hear details of it.

'The future of India,' he said, 'lies not in the hands of those who rule but in the hands of our village people. Their content or discontent will be the factor which will decide who shall rule. Full stomachs will do more to keep the Congress Party in power than any other reform. I rejoice that you will be concerned, if only indirectly, in the alleviation of hunger.'

He smiled at Ajit, and continued: 'Bhim will one day be

a magistrate, perhaps a judge. I have trained him to be incorrupt and to be careful to weight the scales of justice as far as possible in favour of the poorer man. I am happy to think that I have two sons who will be of some use to our patient villagers.' He wagged his finger at his son. 'Never despise a man because he is of lower caste or lives in a mud hut. He feels as we do. Remember!'

Ajit said: 'I do not despise any honourable man.'

This was getting away from the subject of Ajit, however, and the old man asked where Ajit would live and what he would earn.

Ajit explained that he would start on Rs.700. His friend, Chundabhai Patel, had warned him, however, that Shahpur was an expensive town in which to live, as middle-class people were few and the bazaars catered either for the many rich industrialists or for the thousands of poverty-stricken mill workers. There were few districts in which a man of modest means might live comfortably. The Government had, however, found accommodation for the senior staff of the power house, and had allotted to him a small flat in the same building which housed most of the staff of a nearby college. Although the flat was six miles out of town, it was not very far from the power-house site.

'And who will look after you?'

'I thought Mother might have a servant here, who would come with me,' said Ajit guardedly. 'Servants are hard to get in Shahpur – the mills take many men and the building of the power house has attracted most of the surplus labour from the villages round about.'

'Hum,' said Ram Singh, taking out a handkerchief and mopping his face. The weather was already getting hot.

'Doubtless Mother could spare you somebody, but – er – um – would it not be pleasant to – er – have someone else to share a flat with you?'

Ajit said nothing. He saw with horrid clarity the proposal which was about to be made, and he was appalled. Although it was inevitable that his father should have in mind the question of a wife for him, he had hoped that it would have been left unmentioned until he had been home for some time. What in the name of Ram was he to reply to his father?

He stiffened himself. Humility before his father was all very well, but he had some pride. Why should he fear to do what he knew was right just because it was not the custom? He held up his head and again mentally rehearsed the first words of his confession. His father, however, was burrowing in his desk, and from underneath the lid his muffled voice announced: 'I have been thinking of you during your absence – I – er – have not mentioned marriage to you before because I wished you to complete your studies without distraction, but now you are thirty, and – er – your mother and I feel – er – that it is more than time you were married.'

He emerged from his desk looking flustered and clutching a number of papers. Putting down the desk lid, he carefully spread out the papers and smoothed their corners with uncertain fingers.

'Now,' he went on more firmly, 'our good friend and caste brother, Kasher Chand Rana Sahib, has, as you will remember, a daughter a trifle younger than yourself, and it would give us both pleasure to see you united.'

'Father – ' broke in Ajit; but Ram Singh lifted his hand for silence.

'Here is a photograph of her,' he said, as he put into Ajit's reluctant hand a formal studio portrait of a magnificent woman who had the bearing of an Amazon.

'Her father has not pressed her to marry, since she has shown no preference for anyone. He tells me, however, that you would not be unwelcome.' He omitted to say that Bimla Chand Rana's temper was so famous that a number of men had persuaded their fathers to excuse them from marrying her. Ajit knew of it, because ever since he was a small boy he had been teased by his friends about a promise that his mother had made to Mrs Chand Rana, that Ajit should marry Bimla when he grew up.

Ajit looked at the imposing photograph.

'Father,' he said, panic-stricken, 'Father, I can't – I'm – '

'Don't you like the look of her now she is grown up?'

asked Ram Singh, taking up a copy of her horoscope. 'If you really don't like her, I could advertise for someone else. I know we should get some good replies – you are an excellent catch, you know.'

He smiled lovingly upon his son. He wanted him to enjoy his wife – and Bimla Chand Rana was a beauty.

Ajit dropped the photograph on to the divan.

'Father, I can't marry anybody.'

Ram Singh looked annoyed.

'Rubbish,' he said. 'It is necessary to marry. Why can't you marry?'

Ajit bowed his head until it nearly touched his father's knees.

'Forgive me,' he said, 'but I am already married.'

'Married already!' exclaimed Ram Singh. 'When? To whom?' And added without much hope, 'To an Indian fellow student?'

'Last month to an English lady named Margaret Delaney,' whispered Ajit, while a second Ajit inside was praying: 'Ramji, don't let the shock make him ill.'

Ram Singh gasped.

'Not in my family,' he muttered. 'It could not happen in my family. Ajit, you have lain with a foreign woman – you, whom I love above everyone – you have married an English woman.' His voice rose to a wail: 'Ajit, you are joking.'

'It is true, Father.' Ajit could feel the pain of his father, and it was a great pain.

'What will your uncles say? This is impossible.'

Ajit said afterwards that while he sorrowed for his father, he could hear my voice at the time of our parting saying: 'Ajit, darling, don't desert me, will you?' Ajit had not resented my entreaty. He knew of the work I had done amongst bitter, disillusioned women, and he knew, too, that I had learned to love him truly and dreaded that somehow he would be taken away from me, as the other men I had loved were taken.

He had promised passionately that I should join him, and that promise he remembered as he faced the disgust in his father's eyes. The old man's face was flushed and his moustache was trembling. He sat in silence, as he collected his thoughts, and regarded steadily the son who had betrayed his family and his caste.

Ajit awaited judgement, his head still bowed. Far away, he could hear the clatter of Cook Maharaj's tava and tongs as he made bread for the house servants' meal. It was a homely, familiar sound and seemed to string together all the quiet pursuits and gentle relationships of the family. Tears stung in his eyes as he listened.

While he sat, Ram Singh's agile mind had evidently already been at work on the question of extricating his son from what must have appeared to him as a dreadful predicament; for he leaned forward, his face passive, and lifting his son's chin with his thin fingers, he said: 'Weep not, my son. We will untangle this unfortunate knot which you have tied.' He dropped his hand to the desk and fidgeted with Bimla's horoscope. 'We can probably come to some arrangement with this woman, whereby for a reasonable allowance, she would relinquish her claims upon you, and if she desired she could later divorce you. For our part, we will invoke the old Hindu law and simply obtain a second wife for you – a good Indian wife, like Bimla.' The dark flush eased away from Ram Singh's cheeks, as he went on: 'I presume that no one here knows of your English marriage, and for all purposes of inheritance the second wife here in India would be considered the first wife. An English woman would probably have no knowledge of our laws and is not, therefore, likely to make troublesome demands upon the family at my death.'

Ram Singh folded his hands in his lap and looked very satisfied about his solution to the problem. He had propounded the popular thesis that an English woman would do anything for money or jewellery. He waited.

Ajit was flabbergasted at the proposal. Such an idea had never occurred to him. It was so cold-blooded and showed such a disregard for the feelings of the persons concerned, such an inability to grasp what a marriage of love meant, that he was speechless for a moment. Then words poured out of him.

'Father,' he said, outrage in his voice, 'I would never

agree to such a settlement. I have promised her that she shall come to me here, and she shall come.' He looked round wildly, trying to think of a way in which to appease the wrath immediately apparent in his father's eyes. 'I love her,' he shouted defiantly. 'I love her.' And the walls of the big, bare house echoed back mockingly: 'Love her, love her.'

'Ajit!' roared Ram Singh, infuriated at such a show of passion – but Ajit was past caring.

He thrust his face close to his father's.

'I will not marry anyone else,' he said, his voice cold with rage.

Ram Singh stiffened. Such insubordination was insufferable. He picked up the horoscope and slapped it down again on to the desk. The sharp thwack on the desk brought Ajit to his senses, and before his father could say anything he had pulled himself together and was speaking in a carefully controlled voice.

'Forgive me,' he said, 'for marrying without your permission. I know in that respect I have done you a deep wrong. I had intended to come home and ask you first – but Margaret is so beautiful that I was afraid another would make her an offer before I could. I would have been far away, here in India – and she might in despair have accepted someone else for a husband.'

Afterwards he wrote to me: 'When I was arguing with my father, I kept seeing you in my mind's eye as you were on our wedding night. Never had I seen anyone so fair. I ached to touch you – to be with you – to be part of you – away from people who thought of women merely as useful additions to the family.'

Ram Singh apparently did not take in Ajit's last remarks, and his thoughts were concerned only with avoiding the entry into his house of a casteless English woman. Condemnation burst from him.

'I know English women,' he shouted. 'I have seen them – painted, loud-mouthed, immodest. They bare their shoulders and legs so that any sweeper can goggle at their charms. They take all from their husbands and give nothing.' His moustache bristled, and he shuddered. 'They

101

humiliate their husbands with public discourtesy. They have affairs with other men. Do you know what they say about them in the bazaars? In the zenanas, hey?'

'Margaret is not like that,' broke in Ajit indignantly. 'She is a refined, educated–'

'Educated, you say? All the English women I ever met were supposed to be educated. But to what end? Allow such a woman in my family? No, a thousand times no.' And the little man banged his inoffensive mahogany desk to emphasise his words.

'Margaret is as good and kind as Mother,' said Ajit, his voice again rising in anger.

'How dare you compare her with your respected mother? You know what they call them here. Landlady's daughters – a synonym for a leech, sucking away the wealth of good families and bringing them to shame. Shame on you, my son, shame on you.'

Determinedly Ajit held down his anger and managed to say between gritted teeth: 'Father, I have given my word to an honourable woman. She has married me in good faith, and I will bring her to India. I cannot marry anyone else.'

Ram Singh took a deep breath. 'You dare to say what you will do, indeed.' His voice was full of the fury he felt. 'For the sake of our family, I will not have a casteless woman in this house – an English woman, moreover.'

With a gesture that would have done justice to a prosecuting counsel, he pointed his finger at his son. 'Go to your room. Think carefully of the suggestions I have made. Although you have behaved foolishly I am ready to help you.' His voice rose to a near shriek: 'Go.'

Ajit got up and bowed to his trembling parent, who sat very straight and stared at the opposite wall, on which hung a picture of Gandhi. He did not acknowledge his son's bow, and Ajit marched out of the room, speechless with anger.

CHAPTER FOURTEEN

Ajit marched across the drawing-room and into the hall.

Khan was seated cross-legged by the hall door. He had evidently moved from the office door at the sound of altercation.

'What are you doing here?' hissed Ajit, provoked to further rage at the thought that a servant had overheard his father upbraiding him.

Khan lowered the lids of his mild, slanting eyes. 'Burra Sahib said that I must stay within call,' he said.

Ajit grunted, realising that it was not the man's fault if he had overheard.

At that moment there was a roar from the inner room. 'Pani.'

The servant jumped to his feet. 'You see,' he said.

'I understand,' said Ajit with a sigh. 'Get the water for him.'

Ajit walked swiftly along the verandas towards his room. Before he could reach it, however, he was engulfed by a horde of male cousins who had come over from his uncles' house to greet him. He had to stop and sit with them for a while, make jokes and drink tea, which Nulini and Shushila brought as his mother had gone to the cloth bazaar.

He behaved as cheerfully as he could, but Nulini looked at him curiously as she handed round the teacups. She made pan for each man to chew and then withdrew. Shortly afterwards, Ajit was able to escape too, on the promise that he would come soon to his uncles' house to make his obeisances to them.

Thakkur had put chattays over the windows of his room, to cool it. The water dripped down them in a slow, melancholy fashion. The interlude with his cousins had calmed him, but he felt weak as if he had lost a lot of blood from a wound.

He turned on the table fan, kicked off his slippers, and, to comfort himself, sat down on the divan and wrote to me. In page after page he poured out his troubles and his love. He wrote with the blissful trust that I would surely understand him. And I did understand.

He wrote that the reputation of English women in India was unfortunate. Everybody could quote at least one scandal that had been created in times past by marriages contracted by young Indians sent to study in England. Many students had never mixed with women before going to England, nor had they ever had to think for themselves, since autocratic parents had always arranged their lives for them in detail. The sudden freedom from parental control was often too much for them; they experimented with everything that came to their notice; they smoked, they drank, they had affairs with women.

The fairness of the women was intoxicating and they often fell in love and married a white skin, regardless of the type of woman to whom it belonged, and some proud Indian families had been faced with prostitutes, or little better, as daughters-in-law.

'I am not alone in my fight to choose my own wife,' he wrote. 'There are men here, who, estranged from their families, are facing near-ruination as their parents try to prevent or break up their marriage. But do not fear, my Rani, we shall not go hungry – and I hope that my father will see sense soon.'

There was a break in the letter here as if he had left it unfinished and then come back later to complete it. It continued: 'He has, of course, brought up the question of caste, as you are in our society casteless, and he thinks it is wrong of me to marry outside our caste. I cannot tolerate this point of view. Caste is obsolete and must go. People like us should make the first moves towards its abolition; in fact, many already have. I cannot think of a single acquaintance of mine, who is under fifty, who would hold aloof from you because you had no caste, and you need not fear insult because of it. New ideas are clamouring at our gates and we must let them in.

'Our strength – yours and mine – lies in that we are

financially independent of Father. I have saved and so have you and this can be our capital. Never fear, dearest one, that we shall come to real harm – only I would be infinitely happier if Father acquiesced to our marriage.'

And so on, assuring me of his eternal love. I wondered, and I feared. Was he telling me the truth? Could his father ruin us in the same way that other fathers had their sons?

I remembered the dark velvet of his skin and the matching deep timbre of his voice, and I ached for my husband.

Ajit put down his pen. Again and again, he had got up from his chair, to pace up and down the room, and then gone back to write more. How could he explain to me the formal, yet deep, relationship between parents and children in India, the invisible ties which made families and caste more important than the State or the country.

Thakkur came to say that tea was ready, but Ajit said he did not want any. Later, Thakkur brought his dinner on a brass thali and again he refused to eat. Thakkur removed the tray and went away grumbling that Maharaj had made all the dishes his young master liked and now they would be wasted.

Ajit laid his head on his desk. Thakkur made him feel like the unrepentant boy, who had on many occasions been banished to this room to do his homework. Depression flooded through him.

He moved to his divan and lay down on it, and watched listlessly as a few flies danced in the failing light. They would soon die in the summer heat, he thought. How would I endure the heat of summer? Shahpur was hotter than Delhi; he would have to take care that I observed caste rules of cleanliness, so as to lessen the chance of my falling sick. As he thought of me, desire throbbed in him, desire to see, touch and hear me. What was the use of writing? What was the use? He turned over on to his stomach and beat his pillow with one fist.

When there was a sharp swish-swish of skirts brushing along the veranda outside the room, he imagined for a second that the intensity of his longing had brought me to him. But when he looked up, it was his mother who stood uncertainly on the threshold.

He sprang up and went to her, as she surveyed him anxiously.

'Ajit, Thakkur is right – you have a fever – your eyes are too bright – I thought you were studying – otherwise I would have come to see you earlier.'

She entered, and with a graceful movement, sat down on the divan.

'Is it malaria? You have not eaten all day.'

Ajit sat down beside her, and she turned the table fan so that it did not blow directly on him.

'No, Mother,' he said, with a wry smile, 'I have no temperature.'

She took his hand and felt his pulse. 'No,' she said doubtfully, after counting carefully, 'there is no fever.'

She made herself comfortable by tucking her feet up under her and arranging her sari. It was clear to Ajit that she knew something was wrong and wanted to hear more about it. He imagined that his father must have told her at least in part of the quarrel of the morning, and his heart sank. That meant the news would go through the family like a cholera germ. To his surprise, however, she did not mention the matter. She said instead: 'Tomorrow is Holi. We are having a tea party for you and I have asked all your old friends. Your uncles are coming and Dr Chand Rana is bringing Mrs Chand Rana and Bimla. Bimla has grown into a great beauty since you last saw her – I think you will like her.'

'Ji, hun,' assented Ajit without enthusiasm. He shivered slightly. Beautiful, certainly – beautiful as a volcano – liable to eruption.

'Shushila has been buying powder for days, so that she can play colour with you,' went on his mother, all the time watching his face through her veil. He could feel her eyes taking in every slight alteration in his expression. She must have noticed him shiver at the mention of Bimla.

The tension in Ajit eased as he heard of Shushila's preparations for the Spring Festival. Of course, he would play with her. They would have tremendous battles with the small boys nearby, each one of them armed with a pail of coloured water. Honour would not be satisfied until every shirt in the neighbourhood had been drenched with rainbow colours. Her day should not be spoiled by his perplexities, he vowed to himself.

'Of course – both Bhim and I will play with her, Mother.'

Mrs Singh chatted on, her lively hands from time to time flashing out from her lap to emphasise a point. She took Ajit's silence for granted – he was being courteous in allowing his elder to speak uninterrupted, and he let her run on until finally she had exhausted her news. Then she tried to persuade him to take some food, but he declined gently.

Then she said: 'Tell me about England. How do ladies live there? How many servants do they have?'

He did his best to describe to her a servantless country, where even high-caste, rich ladies ofted did their own cooking, swept their own floors and made their own clothes, and even went to the bazaar by themselves.

All this Mrs Singh could visualise better than many ladies of her caste and class. She herself had been brought up in a village, the daughter of a small landlord, and had been married to Ajit's father when she was thirteen, long before his grandfather had made the money which had laid the foundations for the remarkable prosperity of his sons. She could herself cook, and had as a very young girl worn the blouse and skirt of a village woman and played in the fields, at harvest time. She had known more freedom in her native village than she knew now, in spite of her husband's lifting of her purdah.

She sat and contemplated her sandal which hung precariously from one of her straight, soft-skinned toes.

'Do they wear bracelets?' she asked, fingering the golden collection on her wrists.

Ajit thought of the gold bracelet he had bought for me, at the time of our engagement, and my pleasure at the gift.

'They do wear them,' he said. 'A gold bracelet is much valued.'

His mother must have noticed a sadness in his voice, because she said fearfully: 'My son, you are ill,' and she flung her sari back from her face and looked at him closely.

He lifted his eyes to hers, and all the pain and worry must have been shown to her.

'Ajit, what is this? What is the matter?'

His eyes flickered and then moistened.

'Mother,' his voice faltered. 'Mother – oh, Mother,' he cried and flung himself full length beside her. The misery in him welled up and regardless of ceremony he wept.

She was shaken by the outburst, but she lifted his head on to the lap made by her crossed legs, and stroked the smooth, black hair. For a time she just crooned softly to him, rocking herself as if she were nursing a baby, and wiped away the tears with the end of her sari.

'Say, Ajit, say what is the matter. It is my privilege to love and counsel you.'

'Has Father not told you?'

'Told me what?'

'About Peggie.'

'About Paickie. No. What is Paickie?'

He realised too late that his father had said nothing to his mother, but he could not withdraw and, in any case, she would have to know sooner or later.

Thakkur came to arrange the mosquito net over the divan for the night, but Mrs Singh gestured him silently to go away.

'What is Paickie?' she repeated.

Hiding his face in the folds of her sari and holding her hand in such a tight grip that it must have hurt her, he told her the whole story. He admitted his wrong conduct and asked her forgiveness.

'She is beautiful and good, and she would serve you well, Mother,' he finished up.

As she later told Bimla Chand Rana, she was shocked beyond imagination, and her first instinct was to say that he must accept his father's advice, get rid of the foreign woman and marry Bimla his caste sister.

Then she remembered suddenly, she said, a similar occurrence in Jaipur, where her sister lived. A young man, Mohan, had come home from America and had asked his parents' permission to marry an American. The parents had refused permission, and, as they held the purse strings, they had been able to insist that he must marry a woman of their choosing. Mohan had shut himself up in his room and had fasted for days. One night, he had emerged when the family was asleep, and the next morning he was found dead among the trees at the far end of the compound, dead from a cobra bite, although none knew that a cobra was in the vicinity. It was said that God Shiva had taken pity on him, killed him and taken his spirit to himself, so that he might be spared rebirth.

During his mother's silence Ajit lay with his head in her lap. He could hear the kitchen boy scrubbing the brass vessels used at dinner; he was slamming them on to the stone floor as he turned them round and round, in order to scour every corner with sand and coconut fibre.

The first words his mother said were: 'The new thalis will be dented – I must tell Gopal to be more careful.' Then she said cryptically: 'Shiva shall not have you – no, not even if you have three English wives.'

Ajit looked up somewhat astonished at the remark, and she smiled down at him and stroked his head.

She began to ask him questions, surprisingly shrewd questions, considering that she had seen little of the world and could not even read very well.

'What is the custom of marriage in England?' she asked. 'Do the parents arrange it? How is a girl brought up? How do they deport themselves?'

Ajit fumbled for his handkerchief. No pockets in a dhoti, he thought irritably. His mother picked the errant piece of linen out of his shirt pocket; he took it and blew his nose. Then he sat up, cross-legged, took his mother's hand in his again, and carefully and in detail he answered her questions, just as he had about a month before answered my father's questions.

'What is Paickie like?'

He slipped off the divan, went to his desk and picked up a battered envelope. From it he drew a photograph of me, which he had taken himself. He had draped a silk scarf over my head and had demanded that I should not smile. The resultant portrait was oddly un-English.

Mrs Singh took the photograph, examined it closely and

said that I did not look like the English women that she had seen before.

Ajit affirmed promptly that I was fair like an English woman, but had the disposition of an Indian girl, quiet, modest and loving.

On finding that she was not trying to dissuade him from continuing the marriage, he went on to extol my virtues, until I would have found difficulty in recognising myself from the description. His mother heard him out patiently, her forehead creased deeply as she concentrated on what he was saying.

When he had finished she continued to sit in silence, twiddling her gold bracelets. Ajit quietly put the photograph, which she had returned to him, back into the envelope and replaced it on the desk.

Eventually his mother raised her head and said: 'It is a pity that your respected father should feel so strongly about Paickie, because he must know – ' her voice trailed off, then gained clarity again as if she had made up her mind to speak out: 'Father must know that Bhim and Nulini are not content. I had expected that he would be more careful over your marriage. Perhaps he fears his brothers' condemnation.' She sighed and added: 'No grandchild yet.'

Ajit's curiosity was awakened by her remark about his brother.

'What's the trouble with Bhim? He looked all right to me.'

'He may be all right – but Nulini is not. She is not happy. Dear Bhim has been so engrossed in being a good partner in his law practice, that he forgets his little partner at home.' Mrs Singh readjusted her sari over her head, and then continued: 'She is a good daughter-in-law – although she does wear such immodest blouses – and I cannot understand why he does not give time to her. A woman needs her husband near her quite a lot – and – and I am fearful of what may happen if he continues to neglect her.'

'What could happen?' asked Ajit impatiently. 'Bhim is a good husband – only last night I saw him give her money for embroidered sandals to match the saris I gave her.'

'Money for embroidered sandals is very well in its place, and Bhim works extremely hard – far into the night – so that she may have luxuries. Yet – I think she would go barefoot, if she could feel that she was necessary to him and not just a pretty doll to be well dressed and politely tolerated.'

Mrs Singh hitched her sari more closely round her, and pursed her lips thoughtfully.

'She is a doll,' she added. 'Not intelligent enough to know how to entice him from his work. Sometimes I long to advise them both – they could be so happy – but I am mother-in-law and must not come between them – I may do more damage.'

'Your wisdom is great, respected Mother. A chance to help them may come when Bhim feels more safely established.'

'Perhaps. I do not wish you also to be indifferent to your wife. It is time there were grandchildren in this house.'

'Peggie will bear children – and they will be fair. I could never be indifferent to her.'

'I was thinking if Bimla was your wife.'

'I will marry no one else but Peggie.'

Mrs Singh suffered the rebuke in silence, while Ajit paced up and down the room. The house was still, except for the occasional cry of the watchman, as he circled round the compound, and the squeak of the gate as he went through to the uncles' compound. Fainter and fainter grew his cry, as he moved up to the far end of the family's property, thumping his staff as he went, to warn all thieves to beware of his coming.

Mrs Singh began to speak – not of Peggie, but of the generations of women of her caste who had gone before her and how they had kept the honour of the family and of the caste, obeying the scriptures and daily making puja, keeping the feasts and fasts, and sharing life's burdens equally with their husbands, as was laid down in the marriage ceremony.

Ajit's heart sank. There was to be no understanding by his mother either, it seemed.

The old lady sighed. These customs were going. Was she

not out of purdah herself? Indeed, yes. Did Nulini keep the fasts? She did not. She could not say that she approved of the modern girl – but then her mother-in-law had not approved of her either. Caste barriers also were going. Did not Ram Singh himself sit down to eat with men of other castes? Why should he fear a casteless daughter-in-law? She would automatically become of their caste by her marriage. What mattered was a kind heart, a forbearing temperament, a suitable humility before the dictates of elders. She sighed again and looked at Ajit when she spoke of the latter requirement.

Ajit laughed quietly in his throat. He wanted to shout aloud. His mother was convincing herself that she could cope with Peggie.

'Did you say something, my son?'

'No, no, Mother.'

She passed her hand wearily over her face, and then said: 'Come here and sit with me. We must decide what to do about Paickie.'

Ajit came and sat beside her, while she opened her pan box, took out a cardamum, peeled it carefully and popped in into her mouth. Then she leaned forward and, speaking in a whisper lest anybody left awake should hear, she counselled Ajit as to how he should deal with his father.

At the end he rose and, bending humbly, he kissed the tiny foot with its swinging sandal. She laughed, withdrew her foot quickly and descended gracefully from the divan. She shook up the pillows, straightened the sheets, and told Ajit to put up the mosquito net and to sleep in peace.

Overwhelmed with gratitude for her advice and understanding, Ajit was dumb, but he went to the doorway with her and held back the curtain for her to pass through. She smiled at him and walked slowly along the veranda towards the kitchen. He felt calmer and leaned against the door jamb. The night breeze caressed him.

A light sprang up in the kitchen and through the big window he saw his mother move towards the small shelf on which the elephant-headed Ganesh sat staring accusingly at her. She struck a match, lit a bunch of incense-tipped sticks and put them into a wire stand before him. Then she stood before the god with hands held out in appeal to heaven.

Ajit had a nasty feeling that she was praying for forgiveness for being an undutiful wife. Her advice to him could hardly be said to coincide with that which his father had given.

CHAPTER FIFTEEN

'I have a headache – I could not sleep last night,' said Ram Singh the next morning to Mrs Singh and Khan, when they arrived with his breakfast.

Ram Singh always had a headache when faced with domestic issues, and the whole house always knew about it. Maharaj always received orders to make special tea, Ayah had to get out the rubbing oil, and the unfortunate clerk, who had followed his master into retirement, was sent hither and thither to bring his work to Ram Singh's bedside.

'What has upset him this time?' asked Thakkur of the clerk.

'I don't know,' said the harassed clerk. 'He gets worse as he grows older.'

Khan might have been able to tell him – but Khan was a very discreet man. He stood by Mrs Singh at Ram Singh's bedside, and silently held out his hand to Mrs Singh for the key to the box in which she kept the aspirins. She took the key off the bunch at her waist, and gave it to him, and he went to fetch the bottle from her room.

'My life is eternally filled with new problems,' Ram Singh sighed, as Mrs Singh massaged the back of his neck to ease the ache.

Mrs Singh made suitable comforting noises, although, as she told Ajit, she was a little amused, since she knew the cause of the headache.

'I could not sleep,' he said again.

Mrs Singh neglected to tell him that she had not even been to bed.

'Here are the aspirins. Khan, a glass of water. Now, just take two and lie back on your pillow for half an hour, and then I'll rub you.'

He lay back comforted. His wife had been comforting him ever since he was fifteen and she thirteen, and there is no doubt that he held her in great affection.

Khan went back to his post outside the door.

About an hour later, Ajit came to his father's room, having heard from Ayah that the headache had eased.

Khan was seated on the floor by the door, surrounded with pink knitting wool which he was winding into balls. As Ajit wished to establish friendly relations with the new servant, he inquired of Khan what he was going to make – he knew that many hill men were skilled weavers and knitters, though normally their wives did this work, while the men themselves went on trading journeys between Tibet and India.

'I am winding the wool,' Khan said softly, 'for Miss Nulini. Last time she bought wool, it shrank after washing, so she asked me to buy for her this time – because my fingers know good quality wools.'

Ajit looked at the small, strong hands as they deftly wound a skein into a ball. The man did not look up from his work – he had not risen at Ajit's appearance, because he had the skein stretched over his two feet to keep it from tangling. Ajit, therefore, gave a little cough to indicate to his father that he was there.

Ram Singh was washing his mouth out, after having managed to eat his breakfast; so Ajit stood just inside the door until the elder man gave a final gurgle and spat into the wash bowl. Then he raised his hands in salute and said: 'Namaste.'

Ram Singh dabbed his lips with the towel.

'Namaste. You may come in. Khan, take away this thali.'

Encouraged by the courteous 'good morning', Ajit moved further into the room, while Khan took away the breakfast tray.

Ram Singh climbed on to his divan, crossed his legs

neatly, straightened his round, black cap, and took up a paper from his desk.

When Ajit had heard about the headache, he had recognised the sign immediately. It invariably meant that his father was upset and torn by indecision over something, usually in connection with the family; so Ajit hoped that his father was feeling less sure that he was right about his son's marriage, less certain that an Indian daughter-in-law was essential to the family. It might also have occurred to his father, who was a very honourable man, that even English marriage vows were meant to be kept, and that it was not right to expect him to break them.

To go straight to the reason for Ajit's visit would have hardly been proper, so Ram Singh asked him if he had seen any of his friends yet. Ajit mentioned the visit of his cousins, and that there was to be a tea party that afternoon. He had already played colour with Shushila and the neighbours' children, as his blue-stained hands testified.

At the mention of a party, Ram Singh unbent a little. Ajit knew that, despite his efforts at prayer and contemplation, Ram Singh still enjoyed a party, especially a tea party, with lots of hot, spiced samosas and sweet hulwa to nibble.

'The courtyard must be swept,' Ram Singh said promptly. 'Tell Pratap to make sure there are no snakes or scorpions there – it will be full of children this afternoon.' He thought for a moment, and then said: 'No. I will instruct Khan.'

Khan was still winding wool outside the door, and came immediately his master called. He was given the message for Pratap and instructions to help Mrs Singh and Thakkur to put out extra divans for the many matrons who would invade the drawing-room.

'They will enjoy talking scandal – scandal – ' he trailed off. Ajit felt sorry if he was thinking what a scandal his son's marriage could prove to be. At best at such a party there would be lots of jokes about the return of a marriageable son – and Bimla's presence would make all the guests surmise. The samosas would taste flat and greasy to his father during this party.

Ram Singh absent-mindedly picked up a glass pot of wheat seeds which had been lying on his desk, and turned it slowly round in his hands, gazing unseeingly at the contents as they slithered round the pot.

Wishing to divert him, Ajit asked if he was considering planting wheat on some of their land.

'Yes, I am,' said the elder man. 'If this strain does well, I will import some more and distribute it to the cultivators round about. They might get a heavier yield.'

Ajit was interested, and an amicable conversation ensued.

When at last the discussion languished, Ram Singh asked guardedly if his son had considered their conversation of the day before. He asked in the soft, melodious voice that had deceived many a lawyer in the courtroom into thinking that his client had the sympathy of the magistrate.

'Yes, Father,' Ajit replied. 'I have given deep thought to it, and I appreciate the kindness of your offer to help me out of the alliance which I have made.' He paused.

Ram Singh relaxed. So the boy would agree to his suggestions.

'Then?' inquired Ram Singh.

Ajit plunged in: 'Father – I should like to make some other suggestions, if you have no objection.'

The father looked exasperated, but nodded to his son to go on.

'In a week's time I must go to Pandipura to start work – and there also I have a flat. There also live but few of our caste brothers to speak to our family of what I do. I suggest that I send for Peggie and take her there.'

He stopped to take a quick look at his father's face. The expression was wooden and the moustaches stuck out belligerently as if the mouth beneath was compressed with disapproval. Ajit felt his cause was hopeless, but fortified by his mother's advice he continued doggedly.

'Let us stay there for a couple of years. In that time Peggie can easily learn enough of our customs never to offend your good taste and to enable her to fit into this house quite well. Unfortunately, it is not likely that at any time during my working life I shall be able to stay long at

116

home here. When the power house is finished and I have worked there for a few years, there will be better posts in other parts of India.'

Ram Singh was contemplating with great attention the activities of a fly walking on his desk.

'I cannot believe that your objection to my marriage is based entirely on Peggie's lack of caste. You have on many occasions denounced its evils. Rather you must fear the scandal if Peggie should misbehave or should leave me.'

The fly was cleaning its wings.

'If she came straight to Pandipura, you would not have to associate yourself with the marriage.

'If it was not a success and Peggie left me,' Ajit swallowed hard, 'would you – in your goodness of heart – forgive me for my rashness? I would humbly admit myself in the wrong; and our family would feel that you had judged rightly, that I had been headstrong and you had wisely let me learn my lesson in this hard way, rather than cast me off.'

At the words 'cast me off' Ram Singh looked indignant – as if any good Indian father would dream of casting off any of his family, no matter what they had done.

'Nothing was further from my mind than casting you off,' he said defensively.

'If our marriage was a happy one – and I believe it will be – then – ' Ajit hesitated, 'perhaps you and Mother would receive Peggie into the family, forgiving us for our hasty marriage and taking pleasure in your grandchildren.'

He added: 'Thus all would be well. Our respected uncles could not condemn you as lacking in wisdom. They cannot, at the worst, say more than that I have been a very foolish young man and have a very benevolent and long-suffering father. The ladies of our household will not be troubled by someone who does not know their ways; and any scandal would not reflect much on our family as a whole, as it will take place six hundred miles away, in a distant province, and people would hear only vague rumours.'

Ajit stopped, having nothing more to say. He wondered agonisedly if his mother was right in her belief that a compromise could be reached.

Ram Singh brushed the fly off his desk and leaned his elbows on the hard surface. The room was very still. Ajit would have given his meagre bank balance to know exactly what his father's thoughts were, as he stood before him, and he was quite unprepared for the question which his parent suddenly asked.

'Is a child expected?' he asked, his eyes narrowing shrewdly.

Ajit smarted under the insinuation.

'It is unlikely,' he said sharply. 'There has hardly been time.'

'It would be as well,' said Ram Singh reflectively, chewing the end of his moustache, 'if no child arrived for eleven months from the date of the marriage.'

Ajit sighed with relief. His father might be willing to agree. Of course, if there was no child during this period, one subject of gossip would be eliminated. No one could say that Peggie had trapped him into marriage or that he had fathered the child of another man.

'There is also the question of the gold and silver which my daughters-in-law will expect at my death,' said Ram Singh from between bits of moustache. 'Your wife shall have her share, but in practice her sister-in-law may make it difficult for her to claim it.'

Ajit interjected: 'Father, do not think of death – you will be with us many years yet.'

'My son, it is my duty to consider the well-being of all of you at all times. I will specifically mention in my will what she is to have.'

'Father, you are indeed kind. You will not regret my marriage to Peggie.'

'We shall see, we shall see,' said Ram Singh testily. 'In the meantime I have to tell Rana Sahib that I withdraw my offer for Bimla – and a good dowry will be lost, too.

'Shall I never know peace in my life?' he added savagely. 'My sons never consider my feelings – never realise what their foolish actions mean to me.'

Ajit hung his head, and muttered: 'Perhaps one of uncles' sons would do in my place.'

'Possibly – and there is another problem. No mention

must be made to your uncles of this woman you have married.'

'No, Father.'

While they had been talking, Ajit had been standing up, since his father had forgotten to tell him that he might sit. His father now said: 'Sit down, sit down, boy. Why do you stand gawking at me? Here I am, trying to mitigate the result of your hotheadedness, and what do you do – you stand and say "No, Father".'

Ajit sat down hastily on the edge of his father's divan.

'Khan,' shouted Ram Singh.

The rapidity of Khan's entrance indicated that he had been very close to the door, and Ajit hoped the servant was as discreet as his looks implied.

'Bring tea,' demanded Ram Singh, 'with nutmeg and cinnamon in it.'

The old man is making peace, thought Ajit; he must be regretting his hasty words of yesterday.

It did indeed seem as if Ram Singh was anxious that Ajit should be right in his remarks about his marriage and that, having tentatively agreed to my coming to India, he wished that Ajit should not suffer more than was necessary from his 'mistake'. He spent some time in counselling his son on the proper management of his affairs, both financial and matrimonial, and he lavished as much thought in lecturing him on the care of his wife as most English fathers would have done in advising their sons on the care of a pedigree dog.

While they drank tea, Ram Singh dealt with the details of the duties of a householder, ranging from the keeping of household account books to the saying of prayers twice daily; and as he went on his temper improved. It was apparent to Ajit that he feared a scandal most of all, and once the chances of that had become slender he was willing to co-operate with his son, to a degree.

When at last Ajit was dismissed, Ram Singh's anger had evaporated and only a distinct coolness showed that his son was not yet restored to parental favour.

Mrs Singh was summoned to her husband's room and informed of the marriage. She looked suitably surprised,

119

murmured that Ajit was a sensible boy and that his father should be complimented upon his wisdom in not being too hard on him, at which Ram Singh cleared his throat and looked embarrassed.

'May I give daughter-in-law a wedding present? And may I tell sisters-in-laws about the marriage?'

'No,' roared Ram Singh, so that Mrs Singh jumped.

'No present?'

Ram Singh shook his head irritably, and dismissed the present with a wave of his hand: 'You can give a present if you wish – but on no account is anybody to be told about this misalliance. Nobody must know of it – it will cause trouble enough without people speculating about it now. I shall speak to Bhim about it, after which the matter will not be mentioned either in my presence or in my absence.'

'Ji, hun,' said Mrs Singh.

'I have only agreed to it, because I do not want my son to go away to England again and perhaps never come back.'

'Ji, hun,' said Mrs Singh, rising to her feet.

'I don't know what the younger generation is coming to – defying their parents as they do.'

'Ji,' said Mrs Singh as she moved towards the door. 'Would you like some more aspirins?'

'No,' snapped Ram Singh, and added as an afterthought: 'One sari will be sufficient present.'

'Ji, hun,' said Mrs Singh.

CHAPTER SIXTEEN

In spite of the silence imposed by Ram Singh upon his family with regard to Ajit's marriage, there was an undercurrent of sly whispers amongst the ladies present at the tea party. When Mrs Singh approached a group, the conversation ceased or the subject was changed.

Ajit also felt that his private affairs were the subject of gossip, so he sought the company of Shushila and the other children playing in the courtyard, and left the entertaining of the younger men to Bhim.

It is likely, he thought, that Bimla has heard of father's negotiations with Kasher Chand Rana and has confided her hopes to her girl friends, and it has caused some speculative gossip. In any case, it was well known that the two mothers had been friends in their youth and had declared that their children should marry each other. He had felt all eyes upon him when he made his bow to Bimla, who was gorgeously dressed for the occasion. Her jade-green shirt and trousers were silk and the matching veil was embroidered in gold. She turned languorous, brown eyes upon him and her voice was unusually soft, but Ajit felt cold at the idea of marrying her, and he excused himself and left her to his cousins, who were happy to take his place and flutter round her with tea and sweetmeats. Moths round the candle, thought Ajit.

The tea party was soon forgotten by Ajit as a minor unpleasant experience, in the rush of visits he had to make to old friends. He spent a considerable time playing with Shushila and in talking to his mother; his father avoided him as much as possible.

On the morning after the tea party, he accompanied his mother to the bazaar. She could easily have asked merchants to bring goods to the house for her to see, but Mrs Singh preferred to go to the bazaar herself. She was still near enough to her days in purdah to feel an exhilarating freedom in walking in public, and a certain wickedness in having her face unveiled and her head uncovered.

She and Ajit wandered in and out of sari shops together. Mrs Singh made several purchases of pieces of cloth for blouses. She bought no saris, however, and Ajit remarked on this as she usually bought sari and blouse piece together.

She said with a smile that she had plenty of saris.

When they returned home they washed the dust off their feet and Mrs Singh asked Ajit to carry her purchases to her room. He did so, and laid them carefully on a side table.

Mrs Singh took her keys from her waist, unlocked the storeroom which led off her bedroom, and vanished inside. Ajit sat down and switched on the fan. He was daydreaming when his mother came back loaded with multicoloured silks.

Taking a pale-blue blouse piece from amongst those she had just bought, she lifted from the pile of silk a length of almost exactly matching colour, ornamented at one end with silver embroidery.

'One,' she muttered, her forehead lined, as she peered at the colours to make sure they matched.

She did the same with a length of red silk, heavily patterned with geometrical designs in yellow and green, and then she added a third of yellow with a border of brown flowers and touches of gold embroidery.

'Help me to fold them up,' she commanded.

Ajit did so, and she lifted the neat pile and put it into his arms.

'For my daughter-in-law,' she said.

A lump rose in Ajit's throat as he received the first wedding present from his family. Eleven saris might have been expected as the usual gift; but, as his wife was not being recognised by his family, his mother was obviously giving from her own wardrobe three of the best saris she had.

She turned to lock up the storeroom, placidly chatting at the same time about the fashion in which Peggie should wear the garments; and Ajit was filled with gratitude towards his simple, but astute, mother, who had not once upbraided him but had heaped kindness upon kindness.

He put down the saris and, with a sharp movement, went to her, and bowed to touch her feet. She lifted him and smiled and patted him.

'My son,' was all she said, but it expressed all her devotion and all her desire for the real happiness of her child. However much she feared for him in his strange adventure, she was doing her best not to make it harder for him than it already was.

'Mother,' he said, 'Peggie will honour you, and I think she will always remember that her Indian mother was sympathetic towards her when she was new to this country.'

The bedroom door creaked, and they both jumped.

'Respected Mother,' said a silken voice, and Nulini slid

into the room, 'if you are agreeable, I will call on Bimla this afternoon.'

Mrs Singh hooked her key holder back on to the waistband of her petticoat, and said: 'Yes, go. Take Ayah with you – Shushi can go too, if she has done her lessons.'

Nulini was dismissed, but she lingered, leaning against the door, her sari swaying in the draught. Ajit, who had stood silently behind his mother, noted her daringly short blouse, which hardly covered the generous curve of her breast and left her waist naked. He wondered that his mother did not demand that she should wear longer blouses – perhaps she hoped that Nulini's modern dress would attract Bhim to her. In any case, there was no one else in the house who could be enchanted by a slim, bare waistline. She rarely met any men from outside the family and was invariably chaperoned wherever she went – it was doubtful if she had at any time been alone with a man other than her husband. His thoughts rambled on: 'I suppose Mother is wise in not criticising her and spoiling the affection which seems to have grown up between them – Nulini probably realises that she is lucky to have as much freedom as she has and that she owes it to Mother's understanding of her.'

'What a fine blue silk you have there, Mother. I have not seen it before – it would look well on you,' remarked Nulini, eyeing the sari covetously.

Mrs Singh looked guilty and said: 'Yes, I have not worn it for years. Now go on your visit,' and she turned away to open the window.

Behind his mother's back, Nulini made a little moue with her mouth at Ajit, and then went out as quietly as she had come, leaving Ajit thoroughly shocked. Sisters-in-law, he wrote to me indignantly, should hardly look at their brothers-in-law, and in many houses they still covered their faces at the approach of their husband's brothers.

Mrs Singh sighed. 'Perhaps Paickie will also be a good friend to Nulini – and to Bimla. Bimla has a great capacity for friendship.' She sat down on a mattress and tucked her legs under her slowly, as if they ached.

Ajit knew perfectly well what his mother was thinking

123

about, and said: 'I am sorry about Bimla, Mother.'

'Arree, don't worry about her – she is not in love with you.'

Ajit laughed, and picked up the saris.

'Shall I bring you some cool water to drink?' he asked.

She nodded assent.

He brought the water for her, and found her gazing abstractedly into her mirror. She put down the mirror and took the glass from him.

'Your children will be very fair, Ajit?' she asked.

'They will be as fair as the women of Peshawar.'

'Indeed? Ramji, that is very fair – and lovely.'

Ajit smiled and left her. He went to his room, and sat down to write to me.

Nulini, escorted by a grumbling Ayah and a jubilant Shushila, went to call upon her friend and confidante, Bimla Chand Rana.

Bimla found Shushila some coloured shells with which to play, and sent Mrs Singh's Ayah to join her own Ayah in the shade of a nearby mango tree, then she sat down with her friend on the swing which hung from the veranda roof.

'And how are things with you?' asked Bimla, tossing back her long plaits. Nulini seemed to be more on edge than usual.

'I am so bored,' said Nulini, pulling irritably at the cushion under her.

'Why? You have a good young husband.'

'Hmm,' sniffed Nulini, 'I have told you many times that I might just as well be single. I wish I was back in my father's house.'

'You should say to Bhim that he must take you out – he is modern – why, you could even dance together, as long as Singh Sahib never found out.'

'How can I tell these matters to a husband I hardly ever see alone? He never comes to my room – anyway, Shushila shares it with me – and he has asked that I should not go to his room unless he sends for me, as it interrupts his studies. Studies! Books!' She almost spat out the last word.

'He will be a great man one day.'

'A great man? And what am I to do in the meantime, pray? So rarely he sends for me and when he does he has an abstracted air, as if he is thinking of something else. He gives me money and tells me to buy myself something pretty. I do not care about money – it will not buy me a son.'

She looked down at her flat stomach and tears came into her eyes. Her voice was bitter as she said: 'Singh Sahib should not have insisted upon his marrying yet – he does not want to be bothered with a wife or children. I could have been enjoying myself, dancing at the club at home or playing bridge – instead, I waste away sitting on the veranda and knitting.'

Bimla put her arm round Nulini. 'If I were you, I would make him take an interest in me,' she said stoutly.

'You are different – you are not afraid of anybody.'

'Just wait until I come to the house – I will change all this – Ajit will eat out of my hand. Together, we will make the brothers less stuffy.'

'Arree, Bimla, troubled with my own woes, I forgot,' and Nulini caught her friend's hand. 'Such an uproar there is over Ajit.'

'Why, what has happened?'

'He has married an English woman.'

Bimla was off the swing in a flash, her face contorted with dismay.

'You lie!'

'I do not. It is true.'

Rage enveloped Bimla. She grasped Nulini's wrist.

'How do you know?' she hissed.

'Let go, Bimla, you are hurting me.'

'How do you know?'

'I was told.'

'By whom?'

Nulini twisted away from Bimla, and shrank into a corner of the swing.

'I will not tell you.'

'Have you been trying to win Ajit – and he has told you this to get rid of you?'

'No, no, Bimla,' said Nulini indignantly, as she rubbed her wrist.

'Did Mrs Singh tell you?'

'No.'

'Then how do you know and how do you know it to be true?'

Nulini blenched. 'Someone whose word I can trust told me.'

Bimla's rage left her as quickly as it had come and curiosity mixed with vague suspicions took its place. A small flickering fear for her friend warned her not to press her further. She asked no further questions and accepted Nulini's word that she had spoken the truth.

'Put an English woman in my place,' she muttered. 'How can I face my friends in such a situation – the humiliation of it. Father must demand that Ajit put her away – why, everybody knows he is going to marry me – the humiliation!' And she burst into tears.

CHAPTER SEVENTEEN

When I received from Ajit the letter in which he told me of the agreement reached with his father, I felt as humiliated as Bimla Chand Rana must have done when she found she had been superseded by me. I was most indignant at having to serve an apprenticeship before Ajit's parents would acknowledge my existence, and it was two or three days before calmer feelings prevailed and I thought comfortably that I should be living six hundred miles from them, so recognition did not amount to much. I could not know then what a comfort it was to be part of a tightly woven family in a country where any other protection from disaster was negligible.

On my next free day, the spring weather tempted me to pay a surprise visit to Angela, and I caught the mid-morning train down to Pentecost.

When I arrived at the farm, I was met at the door by the farmer's wife. Miss Delaney, she said with a faint air of disapproval, had gone for a walk with a Chinese gentleman, who was staying at the George and Crown. I assured her that Dr Wu was an old friend of ours, and her disapproval melted into curiosity. 'He's the first Chinese I ever saw,' she said. 'Is he living here for always? Would you like some lunch?'

I accepted the offer of lunch with alacrity and sat in the kitchen while she prepared the meal. As she beat eggs and peeled potatoes, I entertained her by telling her about the people who came from all over the world to study at Wetherport.

There was a peal of laughter from the direction of the front door, which was open.

'That'll be your sister.'

I nodded and walked down the hall to the front door.

Angela was sitting on a garden seat, and Dr Wu was doing an excellent imitation of Dr Gantry in a bad temper. I laughed and ran to Angela.

'Pegs,' cried Angela, flinging her arms around me in unusual exuberance, 'see who is also staying here.'

'Yes, dear,' I said. 'Dr Wu, I am really glad you decided to take a holiday.'

Dr Wu bowed. 'My holiday has been embellished by Miss Delaney's company. We met in the lane only yesterday.'

Wu smiled and walked on into the house, to give us time for a word together.

'Has Wu told you what has happened to him?'

'No.'

I told her what I had learned at the club and from him personally.

Angela stood stock still.

'I would never have guessed at such a tragedy,' she said. 'He has been so cheerful – what misery must be inside him? Poor man! All his dreams and beliefs lost . . .' She scuffed on the path with her shoe. 'Thanks for telling me.'

The farmer's wife came to the door: 'Lunch, Miss,' she called.

I slipped my arm into Angela's and we went together into the house.

*

At half past eight that night I put the key into the lock of our front door and turned it wearily. Entering, I flung my hat on to the hallstand as I had done ever since my school days. Mother called: 'Hullo, is that you, dear?' as she always did, and I was grateful for the routine sanity of it.

'Hullo, Mum,' I called. I was very tired and I wanted Ajit. The world had been a topsy-turvy place during the past month. There had been the hurried preparations for my marriage, then the exquisite peace of my honeymoon, to be followed by the rushing back and forth for passports, permits, passages and all the impedimenta of travel, the uncertainty about Ajit, the finishing up of my work at the club. It all added up to an enormous expenditure of nervous energy.

I went into the kitchen, sat down thankfully on a primrose-yellow chair, and rested in the gentle stream of Mother's inconsequential chatter.

Three weeks later I abandoned the safe refuge of our old, Victorian house, and the parents who had, if anything, sheltered me too much from the rigours of life, and embarked for India.

It was then I discovered that the pain of departure is a real pain, a physical racking as if part of one is being torn away. As the three beloved figures waving from the dockside grew smaller and smaller and the tugs moved the great ship out into midstream, even the thought of Ajit's waiting for me could not ease the cruel wrench, and I clung to the ship's rail feeling that I would collapse if I let go.

During the upheavals of the war, I had been blessed by being allowed to stay at home, and the fact that my present banishment was self-imposed did not make the leaving less painful. Until the night came down and there was nothing to be seen except the foam falling away from the ship's bows, I stood in anguish by the rail; and then a kindly stewardess came to inquire if I was Mrs Singh, and when I said I was, she said she had put in my cabin a bouquet of flowers sent by a Dr Wu.

I went downstairs. A bouquet of daffodils lay on the

dressing-table in my cabin and attached to it was a note. I opened it and read:

> 'Deep is the water in the Peach-blossom spring,
> Deeper still is our hearts' feeling
> When good friends are leaving.'
>> Best wishes for your happiness.

It was signed simply 'Wu', the name by which he had always been known to me.

CHAPTER EIGHTEEN

Shahpur station is big, but when our train drew into the platform at the end of a hot May day it was crammed to capacity with a shouting, milling crowd and with immense piles of luggage, amongst which strode the railway police with their rifles slung over their shoulders.

A thin, red-shirted, red-turbaned porter piled on to his head our tin trunk, two pigskin trunks and a bedding roll, took a suitcase in each hand, and then motioned us to lead the way to the ticket barrier. Ajit, tickets in hand, pushed a way for me through the crowd, and I followed, clutching my unaccustomed sari closely round me.

Ajit had been waiting for me on the wharf when my ship docked at Bombay. I had dressed myself in the sari he had given to me at our engagement and when I took a last peep at myself in the cabin mirror, I had been surprised. The restful voyage, together with better food than I had tasted since before the war, had helped my figure and cleared my complexion, and the scarlet sari became me. Ajit had bounded up the gangway as soon as he was permitted to do so, caught my hands and looked into my face, while porters and passengers fought around us. Words did not come easily to either of us, but we both knew a wave of feeling. I knew I had come home.

'You – you look wonderful,' gasped Ajit at last.

'It's wonderful to be with you,' I said, slipping my arm into his and clinging close to him, as we became engulfed in deckhands and customs officers.

We managed to get the luggage through the customs quickly enough to enable us to catch the day train up to Shahpur; and I sat through the day in a semi-daze compounded of intense heat, great happiness and a terrifying flow of new experiences. So I walked out of Shahpur station following Ajit closely, while my new fellow countrymen looked at me with great curiosity.

Immediately outside the station we were buttonholed by a rogue in a red fez. He was carrying a long whip and he thrust his bearded face into Ajit's and shouted: 'Tonga, Sahib? Where to?'

'Pandipura. How much?'

A dismal expression was promptly assumed by the tongawallah. 'Arree, Sahib,' he whined, 'Pandipura is a long way, fully seven miles over poor roads. It will cost four rupees.'

'Three rupees,' countered Ajit, although he was swaying with weariness, having spent the previous night travelling to Bombay; his khaki shirt was black with sweat. I kept very close to him and clutched my handbag firmly.

Other tongawallahs were closing in upon us, attracted possibly by foreign suitcases on the head of the porter, who stood patiently near us, his eyes averted from me.

I pulled my sari well over my head and face, to avoid the stares of the passers by, and concentrated on the conversation. My weeks of study had not been in vain. Provided the sentences were short, I understood the gist of the tongawallah's speech. Ajit was answering him in Hindi, which the man apparently understood.

The tongawallah saw his rivals bearing down upon us and struck a hasty bargain at three rupees and four annas. The porter heaved some of the luggage into the high-wheeled horse carriage, and reverently laid my pigskin cases on one side of the driver's seat. Then he straightened his back, spat into the dusty, cowdung-strewn courtyard, rubbed his hands on his loincloth and held one out for his tip. Ajit paid him and he salaamed low.

The tongawallah saw the salaam and immediately became more obsequious. He must have realised that Ajit's tip was generous and thought that we were people of importance. He let down the steps at the back of the carriage, wiped the seats with the sweat rag from round his neck, and held the door open.

I put my hand into Ajit's and was helped inside. Out of the corner of my eye I saw the tongawallah gape as he saw my white hand, and his eyes shifted to my sandalled feet. It had dawned on him that one of his passengers was a Memsahib, and to him that meant that Ajit must be at least the son of a Raja – only a man as rich as a feudal lord could afford to keep a white wife.

Ajit climbed in and the tongawallah absent-mindedly folded up the steps, shut the door, walked round to the front of the carriage and laboriously climbed on to the driver's seat. He gave his horse a flick with a whip, and we were off.

The name of the owner-driver of the tonga, with his registration number, was painted on the back of the carriage, and as Ajit helped me to settle myself on the narrow seat, I asked him: 'Is Mohamed Ali a Muslim name?'

'Yes,' he said, looking surprised at the question.

'I thought all Muslims had gone to Pakistan.'

'No, no, there are more Muslims still left in India than are in Pakistan.'

'And are they safe? Do you still have riots?'

'Hindu-Muslim riots are becoming rare now. The police do their best to stop any disturbances before it becomes a riot.' He mopped his brow with an already sodden handkerchief. 'Ten thousand Muslims live in the middle of Shahpur, surrounded by Hindus, and I think Mohamed Ali would tell you that he does not take any more precautions for the safety of his family than a good father in India has always done.'

I was impressed. I knew of the religious and economic contentions between Hindus and Muslims – and I knew also that in West Pakistan very few Hindus were left.

The carriage was clattering over the cobblestones of the station yard, the driver shouting to people to get out of the way; beggars, fruit vendors and children scattered in all directions. The driver leaned down and said something rude to a turbaned taxi driver, who was trying to manoeuvre his vehicle through the yard gates. The taxi driver retorted angrily.

Ajit saw the incident, and said: 'Most of the taxi drivers here are Sikh refugees from West Pakistan, and they naturally hate the tongawallahs who are their competitors as well as being Muslims.' He grinned, as with a fine flow of language the taxi driver got through the gate and passed under the nose of Mohamed Ali's horse. 'Most of their fights are verbal,' he added.

As the tonga plunged into a narrow side street, I glimpsed a forest of mill chimneys sticking into the sky. Then we were ploughing through the cloth bazaar.

I leaned my head against the awning support and gazed in bewilderment at the packed street. A human flood eddied and flowed against the carriage wheels. The pavements were packed with people and crowds walked in the middle of the street. Each shop entrance was the centre of a small whirlpool of purchasers; and even the verandas overhanging the streets bore a burden of lounging women and children.

Our tongawallah frequently exploded into speech, as children ran nearly under the horse's hooves or a cyclist cut across the animal's nose, causing it to snort with fright. Once we had to stop while a string of camels, walking with the aloof air of mannequins at a fashion show, swayed across the road and vanished down a side street.

I laughed at their enormous dignity and said: 'It's a little different from Regent Street.'

Ajit rubbed the sweat from his forehead. 'It is,' he said. 'I hope you will be able to manage here, darling. I wish we could have settled in the north instead of in this stinking hole – but Pandipura is a little cleaner and quieter than Shahpur itself. The noise here is dreadful.'

The noise was indeed worse than the heat or the overcrowding; car horns vied with the shouting of vendors; the harassed clang-clang of temple bells competed with blaring radios; and bicycle bells and camel bells seemed to ring in my head.

'I'll get used to it,' I said, with more determination than conviction.

'I won't,' said Ajit gloomily. 'The whole town ought to have been razed to the ground two hundred years ago and then rebuilt. It's so squalid.'

'We've plenty of squalor in England,' I said, 'and at least people here look aboundingly alive and their diversity is amazing. Just look at that old man over there,' and I pointed to a countryman, dressed in the traditional white jacket and loincloth and red turban. He had one arm round the shoulders of a boy about twelve, who was supporting him as he walked. The old man also carried a staff to aid him in his slow progress through the crowd. The expression on his face, as he looked down at the boy and addressed him, was one of great tenderness; every wrinkle was softened and even the bushy, white eyebrows had a gentle curve. The boy's face had a clear, innocent look long since missing from Western faces.

Seeing that I was not horrified by the dirt and the turmoil, but only sympathetically interested in the people swarming about the tonga, Ajit lost some of his gloom and after a quick glance to see that the tongawallah was minding his own business, he took my hand and squeezed it, and as we jogged along he pointed out whatever he thought might interest me.

We passed a marble building smothered in intricate carvings. Its metal door gleamed dully in the fading light, and, though crammed between narrow, dirty shops, its beauty was obvious.

'What is that building?'

'It's a Jain temple built hundreds of years ago – the door is solid silver.'

'If the property round it was cleared away, it would look exquisite,' I said.

Ajit laughed. 'You will find that throughout this town beauty is buried beneath rubbish and dirt. Cotton and chemicals and the money they make are all that matters here.'

'That is not true. Somebody keeps the temple – its steps had been swept.'

'You are too observant,' Ajit said. Then he changed the subject and told me about our flat. He said it was a good flat by Indian standards, one of a block of eight built by the Government to house some of the staff of a new University. Except for the University itself, there was no other building for nearly a mile in any direction.

'I do not know why they built these accommodations in such an isolated place – unless they want to encourage building in that area.'

We passed out of the town and bumped along a dirt road. The tonga moved more and more slowly and, finally, after a particularly hard bump, it came to a stop.

'Sahib,' came a plaintive voice from the direction of the driver's seat, 'this is the Pandipura road. How far along is your bungalow?'

'At least three more miles. Drive on.'

'I must light my lamps, Sahib,' said Mohamed Ali, and sighing copiously he got down and lit the oil lamps on either side of the carriage. 'By the Beard of the Prophet, this is a very bad road.'

The tonga started off again and creaked its way through the near darkness. There was a breeze and its coolness was welcome. Far off, I could hear drums being beaten in an exciting rhythm.

At the end of twenty minutes the tonga stopped again.

'Sahib,' said the mournful voice, 'the horse can go no further. The road is too bad.'

Ajit leaned out. 'This road is no worse than any other road outside the city,' he said sharply. 'Get a move on.' And he sat back in his seat; but the tonga did not move.

'Arree, Sahib, this is the worst of roads and the horse is getting lame; if the horse is lamed how can I work? – my children will starve.'

'Don't be foolish,' snapped Ajit. 'The horse has travelled over worse roads than this.'

Resignedly, Mohamed Ali gave the horse a light flick with the whip. The horse stirred uneasily but did not move forward. It was now quite dark and the jackals were beginning to howl among the bushes, which reared man-high at the side of the narrow path.

'See,' said the driver, triumph in his voice. 'The poor animal is exhausted. I must go down and walk with him.' And he got down and went to the horse's head, but still the carriage did not move.

'And Sahib,' the voice floated ghostlike out of the darkness, 'the harness is strained. Supposing it snaps with the jolting – how can a poor man like me expect to buy new? Truly this is an unlucky day for me.' The voice trailed off.

The drums sounded menacing and there was a horrid smell about the carriage; later I was to know that smell well. It was the stink of a jackal. One must have been quite near us. Why, in heaven's name, could we not move?

I had followed the main theme of the conversation, and said to Ajit: 'Why not offer to pay a little towards the cost of the harness if it breaks?' I drew my sari closer round me, as a protection against the insects which bumped into me as they flew towards the oil lamps.

'All right,' said Ajit to Mohamed. 'If the harness breaks we will pay eight annas towards its repair.'

'If the Sahib would give a few more annas, I could feed the horse well tonight and could risk working him hard now, since with a good feed he would recover by morning.'

Such solicitude for the ill-used bundle of bones he called a horse struck Ajit as funny and he laughed.

'How much?' he asked.

'Another four annas, Sahib, would mean a good feed for him tonight.'

'That makes four rupees altogether,' said Ajit ruefully. 'I agree.'

Mohamed Ali climbed back on to the driver's seat with remarkable alacrity, gave the horse a merciless thwack with the whip, and the carriage lurched forward. I clung to Ajit, to save myself being thrown out, and began to laugh. Ajit clutched me, and gasped: 'Play-actor – all that trouble to get twelve annas.'

'Such a waste of time,' I said, trying to look sober.

'Oh, no,' said Ajit, 'he earned twelve annas.'

So I had my first lesson in bargaining in a country where time is plentiful and cheap.

Ajit had told me on the train that he had obtained a boy servant for me. He had had great difficulty in getting one, as most labour was taken up by the mills; and his parents had not been prepared to send one from their house because they wished the marriage to be kept secret. He had, however, talked to the headman of the nearest village, and, knowing that Ajit was working at the power house and not wishing to antagonise a man who, if offended, might cause some of his people working on the power-house building to be dismissed, he had sent Ajit to the grain bazaar to see his brother, who dealt in lentils.

The brother was a wily-looking individual; he had none of the upright, honest air of his country brother, but he had recommended a boy who had just been dismissed by Shah Vakil.

'Why was he dismissed?' asked Ajit.

The grain dealer ran his fingers through some lentils lying in a sack by his side. 'The Vakil said he was a thief, Sahib, but in my opinion, that Shah Vakil's law practice is shrinking and he wished to get rid of the servant without loss of face.' The lentil dealer spat on to the pavement. 'The boy is honest, Sahib, and he can cook. He is an agriculturist by caste – a Patel – but, Sahib, you cannot expect to get a servant of your own caste in this town,' and he shrugged his shoulders hopelessly.

The Sahib agreed with all the grain dealer had said, so Babu became our servant, and Ajit had been coaching him in his duties for a couple of weeks before my arrival.

Now, as the tonga tore along the narrow track, swaying perilously from side to side, Ajit said irritably that Babu should have put the front lights on in the flat, so that we could find our way. All the other tenants were spending the hot weather in the hills, so there was no other light to guide us. 'Big building on the left?' shouted Mohamed Ali, reining in.

'That's it,' said Ajit, with a sigh of relief.

The tonga stopped and a hungry, weary couple made their descent. We had been travelling since early morning – but for me this lonely spot was the end of twenty-one days of journeying.

'Babu, come and help Memsahib,' yelled Ajit, 'and take the luggage.'

The walls echoed back the cry and no one came. Outside the ring of light from the tonga lamps, the darkness encircled us like a wall. I moved closer to Ajit while he paid the driver, and they got down the luggage and dumped it into the sand.

'Babu, chelo!'

But Babu did not come, and there was not a glimmer of light from the flats. The tongawallah whipped up his horse, quickly turned the carriage in the clearing near the house and started back to town.

Ajit struck a match and we picked our way through odd bricks and builder's rubble, round to the entrance of the flat, which was on the ground floor and had a separate entrance.

'Babu,' shouted Ajit with real annoyance in his voice.

Only the echo answered.

'He must have fallen asleep,' said Ajit.

A flight of stone steps led up to a small veranda. Ajit ran up the steps ahead of me, but pulled up short at the top.

I too could see that the front door was open, and I too realised that in such a deserted spot any servant left alone would surely have bolted it shut. There was no light within.

Ajit backed quickly down the steps.

'Peggie,' he said softly, 'just wait here quietly while I see that all is well.'

CHAPTER NINETEEN

I stood in the lonely dark and was dreadfully afraid. Far, too far, away, I could hear the jingle of the harness bells on the receding tonga.

Ajit bent down and picked up a brick, then glided up the steps with it poised for action. He paused on the top step and then moved swiftly to the entrance, and, standing on one side of the doorway, so that his body was shielded from any missile discharged from within, reached round into the room and switched on the light.

The light sent a pariah dog speeding away with fright, but I felt better now that I could see; and I picked up a brick and followed Ajit.

He had meanwhile peeped into the room, seen that it was empty, and crossed quickly to a second room which led off it; it was also empty. He turned to the other door leading off the main room and went through to the kitchen, and then to the bathroom and storeroom. Both were empty. In the kitchen a charcoal fire still glowed faintly in a tiny stove on the floor, and round it were grouped open cooking pots full of food. The back door was bolted.

He was puzzled. I stepped up behind him and he whirled round, brick raised to smash down on the intruder's face.

'It is only I,' I said. 'Don't look so grim.'

Relieved, he lowered the brick and said: 'It was not good that you followed me.' He looked round. 'I cannot understand. Babu has cooked – everything is in order – but where is the boy? Unwise to leave the front door open like that – dogs might have eaten our dinner.' He laughed nervously, and put the brick down on to the floor.

'I will bring in the luggage.'

'I'll come and help.'

'You are to stay here,' he commanded.

I started to object, but the look on his face was that of a man who expected to be obeyed, and I found myself acquiescing.

'OK, Chief.'

He grinned and pinched my cheek, but he shot the bolts of the kitchen door as he went out so that I could not follow. I heard him cross the living-room and then a muffled exclamation. I ran to the bolted door.

'Ajit, what is it?'

'All is well. It is Babu. Babu, what have you been doing?'

'Sahib,' said a feeble voice. 'Arree, Sahib.'

Ajit came and unbolted the door, and I nearly fell through in my haste.

'Good heavens!' I exclaimed.

A figure stood at the front door. It was clothed from head

to foot in thick mud, out of which stared a pair of weeping, bloodshot eyes. A horrible odour rolled into the room and wrapped itself round us. Mud splodged on to the veranda, and there was a trail of it leading into the darkness.

'What has happened?' I gasped. 'He can't come in while he is like that.'

'He can't,' said Ajit, his eyes twinkling.

'Tell him to sit on the steps for a minute. My God, how he stinks.'

'Betho,' said Ajit, pointing to the steps, and Babu still weeping loudly sat down with a plop.

I flew back into the kitchen to fetch some water, but could not find a bucket. There was, however, a large earthenware jar on a stone stand. It was already full of water, so I staggered out on to the veranda with it.

'Close your eyes. I'm going to pour water over you,' I said, feeling that drastic action was necessary to clear the main coating of mud; and I tipped the water over his head.

Unthinkingly I had spoken in English. Babu had not, of course, understood, and I had acted too quicky for Ajit to intervene.

The boy leaped up with a shriek, as I cascaded carefully cooled drinking water over him. Gurgling and choking he fled down the steps and stood in the darkness, howling like a young animal, so that the pariah dogs, startled from the hollows in the sand where they slept, barked alarmedly.

'Babu, Babu,' shouted Ajit over the lamentations, trying hard to contain his laughter. 'Come here. You must have a bath. Come now. Memsahib will not pour any more water.'

Snuffling and rubbing the mud out of his eyes, Babu came slowly back to the veranda. The water had had some effect. His face and shoulders had emerged from their covering, and he proved to be a dark, low-foreheaded lad of about fifteen.

I said penitently to Ajit that I was sorry I had frightened the boy. 'What shall I do? I had no idea the water was so cold.'

'There is a bucket in the storeroom. Fill it with water from the tap – the tap water will be warm from the sun –

and bring it here with an old cup and any soap you can find. I will stay here and calm him.'

I hurried to do as I was bidden, and when I returned with a bucket of water, Babu had stopped crying and was talking to Ajit in a slow, sulky voice.

Ajit stopped him and commanded: 'Go to the foot of the steps. Take off your shirt and have a bath.'

Babu looked at me resentfully, took the bucket from me, scooped up the water with his hand and washed out his mouth. After spitting over the veranda rail, he carried the bucket down the steps and a moment later the splashing of water announced that the bath was in progress.

'How will he take a bath out there?' I asked.

Ajit smiled. 'It will be somewhat cold, but he will use the cup to pour water over himself, then he will lather himself with soap, and rinse it off by pouring more water. Give him another bucket of water – and an old shirt and pyjamas of mine to wear. I think he has no clothes other than the ones he was wearing – I promised him two suits of clothes as part of his wages – I must order them.'

'Won't that be very costly?' I asked, as I delved in the cupboard for clean clothes. The cupboard was in chaos – clothes, blueprints, detective novels and bars of soap, mixed with crumpled bed-linen and my letters to Ajit.

'No,' said Ajit, 'it means only two each of shirts, cotton pants and vests.'

He fetched another pail of water and took it outside, with the garments I had found.

When he came back I was sitting on the floor in the kitchen, trying to coax the charcoal stove into burning again.

'What happened to Babu?'

Ajit fetched some more nuggets of charcoal from an old kerosene tin in a corner, before answering. 'I shall tell you – don't trouble with the fire – Babu will make it burn when he comes in, but these coals will keep it from dying in the meantime.' He sat down on the floor beside me and put his arm round my shoulder. He looked very tired, his eyes black-ringed.

'Babu has a friend who is a shepherd,' he said. 'This man

came to ask Babu for one or two bilis – the brown cigarettes village people smoke – and as dinner was ready, Babu sat on the veranda with him and they smoked, while the goats grazed around the house – at this time of year fodder is so scarce that they graze one herd during the day and another on the same ground during the night – anyway, the shepherd had a goat lying away under the trees at the back of the house, and it had just given birth to three kids. Two kids being the normal yield, Babu's interest was aroused, and, forgetting that our door was open, they walked off to have a look.'

He paused to look down at me. Hunger had made me weak and I had laid my head on his shoulder. I did not really care about Babu as long as he was not hurt; all I wanted to hear was the rich cadences of Ajit's voice and to feel him close to me.

Ajit sighed. 'Babu saw the lights of the tonga flash as it turned, realised what it was and started to run back to the flat, hoping to get in before we spotted his absence – but he forgot about the sewage pond, and in the darkness he plunged into it. It is not deep – but the banks are slippery and it would be hard to get out of it.'

I smiled, roused myself and stretched. 'Poor Babu,' I said, 'I think I should heat and serve this food – we are both hungry, and Babu must be exhausted.'

'Babu exhausted? He is a village boy – very tough. Besides, my Queen, you do not know how to make the bread.'

'That is true – I don't know.' I had heard about the bread-making which is the bane of every Indian household, but I had not been able to find anyone in Wetherport to give me a cooking lesson.

We resigned ourselves to being hungry a little longer. I felt as if I had been pummelled by new experiences and I resumed thankfully my former position with my head on Ajit's shoulder, while he whispered into my ear that he loved me.

It was thus that a clean, damp Babu first saw us properly, as he stepped noiselessly into the kitchen, his master's old shirt flapping round his knees. He looked at me with great curiosity, and then cast his eyes down.

'Goddess Rhada's sister, namaste,' he said softly, putting his hands together in an attitude of prayer.

I sprang away from my husband. 'Namaste, Babu,' I said gravely, and feeling uncertain of my Gujerati I asked Ajit to tell him to serve dinner. 'We shall all feel better when we have eaten.'

Ajit broke into Hindi, which Babu apparently followed quite easily; and, none the worse for his adventure, he moved stolidly about the kitchen collecting trays and brass cups, while the charcoal in the stove caught alight again.

'No drinking water, Sahib,' he said mournfully. 'I boiled it specially for Memsahib this morning, and now she has thrown it away.'

Ajit looked anxious, and then said: 'Make another fire and boil some more water; you can give me unboiled water.' He explained to me that being English I was more likely to get dysentery than he was, so tonight I would have to drink tea, since there was no means of cooling the newly boiled water quickly.

'Babu, Memsahib will show you how to make tea as it is done in her country.'

I acquiesced, and Ajit led me first to the bathroom to wash my hands – it contained only a small sink and an additional tap set shoulder high in the wall, and was neither very clean nor tidy. The towel was grey, so I wiped my hands on a clean handkerchief. We went back into the front room. Except for four straight chairs and a table, it was bare. Ajit closed the kitchen door and turned on the ceiling fan. We stood under its welcome coolness; and Ajit kissed me as I had dreamed of being kissed for many weeks.

There was a final clatter of cooking pots from the kitchen. Babu shouted: 'Khana heh, Sahib.'

We let go of each other, chuckling like conspirators.

'Food's ready,' said Ajit, and we sat down at the bare table, our weariness relegated to the background, each knowing that we had found again the sweet intimacy of our days in England.

Although I was so hungry, I viewed the coming meal with trepidation. I had tried to eat curries aboard ship but the mass of spice had nauseated me, and since then I had eaten English food both in the ship and on the train. This was my first Indian meal with Ajit, and I feared I would not be able to eat it.

I gathered up courage, as Babu, moving fast for once, came in with two large trays and set one before each of us. He paused anxiously. There is no doubt that he had cooked the food and arranged the trays with the greatest care, but he was not a professional cook and could not be sure whether his efforts would please me.

'He is probably wondering if he can possibly please a Memsahib,' said Ajit, sniffing appreciatively at the good odours coming from his tray. He motioned Babu back to the kitchen. The boy sighed and shot back to his breadmaking.

The tray in front of me was of well-polished brass and on it were three small, brass cups, each of which held a different curry. There was also a saucer with slices of raw onion, tomato and green chillie in it. A small heap of hot rice lay on the tray itself and by it a wafer-thin, hollow ball of pastry.

'Bread,' said Ajit in explanation of the latter, as he tore apart his own little ball and with a piece of it deftly lifted some curry from one of the brass cups and popped it into his mouth. 'Babu,' he shouted cheerfully, his round face beaming, 'Babu, bring Memsahib a spoon.'

Memsahib was, however, trying to emulate her husband and managed to convey a little food to her mouth.

I do not know how to describe the bliss of that first mouthful of food in my new home. To my astonishment it had a delicate flavour compounded of potatoes, peas and tomatoes. No burning chillies seared my throat, no heavy, fatty taste cloyed my mouth. It was very different from the curries of the ship, and, as I delved into the other little cups, I remarked on this difference.

'They probably had Goanese cooks on board ship. They tend to make food very hot and rich. This cooking is nearly the same as that of my home – it is North Indian food. I also told Babu not to put many chillies.'

'This is going to be fun,' I said, more relieved than words

can express. 'If I can eat, I can face anything.'

'I'm not going to starve you, darling,' said Ajit, rather taken aback. 'Even if you are not allowed to eat flesh here, you will not starve.'

'Not allowed to eat flesh! – you always ate meat in England.'

'We are living, my Rani, in a Jain community and they are against the taking of life. They tolerate us here only if we become vegetarians. That means no fish or eggs either.' He paused to shout to Babu for more bread. 'All the families normally living in this building are Jains, and since I am not from this province they asked the Government Agent, when they learned I was coming, to make it a condition of my tenancy that I would be a vegetarian.'

'This is going to make life awkward,' I remarked as I licked my fingers.

'I know. It means a purely Indian diet for you – I had to agree, as this is the only vacant flat within two miles of the power-house site.' He went on hopefully: 'If Babu would agree to its being brought into the kitchen, we could buy some meat at present, from the Muslim bazaar, and you could cook it, as the other tenants have gone up to the hills for the summer. They all work in a Government College near here and get months of leave.' He added regretfully: 'We shall get exactly three weeks.'

I giggled at the idea of asking Babu's permission to hold meat-eating orgies. 'Don't worry, darling,' I said. 'If all vegetarian food is as good as this, I shall not come to harm. If other wives can manage, I am sure I should be able to.'

Ajit blew me a kiss across the table.

When we could eat no more, Ajit produced cigarettes, and Babu took away the trays. I looked out of the barred window. The moon was high, lighting up a bleak, flat landscape. It looked cool.

'Could we walk outside?'

'Of course,' said Ajit. He went into the kitchen and told Babu to bring in the luggage, which had lain undisturbed in the sand where we had dumped it, and to wash the mud off the veranda.

'Come along,' he said.

We went out through the front door, carefully avoiding the smelly mud which Babu had deposited, down the moonlit steps and across the builder's rubble which had been left in front of the flats, to the track along which we had driven earlier. We paced up and down.

The scene was wild and lonely, but the silence was soothing after our hectic day. Only the drums still throbbed far away, although there was little sign of habitation other than our own; the track on which we walked continued across the plain, winding in and out of clumps of bushes and trees, and it alone hinted at the presence of others. In the sky above there was no mist or cloud and the stars seemed close enough to touch. On the wind came the smell of ripened crops, dusty sweet. My weariness fell away from me.

'Why are the drums being beaten?' I asked.

'It is the season of marriages.'

'I have come at the right time.'

'You have indeed, my love; the drums are beating for the farewell of the bride to her parents as she leaves to go to her husband's house.'

He bent and kissed me lightly. Arm in arm we went slowly back to the flat, and the happiness on Ajit's face as we passed through the shaft of light from the window was a full reward to me for coming to India.

CHAPTER TWENTY

I lay in the curve of Ajit's arm and watched the sparrows swinging on the window bars in the morning sunlight; their steady cheeping reminded me of my own cosy bedroom at Wetherport, so different from the almost empty stone room in which I lay. No curtains, no pictures, no cushions, no dressing-table spread with silver brushes, nothing of beauty in the whole room, except the sleeping man beside me: but I felt drowsily content, with my husband's arm as my pillow and a cheap cotton sheet to cover me.

I had left my watch in the living-room and had no idea of the time. Ajit had taken only twenty-four hours' leave when coming to meet me and had to return to work that day, so I eased myself gently away from him and got up. He stirred but did not wake. I covered him with the sheet and kissed him; then put on my dressing gown and went into the other room, shutting the door quietly behind me.

My watch said six o'clock.

I wandered into the kitchen, and looked round a little helplessly. Through the open door of the adjacent storeroom I could see Babu spreadeagled on a mat laid beside four large grain bins. He wore only his master's old pyjama trousers and his naked chest looked as thin as a feathered pullet's. Followed by the sound of his snores, I crossed to the back door and pulled back the heavy brass bolts. The snoring ceased, but after a pause it was vigorously renewed. I chuckled to myself.

The door opened on to a new world. There was no compound wall, and stretched before me was what appeared to be a desert. Right to the horizon the sand stretched, almost without undulation. There was a little foliage; round bushes of cacti flourished, and the sewage pond, in which Babu had taken his unexpected bath, was marked by a circle of remarkably green grass and shrubs. I saw that an open ditch led from the building to the pond and this was also fringed with greenery. An unpleasant odour of old soap drifted up from the water, and I was relieved that the lavatory, at least, was connected with a closed cesspool.

To my right, prickly cacti had been arranged as a hedge and from behind this came the sound that was to be the constant accompaniment of my life in India – a steady creak-creak as a tethered ox walked up and down to draw water from a well to irrigate the land. I could just see over the hedge a man standing on the lip of the well and tipping the filled water-skin, so that it discharged its contents into the irrigation channel below him; when the skin had emptied I saw the ox's horns as it turned to walk back up to the well so as to let the skin fall again into the water far below.

An occasional mango or neem tree was silhouetted against the brilliant blue sky, and under one of the trees sat a shepherd boy dressed in a red turban, white frilly jacket and loincloth. He was surrounded by goats munching cactus leaves, and, as I leaned against the door jamb, he took out a flute and began to play. Above his head, in the mango tree, there was a flash of grey bodies amongst the leaves. Monkeys, I thought, with childish delight!

A snuffling at my feet made me jump. A dog, like a greyhound dyed brown, was sniffing round me, ready to take flight at any moment. I bent to pat him, but he cowered down, and I saw to my horror that he was covered with swollen ticks. I hastily withdrew my hand and retreated to the kitchen.

'Babu,' I called softly.

Babu just snored.

I wanted some tea, but had no idea how to light the charcoal stove. I prowled round the kitchen. It was a bare room, stone-walled and stone-floored, as was the rest of the flat. A built-in cupboard with a mesh door presumably held food. On some shelves in an alcove was a collection of brass trays, cups and cooking pots, such as I had seen at dinner, together with some thick china cups and saucers. On a stone stand was the earthenware water pot, the contents of which I had emptied over Babu; a water tap dripped in one corner and in the floor beneath it was a grid over an open drain. The floor looked as if it had been recently scrubbed.

'How on earth does one wash dishes?' I wondered. 'No sink, not even an enamel bowl, and no means of getting hot water quickly. Instead of walking, I should have watched Babu last night.'

Feeling very incompetent about housekeeping, I decided that Babu must be awakened, which I did by shaking him by the shoulder. I think he had not been asleep for some time but had been watching me furtively. He gave a most realistic jump, however, and ceased his snoring.

'Rhadabahin,' he said politely, as he rubbed the sleep from his eyes. He rose and yawned hugely, opened a creaky tin trunk, and took out a twig and a comb. I did not

147

wish to disturb his normal morning routine – time enough for that – so I decided not to ask for tea but to await events.

Events were very slow.

He filled a bucket with water, took it outside the back door and, with much splashing and snorting, bathed himself. He squatted on his heels and while the sun dried him, he took out the twig and fluffed one end of it. Using it as a toothbrush, he cleaned his teeth. He scrubbed and spat into the sand and scrubbed again. He polished and rubbed until I began to give up hope about breakfast, but eventually the toilet was completed by a flick of the comb through his hair, and he lit a bili and sat for five minutes more, slowly inhaling the smoke.

I decided to take a bath myself and went to the bathroom. In the hurry of the previous evening, I had not noticed that, apart from the sink and the extra tap in the wall, it contained a bucket, a two-inch-high wooden stool and a couple of shelves which were littered with old bits of soap and rusty razor blades. An aged towel was looped over one of the bars of the window and a crow was sitting on it. He flew out at my entrance.

Not wishing to disturb Ajit by looking for a clean towel, I splashed myself all over with water and smoothed it off with my hands as best I could, realising with a sense of shock that the last time I had taken a bath had been on the train from Bombay. I wrapped myself in my dressing gown again and combed my hair with a broken comb which I found among the razor blades.

When I returned to the kitchen, Babu was stuffing newspaper into the lower half of a stove filled with charcoal, and I said hopefully in Gujerati: 'Food?'

Babu nodded, picked up the stove with a pair of pincers and took it outside the back door, where he laid a match to it. He fanned it with a straw fan and soon had a good fire burning, which he then transferred with his pincers back to the kitchen. Water was put on to boil.

There was a shout from outside. 'Dudhwallah,' and a pail clanked down upon the step. Babu picked up an aluminium pan, and the milkman squatted on his heels and carefully measured thin, blue milk into it.

148

The milkman was fat and his face was creased with laughter lines. His handlebar whiskers stuck out in a black fluff, nearly burying a pug nose. A cap which had once been white was kept in place by his cauliflower ears, and a thin shirt over a dirty loincloth completed his costume. He smelled of cows.

He took a quick look at me, as I stood in the middle of the kitchen, and lowered his eyes politely – but in that second the price of milk went up by two annas a pound.

He said in a subdued voice to Babu: 'An English woman? Your Sahib is a Hindu, isn't he?'

'Yes,' said Babu, as he put the lid on the pan. 'Sahib is Indian; Memsahib is English. She came yesterday.'

'He must be very rich to be able to keep an English woman,' remarked the milkman as he clamped the lid back on to his can.

'He gets Rs.700 a month and does not take bribes,' said Babu carelessly.

In order to hide my laughter, I hastily bent down over the fire and lifted the lid of the water-filled saucepan. What would Ajit say if he knew his servant was so well acquainted with his affairs?

Babu was continuing: 'Sahib is an engineer working on the new electric house,' he said proudly. 'He went to school for many years, and Lulbhai – you know, the peon at the electric-house office – says that when he is older he will be a powerful sahib.'

The milkman was impressed and looked as if he would like to ask more questions, but I was too near and he was not sure whether I could understand or not, so he hung his can on the handlebar of his bicycle and wheeled the machine away on to the track which led to the city.

The noise of the milk pail had aroused Ajit and he called me. I went to him eagerly.

'Put a cup of hot water into the bathroom,' he ordered without preamble, as he sat up in bed, 'and unpack my shaving things – and I'll need a towel and a big mug.'

I was shocked at the unexpected stream of abrupt orders, given without previous greeting. They struck me like a series of blows on the face. For a second I stood holding on to the door, trying to steady myself.

'Darling,' I said shakily, but my voice was hardly audible and the object of my affection had lain down again and covered his face with the sheet.

My first reaction was a desire to say: 'Damn you. Get them yourself or ask for them civilly.' Then I thought of our happiness of the night before and that I did not understand the customs of the country, so I crept away feeling very bewildered. Obediently I took some hot water from the pot on the fire. Babu had now lit a second fire, which was blazing underneath the milk pan, and the kitchen resembled an inferno, with a presiding devil whose floured hands whisked black pans, brass pots and food through the air with magical speed.

I placed the mug of water on the bathroom shelf and returned with hesitant feet to Ajit, who had climbed out of bed and opened the front door, only to be driven back by the smell of the mud which Babu had not washed away properly the previous evening. He yelled: 'Babu!'

'Sahib.'

A flood of Hindi poured from Ajit on the subject of servants who did not do their work properly. This was answered by placating shouts from Babu. The words came so fast that I could not follow.

'Dear Lord,' I thought, 'if they quarrel like this Babu will leave. What is the matter with Ajit this morning?'

'Don't be angry with him, darling,' I said. 'He could not see in the dark.'

'Angry?' he said. 'I'm not in the least angry. Get me a clean pair of trousers and a shirt.'

I bit my lip at the rough tone, but thinking it best to give no hint that I was hurt, I said as I went to the clothing cupboard: 'It's a lovely morning.'

'You wait,' said Ajit darkly, as he disappeared towards the bathroom and then reappeared flourishing a shaving brush. 'It will soon heat up.' He stood in the doorway of the sitting-room and lathered his chin. 'This evening when it cools we will go to the bazaar. You must learn to buy – otherwise Babu will cheat you.'

As he turned to go back to the bathroom he saw my face

in the light of the window.

'What's the matter, my Rani?' he asked most gently.

Tears threatened to disarm me, and Babu looked at me as he came past laden with cups and saucers.

Shyness and a quiet pride made me force a smile and say: 'Nothing.' To change the subject I asked: 'How do you take a bath in the bathroom?'

'Come and see,' he said, and led the way. I paused a moment to show Babu how to set out cups and saucers correctly on the table, and then followed.

As I advanced to the bathroom door, a hand came round and flung out a pair of pyjamas. I caught them before they hit me in the face. I peeped through the door. Ajit was sitting on the wooden stool, which he had placed under the tap, and water was pouring down over him as he lathered himself with kitchen soap and sang at the top of his voice, while the dirty water made a gurgling accompaniment as it flowed across the floor and down the open drain in one corner.

The singing stopped abruptly. 'Shut the door,' he shouted through the streaming water. 'You're making a draught.'

I shut it abruptly and leaned against the other side. I was trembling from head to foot, partly with suppressed rage and partly with fear. I fumbled for my handkerchief and blew my nose sharply; the abuser renewed his song and apparently had not a care in the world.

Muttering maledictions against men before breakfast, I went to look for clean linen trousers.

CHAPTER TWENTY-ONE

Ajit ate his breakfast quickly and almost in silence. I could not eat much, although the parathas, a kind of fried bread, were good. I was fuming over Ajit's rudeness, and away down inside me a feeling of panic was stirring. I was so terribly alone in this deserted place to which he had

151

bought me, and I had only him on whom to depend to guide me into a new life. The sharp tones of his voice echoed in my head and drowned the whispers of his usual kindliness.

He licked the last of the chutney off his fingers and suggested that I leave the housekeeping entirely to Babu for the day. It would give me time to unpack and to rest.

I assented listlessly and went out on to the veranda.

He called for water and having gulped down a couple of glasses full, he strode down the steps and mounted an old bicycle which Babu had brought out. He said: 'Take care of yourself. Don't go far from the house. I'll return at one o'clock,' and off he went, the bicycle rattling protests, along an almost invisible track through the cacti.

I watched him out of sight. Already the desert was white in the glare of the sun. In all its great expanse nothing moved except the ox which I could hear walking up and down as it drew up water. Two vultures sat on a rotten tree stump, looking as if they were carved out of the wood. The goats and the goatherd slept under a tree.

The tears welled up in me. What had I done to incur such disapproval? What had I done?

I sat down on the steps, put my head on my knees and cried like a baby. I cried for Mother and I cried for Bessie, to take pity on my helpless loneliness. I cried aloud since Babu was clearing up at the back of the house and there was no one else to hear. But I had not counted on the sharpness of country people's ears. After a few minutes I became aware of a hasty confabulation towards the back of the building. It was carried on in quite loud voices – evidently the speakers thought I would not understand – and at first I could not do so, but as I listened a woman's voice came clearly: 'Who weeps? – has someone died?'

'Memsahib weeps,' said Babu uneasily.

'Memsahib?' queried a woman's voice.

'Yes, Sahib brought home his new bride yesterday.'

'Ah,' the woman gave a sigh of understanding. 'All brides weep at first. Mother-in-law is there to comfort her?'

'No, Memsahib came alone.'

'Ramji,' said the woman slowly, 'these big Sahibs do not understand the suffering of a woman newly taken from her family. Another woman should be here – a sister-in-law to make jokes with her.'

'Truly,' chimed in a male falsetto, 'she must be lonely.'

I had hastily smothered my sobs on hearing the voices, and listened with growing amusement as I was discussed.

'From which province is Memsahib?' asked the woman.

'She is from England.'

'From England? Is she white?'

'Yes.'

'Ramji! She is English and yet she weeps,' exclaimed the falsetto. 'In all my twenty years as watchman in the Civil Lines, I never saw an English woman weep.'

'Foolish one,' said the woman. 'Even monkeys weep.'

There was a sound of footsteps coming round the building, so I dried my eyes and composed myself for the benefit of visitors.

A woman walked round to the front steps, and I goggled at her. I had never seen such a perfect figure or such an exquisite, heart-shaped face. She wore a tight multi-coloured blouse, which, although it had short sleeves, had no back and was kept in place by strings tied round the neck and waist. A red cotton skirt swung about her hips and a light veil hung from her head down her back.

Large almond eyes beneath sweeping eyebrows observed me in a friendly fashion.

'Namaste,' I said cautiously to this vision, thinking at the same time what a sensation she would make if she walked down the Strand. Every man in London would scamper after her.

The woman put down the earthenware pot which she had been carrying on her head. She smiled, showing small, even teeth, and inclined her head in acknowledgement of my greeting.

'Curd?' she said, pointing to the contents of the pot.

Babu, who had come up behind her, said a trifle sourly that he made it daily for the Sahib and that there was no need to buy. I refused to buy, therefore, but asked if she would like to have a glass of water before continuing her journey. She assented and I asked Babu to bring drinking water.

153

While the water was coming, she talked to me. I did not understand all she said but understood enough to discover that she was the daughter of the headman of a village a couple of miles away, her name was Kamala and she was going to the city to sell her curd.

I asked if she was married.

She giggled and said she was not.

Babu came back with a dripping glass. She squatted on her heels and let Babu pour the water into her cupped hands, from which she drank. Very little was spilt.

She stood up, swung her pot on to her head, and with a reluctant 'A-jo', she went on her way to town.

So I made my first friend in India; and I grew to love her and many of the other women of the villages round about – much to the disgust of the middle-class ladies, when they returned to the flats above ours. In their opinion, village women were not people with whom one made friends.

The owner of the falsetto voice had evidently gone round the back of the building and up the main staircase to the other flats. He now came round the front.

Wrapped in a shawl and carrying a staff, he bowed before me obsequiously and said in broken English: 'Me Udharbhai Watchman. Yesterday night sick malaria not come to flats.'

I considered this telegramlike communication and sought for the Gujerati word for 'well'. It came to me and I asked if he was now quite well. He did not understand my bad pronunciation and I asked again in English. He still did not understand, so he grinned all over his unshaven face, said 'OK' rather doubtfully and pottered off into the bush, where I afterwards found he had a small mud house, in which he lived with his mother, who was reputed to be a hundred years old.

Without being asked to do so, Babu brought me a cup of tea, sweet and scented. Evidently Kamala's remark that a new bride should be comforted had impressed itself on his mind.

He held the cup out to me tentatively, as if coaxing a young animal to eat. I exclaimed with pleasure and took the cup from him. Realising that I was pleased, his lips parted to show a set of teeth stained red with betel nut.

As I drank, the exhaustion of crying and the fears of the morning receded. I began to think constructively about my future life with Ajit.

Meanwhile, Babu produced a bunch of soft rushes tied together, and swept the rooms. He squatted on his haunches and shuffled along under the bed and table as he swept with the side of his broom. He swept with slow, steady strokes and sang a little song about Lord Krishna.

Soothed, I got up from the steps and walked through the flat. Although it was not dirty, it was in a dreadful muddle. The shelves were strewn with every bit of junk a bachelor could have collected in a lifetime. The bed, as yet unmade, was a jumble of sheets. In every corner lay suitcases and trunks, the contents sticking out where I had hastily rifled them that morning, and on the veranda the bedding roll still lay; and the steps certainly needed further washing, as Ajit had said earlier, although the mud had dried.

'Bachelors,' I thought grimly, as I wiped my eyes and then took a pinafore from one of my trunks.

Ajit had bought only the barest essentials for the house, pending my arrival, and nothing had been done to make it into a home. I left Babu to sweep and wash, and firmly opened the cupboard door to reveal the chaos within.

'Young woman – not so young woman,' I addressed myself as I unearthed a mass of crumpled shirts and undarned socks, 'your husband has not known much comfort during the past weeks. He has started a new and responsible job in a strange province, apart from arranging for the arrival of his wife, and it is your duty to make him both comfortable and happy – whether you have to do it in Wetherport or in a bally desert – and even if he is a pig in the mornings.'

At one side of a shelf, in a space cleared for it, I found a package wrapped in silk. Unrolling it I discovered a battered envelope and in the envelope a much-thumbed photograph of myself. I wrapped it up again carefully and replaced it on the shelf. I was smiling softly.

CHAPTER TWENTY-TWO

A sweat-soaked Ajit came home for lunch. I heard the hiss of the bicycle tyres through the sand and opened the door for him as he staggered up the veranda steps. He came through the door and sat down in the nearest chair without saying a word, exhaustion apparent in every line of him.

'It's hot,' he said at last, and then as the coolness of the room had its effect, he looked about him and added: 'You have made the room look nice.'

'Do you like it?' I asked, anxious for approval.

'Indeed I do. I am sorry that I had to leave you this morning.' He mopped himself with a towel which I had brought for him. 'I had only one day of leave.'

He pulled me to him and kissed me and I realised that whatever the trouble of the morning had been, it was now past. I chatted about how we would arrange the silver ornaments and the pictures which I had brought from England. Perhaps we could buy some curtains, a wardrobe, and a desk in which to keep his papers.

'We could buy cloth for curtains when we go to the bazaar this evening,' said Ajit.

'You should wear your sari to the bazaar,' he went on, as Babu came in with the lentil soup and rice. He took his place at the table and then got up again suddenly: 'I forgot,' he said, 'Mother gave me a present for you.' He went to a trunk in the bedroom, which I had not yet had time to explore, and brought out the saris which his mother had given to him earlier.

I unfolded them, and was enchanted by their colours and texture.

'I must write and thank your mother.'

Ajit looked embarrassed. 'Father – er – does not know about the present – and he would open the letter.'

'Oh,' I said regretfully. 'Then you must thank her on your next visit.'

'I will,' he said, depression in his voice.

To change the subject, I asked him how his work was progressing, but the depression merely changed to irritation.

'Too many people are making money out of the power house. Only this morning a dealer offered me Rs.500 to pass an installation which I know will break down in no time.' He ground his teeth and waved his spoon in the air. 'I refused. So I have made an enemy who will go to the Minister and tittle-tattle about my corruption.'

I was shocked, and he saw the concern on my face.

'Don't be afraid, darling. I know how to deal with these matters. The Minister is a friend of my father's, and he knows the calibre of our family.'

'Is there much corruption?'

'No more than in many countries in the West – but it makes me angry.'

He finished his meal, went and washed his face and mouth, kissed me tenderly and went back to work, leaving me with much to think about. My respect for my husband increased considerably.

After he had gone, I washed the sari that I had worn the previous day, and watched fascinatedly as it dried on the veranda rail in a few minutes.

I put on one of the saris which Ajit's mother had sent. There was no mirror in the flat, but when I stood by Babu, who was sitting smoking in a shady corner of the veranda, there was no gleam of amusement in his eyes so I supposed that I had tied it correctly. I prowled contentedly round the flat, occasionally tripping over the front folds of my sari.

In the kitchen, I opened the small store cupboard and immediately recoiled with disgust. Evidently Babu's knowledge of housekeeping did not extend to cupboards. Old tins and bottles lay about in profusion; half a dozen different containers, ranging from an old cigarette tin to a cracked saucer, held dirty bits of fat; a forgotten cup of curd had gained an amazing growth of mould; an old kerosene tin held flour in which I could see black insects burrowing. When I moved the kerosene tin, a family of large, leggy beetles ran for cover, and I stifled a shriek as one ran across my hand.

'Babu,' I shouted.

There was no response.

I went to the veranda. Babu was curled up asleep in a corner.

He resented bitterly the interruption of his afternoon sleep, but I was adamant and made him get up and come to the kitchen. I pointed to the insects in the flour.

He grinned fatuously.

I had a strong desire to slap him.

He made some unintelligible remark, yawned and strolled to the storeroom, from which he fetched a tray. He set the tray on the floor and emptied the flour on to it. Still yawning, he carried it outside and set it in the sun. I followed.

The heat hit me as I stepped into the sunlight. It burned my bare feet intolerably and clutched my body like a vice. Gasping, I covered my head with my sari and narrowed my eyes against the glare, but curiosity kept me by the tray.

The insects crawled out of the flour and off the tray, burying themselves in the sand. I nodded and went back on to the veranda. After a few minutes Babu brought the tray to me. I ran my fingers through the flour and found no sign of life. Wheat was so severely rationed that I dared not throw the flour away, so I motioned Babu to bring the tray indoors.

'We will now make the tin and the cupboard clean,' I said. 'Make a fire and boil water.'

Looking thoroughly sulky at the loss of his afternoon sleep, Babu said that the water in the tap would be hot from the sun. I made him bring me a bucketful and found it was as hot as my hands could reasonably bear.

I put on my pinafore, cleared out the cupboard and scrubbed it, telling Babu to throw away the accumulation of rubbish. I noticed, however, that he secreted the bits of fat in a corner of the storeroom. I presumed he would take them home to his mother and made no comment, but made a mental note that when I gave him a holiday I would present him with a new tin of fat as a gift for his mother.

While I was finishing the cleaning, I told Babu to prepare

Sahib's tea, at the same time cautioning him to look through everything he used and if he found insects or dust he was to tell me.

He did as he was bidden, sighing all the time like a morning breeze. I think he believed me to be mad and was most put out at my criticism of his housekeeping.

When Ajit came home and I told him about it, he roared with laughter. 'Darling, you must daily look at all the food. Keep it also behind locks, because otherwise Babu's family will eat as well as the insects.' He squeezed my hand affectionately. 'You will soon learn everything.'

'Babu,' he shouted.

'Sahib,' came a subdued voice from the kitchen. Babu appeared, wiping his hands on the towel he wore round his neck.

'What have you been doing with my stores, letting insects as big as buffaloes graze on them?'

'Sahib, they were few – the Memsahib does not understand how quickly they come.'

'No insects in future, Babu, do you hear me – and don't let me find the Memsahib having to make your kitchen clean in future – what do I pay you for, hey?'

'Sahib,' said Babu, his lips pouting.

'Memsahib will look daily at the cupboards.'

'Ji, hun,' came the polite assent.

It was getting cooler, so we ate our tea quickly, and after Ajit had given my sari a few hitches to make the hemline straight, we started for the bazaar.

As we walked along the path that led through the thorns to the bus stop a mile away, Ajit swung the cotton shopping bag cheerfully, and a comfortable feeling of comradeship enveloped us.

'Step carefully over those big cracks in the earth,' he said. 'Snakes sometimes sleep in them.'

I stepped very carefully thereafter, although my mind was not occupied by thoughts of snakes.

'Why were you so angry with me this morning?' I asked.

Ajit stopped and looked at me amazedly. 'Angry? Me? I have no anger for you, my darling – only love.'

'You must have been angry,' I said stubbornly,

determined to get to the root of the matter. I gave him a nudge to start him walking again. 'You shouted at me, and asked for things most rudely. You never even said "good morning" or gave me so much as a peck of a kiss. Altogether, young man, you were a perfect pig.'

Ajit looked most distressed; then suddenly he laughed.

'It is no laughing matter,' I said. 'I was hurt.'

He slipped his arm through mine. 'I am a wretch in the morning – but I did not mean to be rude. Here I am at home and I do not modulate my voice as is done in England. We all shout at each other – but not in anger – a loud voice does not mean anger.'

'Hmm,' I said. 'You ordered me about as if I was a slave – bring this – bring that – without a single courtesy.'

'Arree, I forgot you were English – an Indian wife would feel that her husband did not love her unless he kept her near him and allowed her to wait on him.'

'In that case, you are forgiven – and may give me the kiss I did not have this morning,' and I lifted my face to his.

He looked about hastily and, satisfied that there was no one in that barren place to see us, he kissed me heartily.

'You are to tell me,' he instructed, 'when I say words which sound hurtful. My English is not good – and I may not understand always the inference of what I say. Promise this.'

'I promise.'

He took out his handkerchief and dabbed the sweat from my face. 'I do not wish to make your life harder than necessary,' he said. 'You have much to endure.'

CHAPTER TWENTY-THREE

The bus, borne along by a cloud of dust, rattled into the centre square of the town and drew up by a large bus shelter. We descended, while the driver removed his turban and used the end of it to wipe the sweat from his face.

'It is very quiet,' said Ajit, looking round the almost-deserted square. Then he spotted a Thanedar and six policemen standing near. 'Arree, trouble,' he exclaimed. 'See the rifles.'

I looked apprehensively to where he pointed. It was true. All the police were armed with rifles.

'Inspector Sahib,' said Ajit to that dignitary, who had just finished telling the cringing driver of our bus that he was late. 'Has there been some disturbance in the city?'

The Inspector flicked the dust off the brass badge pinned on the pocket of his shirt. When the words 'Shahpur Bus Company' were again legible, he twiddled his moustache ends, stuck out his chest to show his importance, and examined earnestly the top of the only tree in the square. 'A little trouble, I believe,' he said in sing-song English. 'But I am not one to spread rumours. Rumours are the prerogative of Hindus and Muslims.'

Ajit's lips tightened. I looked at the Inspector with interest. He was the first Anglo-Indian I had seen. I hated him on sight. His rudeness was unpardonable.

'What has happened?' asked Ajit patiently.

'A Muslim tongawallah was beaten up on the Pandipura road last night. The Muslims say it was done by Hindus. They are quite capable of it.'

'That is not sufficient to cause the police to be armed.'

The Inspector transferred his interest from the tree top momentarily to me and then examined his patent-leather shoes.

'A Sikh taxi driver's house was set on fire and Muslims were seen running away from it. The house was gutted. The police are looking for the culprits now.'

'I see,' said Ajit, and propelled me across the square towards the main bazaar.

'We will keep well inside the Hindu bazaars,' he said. 'A riot can start so quickly. It may be that the raid on the Sikh's house was retaliation for the beating up of the tongawallah, and the police are being careful to see that the Sikhs don't start any more trouble.'

I nodded. I had heard in England and on the boat coming over of the horrors of the partition riots, and for the first time in my life I was glad to see an armed policeman.

The vegetable bazaar seemed to be functioning normally. It was packed with people, among whom unattended cows and goats nosed their way. Along the pavement sat village women dressed like Kamala. They had round baskets of vegetables set in front of them and they shouted hopefully to likely customers. Each woman had a small, heavy stick by her side, with which she hit the wandering cows if they tried to steal from her basket; she had also a pair of scales which she held up before the purchaser, manipulating them with skilful fingers so as to give light weight to the unsuspecting. Almost all the women had heart-shaped faces and at least one in every three would have been considered a beauty in England. I wondered why Ajit had bothered to bring a wife from England when such beauties were scattered everywhere.

In the bazaar itself, the police were armed only with lathis, and I watched them idly while Ajit bargained. It was apparent that the people feared them. Women lifted their baskets up and retreated a little as they ambled past. There was none of the easy aplomb of an English policeman on his beat. No one spoke to them.

The vegetable women made jokes about my fair hair, and Ajit said ruefully that I had caused a price boom in the market. When bargaining for fruit with a man who had a small shop facing the market, the man said flatly that for someone who had an English wife Ajit drove too hard a bargain.

At last we were finished, and I had received my first lesson in shopping in a market where there was no fixed price for any product. I wondered if I would ever gain enough patience to bargain for every vegetable I bought. Ajit assured me that I should eventually regard it as an amusing game of skill.

We were fortunate in catching a bus immediately we arrived at the square, but by the time we reached the end of the bus route it was dark.

'I forgot to bring a torch,' said Ajit, annoyance in his voice.

A voice from the neem tree which marked the end of the route said: 'Sahib.'

I jumped with fright.

Babu emerged from the shadows. He had brought the torch.

'How thoughtful of him,' I said to Ajit.

'He probably wanted to visit someone down here and sought for an excuse to leave the house,' said Ajit sourly. The bazaar had frayed his temper.

Babu took the shopping bags and Ajit the torch.

We came to a tiny restaurant – no more than a thatched roof supported on poles, with a couple of old iron chairs set under it and the owner's cooking utensils and other small belongings stacked in a corner which had been made by draping sacking from the roof.

Ajit stopped to buy a pan to chew. The panwallah carefully wrapped the tobacco, lime and spices into a green leaf, at the same time chatting to Ajit who was evidently a regular customer. Ajit asked him to make up a very small pan for me, which I took and trustfully put into my mouth, only to spit it out again with a fine disregard for good manners.

'It was so bitter,' I moaned, wiping my mouth with a handkerchief.

The panwallah grinned, and Babu looked regretful at such waste.

The panwallah's wife was squatting before the fire, slapping dough into rounds between her hands, preparatory to cooking it on an iron plate. She said something to her husband.

The man looked worried and spoke rapidly to Ajit, while Ajit chewed his pan and nodded now and then.

'What did he say?' I asked curiously.

'He warned me that a dacoit leader was believed to have come from Kathiawar to the Criminal Tribe village near our house. He said I should be careful that you are not kidnapped.'

'Kidnapped?' I laughed. 'Surely not in these days.'

'Robbery is more likely. This dacoit, Vallabhai, must have come so near to a big town for a special reason. He must know of some travellers passing through or an isolated wealthy house to rob. You must keep the doors locked while I am away, however, and I will tell Chowkidar that he must stay near the flats.'

It sounded like an excerpt from a comic opera, and I could not feel frightened about it; but I promised to keep the doors bolted.

Babu had, of course, heard the warning, and he said mournfully: 'Sahib, tell Memsahib to put away her silver ornaments, not leave them on a shelf. Silver will bring Vallabhai to our dwelling like a vulture to a dead camel.'

Ajit translated. I was amused.

'I am not going to bury our pretty things when the flat badly needs something to make it look more pleasant.' I glanced at Babu. 'Babu is quick to notice. I have only had time today just to unpack – never mind arrange the silver. There is nothing very valuable, anyway.'

Ajit said to Babu that what we had was of little value, and Vallabhai would never know what our house contained.

Babu sulked.

That night while we slept Babu packed his creaky tin trunk with his few clothes, his sacred picture of the Lord Krishna, a tin of cooking fat, a tin of tea, most of our precious wheat ration, and seven rupees and five annas of the housekeeping money. Some time in the early morning he let himself out of the back door, and, with his trunk balanced on his head, he loped away back to his village. Either my mania about insects or fear of Vallabhai or Ajit's complaints about bad washing of the veranda or, perhaps, just a desire to see his mother, had proved too much for him, and away he went, never to be seen by us again.

CHAPTER TWENTY-FOUR

Nulini had visited Bimla Chand Rana on the same day on which Mrs Singh gave Ajit the three saris for me. When she returned home she left Bimla seated on a cushion under a mango tree in her father's courtyard stabbing murderously at a piece of embroidery. Bimla's face was contorted with rage. So, she thought, Ajit has married an English woman, a dirty, casteless English woman. She cursed him with curses that scandalised her long-suffering and bewildered Ayah.

'Do not use such words,' said Ayah. 'They are unbecoming to Rana Sahib's daughter.'

'I know what is becoming,' screamed Bimla, her high Punjabi temper in full vent, and she shoved her needle in and out of the cloth as if it was Ajit she was impaling. 'Go away!'

Ayah had no inkling of what had caused her charge's outburst, and she went and sat a few yards away while she thought about it.

'I, Bimla Chand Rana,' muttered Bimla, as she savagely bit her embroidery silk at the end of a line of cross stitch, 'the handsomest woman in the district, to be bypassed by that pudding head of an Ajit in favour of a vulgar Western female!'

She threw her embroidery at a squirrel, who scuttled up the tree in fright, and sat and sulked. She did not wish to betray Nulini, so she did not go to her father, feeling sure that Ram Singh would be communicating with Kasher Chand Rana about the marriage; but the day came when her Ayah said that Ajit was leaving for Shahpur, and still she had heard nothing from her father. Finally, she could endure the suspense no longer, so one morning she put on her best veil and a new shirt and strode to her father's room, Ayah fluttering after her and longing to know what was amiss.

Swallowing hard, she knocked and entered. Her father was alone, working on his private account book. Taking an old servant's privilege, Ayah slipped into the room as well.

Kasher Chand Rana looked up nervously and pushed his spectacles further up his nose. Both his wife and daughter had high tempers and shrill voices, and there were times when he expressed the opinion that a dumb woman would be a priceless pearl. Mercifully, both women had also a full allowance of Punjabi charm and just enough self-control not to shriek at him in public. He was, therefore, under the illusion that nobody knew that he was third in command in his house. Unfortunately, his servants kept his friends' servants well informed and he was famous as a thoroughly henpecked husband.

He clasped his small, clawlike hands before him and lifted up a face on which trepidation was clearly written.

'Well, daughter?'

The story poured out. Kasher Chand Rana was surprised but not angry. In the background Ayah punctuated the recital with horrified exclamations.

'It is not Dr Singh's fault,' he said. 'It is Ajit's. We must tell your mother – she will not like it.' He sighed and twiddled his wispy moustache. 'And your grandmother, I suppose – what will she say?' He sighed again at the horrid prospect before him. 'How did you find out?'

Reluctantly Bimla told of Nulini's visit.

'How did she know? It may be only a rumour.'

Bimla's loyalty to Nulini made it impossible for her to say how Nulini probably got her information, so she said: 'I don't know. You should go and see Dr Singh.'

'I will inquire,' he said.

'Go now – please, Father,' demanded Bimla.

'Yes, yes, child,' said her father resignedly, and he got up from his chair and shuffled about looking for his slippers. Ayah found them and put them on his feet. 'I will go now – although it is already hot.'

Satisfied, Bimla left him. Ayah brought him water, while he was waiting for his carriage.

'Ayah, no one must know of this yet.'

'Sahib,' she said reproachfully, 'I have served you faithfully for forty years.'

'I have malaria, Ayah. My hands are shaking. And I shall have to start marriage negotiations all over again. It is trying, very trying. And where did Nulini Singh get this gossip – it may well be gossip, Ayah.'

'It is truth, I think, Sahib. Nulini Singh is likely to know the truth.'

'Why?'

Ayah shrank away.

166

'I demand to know,' said Chand Rana sharply.

Ayah whispered into his ear.

He looked shocked. 'Ridiculous,' he said. 'How dare you say such a thing – you are not to purvey such damaging gossip in my house – I am surprised at you.'

'I have seen him look at her with love, Sahib,' said Ayah defensively.

'Absolutely ridiculous,' said Chand Rana. 'Probably her husband told her.'

The carriage came.

Kasher Chand Rana spent half an hour discussing politics and drinking tea, before he could gather courage enough to ask Ram Singh about his son's marriage, and just as he broached the subject Mrs Singh came into the room followed by Thakkur bearing a special sweetmeat which she desired Kasher Chand Rana to try. The servant retired, but Mrs Singh showed no signs of going away again, so he was forced to speak in front of her and to nibble the confection with which she presented him.

He mentioned that he had heard a rumour, a most extraordinary rumour which he felt was unlikely to be true, but as his own family was involved, would Ram Singh be so good as to confirm or deny it?

Ram Singh could not imagine how Chand Rana had heard about the marriage, but it was the only source of rumour which could possibly have driven him to visit his friend in the middle of the hottest afternoon of the year.

'My friend – er – this distresses me very much – er – I cherish your friendship very much – I – er . . .'

'I understand,' said Chand Rana glumly and absent-mindedly took another sweet.

Mrs Singh covered her face with her sari and the study was silent. It was a difficult moment for them all.

At last Ram Singh said: 'I am sure you will have no difficulty in finding another husband for Bimla. However, if you would care to consider another boy from our family, my brother has a son of the same age as Bimla – a fine young man, who will inherit a share in his father's silk mill. He is a handsome boy, nearly six feet tall and of good proportions. If you would . . . if I might suggest . . .', and he looked at his friend slyly, 'I would be very pleased to act as mediator.'

Chand Rana, who had been imagining the screaming fury of his wife when he broke the news of Ajit's marriage to her, was immediately interested. It would be something with which to placate her.

'Six feet tall, did you say?' he asked hopefully, 'and of what kind of nature?'

Ram Singh knew all about the distaff side of his friend's family, and he said: 'Of a most determined nature. He was very disappointed when it appeared that Ajit would marry Bimla. He has seen her here – and I think he would be delighted to have the honour of marrying her. My brothers also would find pleasure in an alliance with your respected family.'

The two men grinned at each other, and behind her veil Mrs Singh giggled with relief.

Chand Rana nodded his bald head. 'Will you arrange a meeting with your respected brother?'

'Certainly.'

They talked a little longer and then Khan was sent to fetch Chand Rana's carriage. Ram Singh accompanied his friend to the front door and paused on the threshold. A little anxiously, he said: 'My friend, at this time, the marriage of my son is a source of anxiety to me and we have decided not to make it known for the time being. May I count on your discretion in this matter?'

'Of course – and I will instruct my family not to mention it until you announce it.'

Kasher Chand Rana told Bimla as gently as he could that Ajit had indeed married someone else. Bimla wept and Mrs Chand Rana's voice reached new heights of shrillness as she held forth on the stupidity of the man that her parents had made her marry.

Kasher Chand Rana waited patiently until Bimla's tears of frustration ceased and his wife's upbraiding had been reduced to a recitation of the foolish things he had done in the past, and then he mentioned casually that he had heard that a most handsome young man was secretly in love with his pretty daughter.

The pretty daughter pushed her ruffled hair back from her face, and with a thread of excitement in her voice demanded to know his name.

Her father settled himself more comfortably on the mattress on which he had deposited himself, and added dryly that the young man would one day be very rich.

His wife's voice snapped off as sharply as if she had been turned off like a radio, and she became very attentive.

'The young man is very handsome indeed,' said Kasher Chand Rana.

The women forgot about Ajit and clamoured to know more.

He refused to say who it was, but promised to make further inquiries, and in the meantime they were to keep Ajit's marriage a secret, for the sake of Dr Singh, who was, after all, their very good friend.

'If a rumour of this marriage comes to me from any corner,' he said threateningly, 'I shall know who started the gossip – and I shall stop all negotiations regarding Bimla's prospects with the young man of whom I have heard.'

At such a dreadful threat, both Mrs Chand Rana and Bimla quailed and promised faithfully that neither of them would mention the subject, and Bimla went back to her embroidery which lay under the mango tree. There she sat down to dream of an admirer as beautiful as a Rajput prince; and her Ayah marvelled at the unaccustomed peace.

CHAPTER TWENTY-FIVE

Babu's departure was a blow to me, but Ajit took it more philosophically.

'They all do it sooner or later,' he said. 'I expect he has just gone home.'

'Gone home – without notice?'

'Without giving notice,' he said, sitting on the edge of the bed and rumpling his hair wearily.

'We must manage for a few days,' he added, 'until I can find another boy. Just make the simplest of food.'

I bit my lips. I had seen very little of Babu's activities in the kitchen, and had no idea as yet how to cook even simple Indian food. Without at least eggs, English food seemed out of the question.

'I'll light a cooking fire for you, before I take my bath,' Ajit said.

He looked so harassed that I bent and kissed him, and told him not to worry, that I would manage. I knew that the amount of work he was doing was growing with the power house and that the Chief Engineer was down with malaria; his load was enough, without domestic difficulties being added to it.

I improvised a breakfast and sent him off to work looking quite happy, but I felt far from happy myself.

The cooking fire had gone out, so I washed the dishes by scrubbing them with sand and rinsing them under the tap, as I had seen Babu do. The water, unconfined by any sink, splashed over the floor and over my sandals. I kicked off the sandals and thereafter went barefooted. I tore up an old sheet and mopped up the water.

My legs ached from squatting on my heels as I washed the dishes, but the rest of the house was full of sand and dust, so I took Babu's bunch of rushes and swept the floors in a kneeling position. The ache extended to my back.

With a stiffer rush broom I scrubbed the bathroom floor, again squatting on my heels. The water from the tap was already warm from the sun.

Leaving a trail of wet footprints across the rooms, I went back to the kitchen. Heat was already invading the house, and my hair was wet with perspiration. My cotton frock was already dust laden and the hem was soaked from my scrubbing efforts in the bathroom. I went to the water cooler for a drink, but it was empty. I remembered then that Babu boiled water in the evening and let it cool overnight; he had evidently not done so the previous evening. I set the clay vessel under the tap and filled it.

To hoist a two-gallon pot from floor level to shoulder height requires some skill. I lifted the pot by the rim, but it was too heavy for me, and I had just decided that I must empty it, put it back on to the stand and then ladle water into it, when the pot settled the question by bursting at the bottom and flooding the newly cleaned kitchen.

'Damn,' I said.

After wringing the water out of the skirt of my dress, I painstakingly swept the pools on the floor down the drain in the corner of the room.

It was getting late, and Ajit would soon be home for lunch, so I hastily piled charcoal into the cooking stove and lit some newspaper under it, then lifted the stove with the tongs and placed it outside the back door so that the wind could fan the charcoal into flame. The wind merely blew the charred paper out of the stove, through the kitchen door and on to the damp floor.

I tried not to cry, but the tears came. How I longed for even an old-fashioned English kitchen range.

More paper was stuffed into the recalcitrant stove. I lit it and it blew out again, and more charred newsprint was added to that already stuck on the kitchen floor.

I sobbed quietly and prepared to try again. I was kneeling on the sand outside the kitchen door, tearing up yet another newspaper, when I realised that someone in that lonely place was watching me. Slowly I looked round.

Almost immediately behind me stood a tall, thin man dressed in the red turban, white jacket and loincloth of a countrymen. He lacked, however, a countrymans' moustache and the face was hard, seamed and very dark. The thin lips were curled in cynical amusement, and, as he stepped up beside me, he fingered a wooden-handled dagger, half concealed in his silver belt.

I jumped up and backed towards the door, but the man lifted his hand from the dagger and made a conciliatory gesture. Slowly he laid his staff against the wall. His eyes, which were almond-shaped and light like a goat's, looked me up and down insolently, as he squatted down in front of the stove.

I stood ready for flight while he lifted half the charcoal

off the fire and at the same time addressed me. Although his language was something akin to Gujerati I did not understand it, and he glanced up at me with a keen, hard glance. I was again reminded of a goat.

He half-smiled. I doubt if he had ever seen such a dishevelled Memsahib as me.

Pronouncing the words carefully, he said: 'Bring kerosene.'

'Of course. Why had I not thought of it before? Comforted by the English words, I ran to the storeroom and after sniffing at several bottles found one with kerosene in it. I took it to him and he sprinkled it over the charcoal and lit it. Deftly he set the stove so that it caught the wind and in a few seconds a fire was roaring. He picked up the pincers and handed them to me, so that I could lift the stove into the kitchen. For a second his fingers touched mine. His face was close to me, and my words of thanks died on my lips. I saw the peculiarly light eyes flicker, and sudden fear gripped me. He made a half step towards me.

With the pincers I snatched up the blazing fire and whipped it between us. In that moment I was more afraid than I had ever been in my life.

'Namaste, Memsahib,' said Udharbhai, as he rounded the corner of the building.

The stranger moved smoothly away from me, picked up his staff, raised his hand in salute, and then, mopping his face with his sweat rag, he passed Udharbhai and swung swiftly down the path to the Criminal Tribe village.

Udharbhai watched him go.

'Who is he, Chowkidar Sahib?' I asked Udharbhai, my voice trembling.

'He is a stranger, Memsahib. The Mem must door lock. Strangers no safe.'

'I will,' I said feelingly, and I took the stove indoors and shot the bolt.

I did not tell Ajit about the stranger, because he had warned me to keep indoors as much as possible and would surely upbraid me. As it was, he was delighted with the lentil soup and boiled rice which I had made and hugged me till my aching back throbbed with pain.

*

Ajit again consulted the village headman about finding another servant, but the headman was ashamed that the boy his brother had recommended had left so quickly, and he was diffident about recommending anyone else. Ajit asked his friends, but they also were finding it hard to get servants. 'The mills take them all,' they sighed. I suggested that we advertise in the local newspaper, but Ajit pointed out that it would be unwise to take into our home a boy not personally vouched for by someone we knew. 'He might open the door to robbers,' said Ajit.

So I learned to keep house by myself, and since there was no one to teach me, although Ajit did his best, I learned the hard way. The fact that we were so far from a bazaar made it even more difficult for me.

Once a week I walked two miles through broiling heat to the ration shop to buy our wheat and rice. I took this home, spread it on a tray and spent several hours painstakingly picking out all the stones and other debris. Then I walked back to the miller, who lived next door to the ration shop, and handed him the precious wheat ration for grinding. I dared not entrust this task to anyone else since they would surely steal part of the ration. It was Kamala, however, who showed me how to avoid being swindled in another fashion. She happened to be in the mill one day and she showed me how to feel the flour from time to time, as it poured out of the grinder into the bag, in order to be certain that I was given wheat flour, instead of some inferior flour from a cheap grain already placed in the machine.

At first, Ajit accompanied me to the bazaar, but as he was on his feet all day, to go into town in the evening became a burden. Further, the city had now relapsed into its usual calm and the police put away their rifles and returned to their traffic direction. Every other day, therefore, I made the trip to town for vegetables and fruit. I soon learned to bargain – but it took hours, and the walk from the bus stop to the flat seemed to get longer as the days passed and the heat and humidity increased.

No washerman was prepared to come so far out of town to collect our laundry, so I learned to wash the clothes, sitting on my heels in the bathroom and pounding the garments on the stone floor; and I got used to wielding an iron while sweat rolled off me.

Life seemed to be an endless circuit of work to be done and heavy loads to be carried; pain in my back and legs from doing all my tasks while squatting on my heels became my constant companion. I searched in vain in the bazaars for dishpans and brooms with handles – no one had ever heard of such peculiar things. Then dysentery struck at me, and with it came a lassitude that made a walk across a room seem too great a task to be undertaken.

Ajit had not been able to show me how to make chupaties properly. It was an art which eluded both of us, with the result that as long as the rice ration lasted, we ate rice with our meals. When that was finished, we made different kinds of fried breads although these were too rich for daily consumption. Kamala showed me how to make village chupaties, but this heavy, indigestible bread was meant for men who worked all day in the fields and was not very palatable to us.

One afternoon, sickened at the idea of again eating rice for dinner, I tucked myself into a sari and went to the city.

The heat was a raving animal that clawed at my hair and clung to my legs so that it was hard to drag one after the other, and I was exhausted by the time I crawled into the bus, but I was determined to buy some European bread, which I knew was sold free of ration coupons in the Muslim bazaar if one was prepared to pay enough for it.

The Muslim baker, whose shop was on the edge of the bazaar, knew me because I had bought biscuits and cake from him once or twice before, and when I said I wanted bread but had no coupons, he merely looked resigned, gave me two loaves and charged me double the usual price.

The loaves smelled delicious and I took up the parcel lovingly and turned towards the door. The door seemed to recede from me, the floor spun under my feet and I fainted.

I heard a man's voice in the distance shouting: 'Ma ji, Ma ji.' Far away, there was a heavy flip-flap of sandals, I was lifted up, and a long time afterwards there was the feel of water on my face.

'Allah be praised,' said a voice in my ear.

I opened my eyes. Three faces floated before me – a bearded man's, a fat female's swathed in dirty veiling, and the Madonna herself.

I shut my eyes again – I was so tired. Someone chafed my hands.

Wearily I forced my eyes open. I could not remember where I was, but I did not care much. If only I could sleep.

Above me was a low, dark ceiling, smothered with cobwebs.

The woman clucked with satisfaction and exclaimed over the light colour of my eyes.

I lifted myself on one elbow. The Madonna became a young girl with a face so innocent that it was not surprising that I had mistaken her for the Mother of God. She was heavy with child, her shirt pulling tightly over her swollen figure.

An old lady was rubbing my hands, her bracelets and earrings jingling as she worked. She smiled like the sun when she saw that I was recovering, her pan-stained teeth gleaming blackly in the poor light.

The man with the beard was, of course, the baker and he retreated to the shop immediately I raised myself up.

I was lying on some sacks in a grain storeroom, and I hastily swung my feet to the floor and made as if to get up, but the two women restrained me firmly.

With their hands upon me, I remembered that I was a Hindu woman in the Muslim quarter, that my value in the white slave market was enormous and that no one knew where I was.

I pushed the women aside and jumped to my feet, but the room dissolved around me and I must have fainted again.

CHAPTER TWENTY-SIX

When Ajit arrived home from work and saw the big padlock on the front door, he realised at once I must be out. I had never failed before to be at home when he returned from his work, and while he unlocked and entered he was already anxious about my absence. He guessed that I had gone into the city – and he remembered the smouldering unrest there. He prowled into the kitchen – no sign of cooking – I must have been gone for some time. His throat went dry, as he remembered the panwallah's warning about the presence of dacoits from the east; it would be easy to kidnap a woman walking by herself in the bush. A sweat of fright redamped his shirt.

He went to the veranda to peer down the track to the city, and reproached himself bitterly for failing to accompany me to the bazaar. There was no sign of me along the path. He looked at his watch – the next bus from the city was just due to arrive at the Pandipura terminus, and, as I might be in it, he decided to wait for fifteen minutes before setting out in search of me – it would take that long for me to walk from the bus stop to a point where he would be able to see my approach from the veranda.

Far away, down the track, two moving clouds of dust appeared above the thorns.

'Bullock carts – or tongas,' thought Ajit. 'I can ask if they have seen a white woman anywhere along the track – or perhaps she has hired herself a tonga.' His fear turned to annoyance – I should have told him I was going out. Irritably, he kicked off his sandals.

To fill in the time until the tongas should approach nearer, he prepared a cooking fire for me, and got out the vegetables and spices from the store cupboard ready for the preparation of the evening meal. If only electricity was cheaper, he thought, he could buy an electric stove and I would be saved so much labour. But our electricity bill was already heavy, for light and the running of the fan. Only when the power house was complete could we hope for cheaper power.

The first vehicle, a tonga, arrived quicker than he had expected; and when he heard its bells, he ran down the steps so fast that his next-door neighbours, the three Misses Shah, who were descending from it, were quite overwhelmed by such an enthusiastic reception on their return from holiday.

When he saw who had arrived, all his fear for me returned and his anger was quenched. Courtesy demanded, however, that he should help the ladies, so he advanced and called as cheerful a greeting as he could.

He was immediately enveloped in a whirl of gaily coloured saris and flying pigtails. How was he? How was his wife? They had had a wonderful rest in the hills; dear papa and mama were happily settled up there. Had he any change with which to tip the tongawallah? Would he mind lifting that trunk out of the way of the wheels?

It was not surprising that he failed to hear the jingling of the second vehicle – another tonga; and he jumped when a horse neighed close to him and a vaguely familiar voice called: 'Sahib.'

To the disgust of the eldest Miss Shah, her best tin trunk was dropped into the sand as if it was a bomb, and their neighbour leaped to the back of the second tonga.

'Peggie,' he cried, 'Peggie, are you all right? Ramji, you do look white. What has happened?'

I was laden with newspaper parcels and I dimpled wickedly at Ajit's discomfiture, as I waited for Mohamed Ali to open the door.

'Of course I'm all right, love,' I said. 'Just help me down and pay this man – he has been very kind.' I handed out to Ajit a large parcel and said cryptically: 'Forbidden fruit – be very careful how you handle it.'

Mystified, he laid it and the other parcels in the sand and helped me down. I was still rather unsteady and clung to him for support, while the Misses Shah, silenced for once, watched with interest.

Ajit produced four rupees from his pocket and handed them to the driver.

Mohamed Ali's beard twitched as if he was smiling and he salaamed, then he shouted to the other tongawallah to be careful while he turned. I hastily grabbed my precious parcels before they were trampled by the horses, and looked expectantly at the other ladies.

Ajit introduced them, and in perfect English they chorused their welcome to Shahpur.

They were plain women, their hair drawn stiffly back from their faces into long pigtails. No flowers were tucked into the pigtails and no jewellery relieved the solidarity of their square faces; and yet they had charm. Unlike most Indian women, they looked at me straightly. No side glances or coquetry for them; plain honesty had written itself into their expressions.

I assured them that I was most pleased to have such pleasant neighbours, and I motioned to Ajit to move their luggage on to their veranda, while I invited them into our flat for tea before they unpacked.

After a polite flutter of refusals, they were persuaded into our living-room where they hopped about like budgerigars from one English ornament to another, while I put the water to boil and brought in cups and saucers. I still felt dizzy and occasionally the floor heaved under my feet, but I was enjoying the sudden feminine invasion very much.

They declared the English method of making tea far superior to their own and smacked their lips appreciatively as they sipped, although I doubt if they really liked it.

Finally, armed with a water pot of cooled water from our kitchen and some boiled milk, they departed to unpack, and I was alone with Ajit.

He also had enjoyed the fresh company, but occasionally I saw him glance at me anxiously over his teacup, and now the flat was quiet again, he asked: 'What happened, old girl?'

I told him, and finished up by saying: 'I thought they were trying to keep me by force and I was terrified, but they were only making tea for me and wanted me to rest until it was ready. They brought me English fruit cake and a cup of spiced tea, and sat on the floor of the granary and talked so sweetly while I ate.

'They afterwards sent for a tongawallah, who is a relation, and it turned out to be the same man who brought us here. He recognised me. The old mother said that it was he who was beaten up, that he had been attacked while driving back from our flat. He believed the attack was made by thieves from the Criminal Tribe village – unfortunately the rumour went round the bazaar that the Sikhs had done it, so some young rowdies burned down a Sikh house. The police made a lot of trouble about it.'

'Thank God you are safe,' said Ajit fervently. 'Anything could have happened in such a situation.'

'I was perfectly safe. No two women could have been more ingenuous. The baker seemed upset at their telling me about the attack on Mohamed Ali – just annoyance over the chattering of women, I suspect – ' and I looked at Ajit with a twinkle in my eye.

Ajit did not laugh. He said: 'You are now to get into bed and I will cook a dinner. The dysentery and hard work have damaged you – tomorrow I will obtain a doctor.'

And in spite of protests, to bed I went. It was a blessed relief to lie down and I must have fallen into a light sleep, because it seemed no time before Ajit was standing in front of me with a hot dish of rice and lentils.

He looked tired, but when we had eaten together sitting cross-legged on the bed, he felt better and said he would walk for a few minutes in the breeze outside. I agreed and lay back on the bed. He lit his pipe and went outside.

The eldest Miss Shah must have been sitting on the steps of her flat because I heard her ask: 'Where is Mrs Singh?'

'She is sleeping,' said Ajit, in English. 'She is not very well.'

'Can I help her?' asked Miss Shah.

Ajit hesitated and said: 'I think not, thank you. The transition from one kind of food to another has upset her.'

'I will come and see her in the morning,' said Miss Shah.

My heart warmed to my new neighbour.

Ajit had told me about the three sisters, whose acquaintance he had made during his first week in the flat.

When the University closed for the summer months, they went away to visit their parents at a small hill station. The family were refugees from West Pakistan. The girls had no brothers or uncles to help them, and the two elder sisters maintained their parents and the youngest sister by lecturing in English. A small cottage in the hills was all that remained of their ancestral property after the partition of India, and there they had established their aged parents, who would have found the heat of Shahpur hard to bear.

Although the sisters lived in Shahpur without the protection of a male relative, they were respected by their neighbours and few scandalous stories had been invented about them.

Ajit came in, kissed me and took the dishes away to wash. I knew that to him the washing of kitchen vessels was a humiliating task, beneath the dignity of a member of his caste and family, and I loved him for doing it.

Afterwards, as I was still awake, he brought pen and paper to my bed and sat cross-legged by my feet while he wrote his weekly salutations to his mother, adding that I was far from well. I protested that he should not bother her with such news, that I would be well by morning, but he insisted that his parents should know something of the struggle I was having.

I must have fallen asleep in the middle of the argument, because the next thing that I remember was awakening to broad daylight and the sound of peasant voices in the kitchen.

The long sleep had done me good, and I got out of bed and wrapped a shawl round me. I saw that a mat had been spread in a corner of the bedroom and a rumpled sheet on it indicated that Ajit had slept on the floor rather than disturb me by getting into the bed.

In the kitchen Ajit was talking to Kamala and a bent, old woman. It appeared that they had just come to an agreement, because Kamala said: 'All right,' with some satisfaction.

A fire was burning and a closed pot on it gave out a bubbling sound. Beside the little stove, on the floor, was a plate of buttered toast and a vessel of hot milk.

'Darling,' I said, a catch in my voice.

Ajit turned. 'Hey, Rani, you are supposed to stay in bed.'

I smiled at him and at Kamala. 'I feel better. What are you talking about to Kamala?'

'I saw her passing early this morning and told her you were ill, so she brought this woman – she is a sweeper and has agreed to sweep the house, wash the vessels, clean the grain and take it to the miller, and make your lunchtime cooking fire. Kamala says that now Miss Shah is back, a sweeper will come daily to clean the lavatory and remove the rubbish, and a washerman will come to collect in a day or two, when the other families get back.'

I was so pleased, and it was arranged that the old woman would return later. Apparently she worked in this manner for several families in the block of flats, and she would go to Miss Shah's first.

I lifted the lid of the pan on the fire. Two eggs were bouncing merrily in it. Ajit had discovered the forbidden fruit with which I had returned the previous evening. I had put the parcel in the cupboard and forgotten about them in the arrival of the Misses Shah. I closed the lid quickly, before Kamala and my new servant saw the eggs. I did not want to lose a friend and a servant at one stroke.

The two women went away, and Ajit made me sit on the kitchen stool while he served me with egg, toast and tea, after which he ate himself. His consideration for me was touching, and I could not eat until I had given him a hug that would have put a grizzly bear to shame.

He asked me where I obtained the eggs, and I told him that while I was drinking tea in the baker's granary a man had come in bringing a great basketful, and I had found my mouth watering and had been unable to resist the temptation to purchase some from the baker. He had offered to supply me regularly.

Ajit looked perplexed. He feared that if it was discovered that we had eggs in the house we would lose our tenancy and have difficulty finding other accommodation.

'I could dry the shells, grind them and throw them out with the ashes from the stoves,' I suggested.

'I suppose that would be all right,' he said reluctantly.

I sent him off to work that day with assurances that I was much better, but in truth my legs felt as if they would dissolve under me at any moment and the dysentery was threatening a fresh onslaught.

The eldest Miss Shah called before going to the college, to inquire how I was, and I assured her I was better. I told her ruefully about my inadequacy as a cook, and she offered to teach me. She cooked daily a meal at ten in the morning and another at about nine at night, so for over a week, as soon as Ajit had gone to work, I went into her kitchen and watched her cook. I learned much which I put to good use, but she did not know the dishes of Ajit's province nor was she able to make good chupaties.

'Dear Mother always made the bread when she was with us, and I have never learned the art. As I have not much time in which to cook we manage by eating rice.'

I nodded sympathetically.

'I find,' I said, 'that all food turns bad within a couple of hours of cooking. Is there any way of keeping food fresh from one meal to another? It would be such a help if I could prepare food in advance sometimes.'

Miss Shah looked disgusted at the idea of keeping food and said: 'Indeed, no. All food must be prepared freshly for each meal, including bread. It is dangerous to eat old food.'

Reluctantly I agreed with her. Only the previous evening I had put some lentil soup into a covered bowl in the hope that it would stay good until morning, and had found upon getting up that it was rotten throughout. Refrigeration would be the only safe way in which to keep food fresh – and a refrigerator was beyond the dreams of avarice.

Letters from my parents had been awaiting my arrival, but it was on the day of Miss Shah's visit that the postman brought me the first letter from Angela. I tore open the envelope before the postman's slippers had given a final flip-flap on the bottom step of the veranda.

After saying that she was glad I had arrived safely and how much she missed me, she wrote: 'Wu has been very kind. He has called several times bringing flowers, which

amuses me very much. Father does not like him at all –
keeps saying he wishes the fellow would go away – and yet
he is so courteous that Father cannot snub him. Personally
I find him refreshingly charming – he is a realist and a poet.'

I remembered the careful arrangement of the room Ajit
and I had shared at the inn on the first night of our
marriage. A poet and a realist had combined to arrange it.
I scanned the letter again. I was pleased that Wu's
friendship with Angela was progressing, but as for Father
– poor Father must be afraid of losing another daughter to
an oriental.

Having a woman to help me, dirty and inefficient as she
was, proved a great comfort, but lead weights dragged at
my legs and the dysentery did not lessen. Even to cook and
to go to the city to shop became nightmares of effort, and
I did not protest when a few days later Ajit brought a
doctor home with him.

'This is Dr Venketraman,' he said as he ushered into the
living-room a tall, black man.

I bade the doctor seat himself, which he did after placing
his bag carefully on the table. 'And now, Madam,' he said
as he removed an outsized pair of horn-rimmed spectacles
from his nose, 'how can I help you?'

His dark face creased with polite solicitude and his
extraordinarily black eyes ranged over me as I explained
my symptoms.

He diagnosed dysentery, asked us to send our non-
existent servant to his dispensary for medicines, and
decreed a diet of curd and rice.

'What a queer man,' I said, as Ajit shut the door behind
him. 'Is he a Negro?'

'No. He is from the south. Many of them are dark and
curly-haired.' He put his arm round my waist and kissed
me. 'I will fetch the medicine after dinner.'

For weeks the doctor and I waged war against dysentery.
Sometimes it left me for a few days only to come again with
greater vigour. I grew thinner and weaker, while Ajit
became more and more worried.

The other tenants of the flats returned from their
holidays and, without exception, curiosity drove the ladies

183

to call upon me, regardless of whether they were elderly, orthodox and disapproving or young and highly experimental. They all knew different cures for dysentery but none of them cured. Many of the ladies, as the dampness of the rainy season approached and the mosquitoes came out of hiding, went down with malaria, but I was spared this as I did not fear to take modern drugs.

The unremitted kindness of people round me, from Kamala, who often shopped for me in the city and charged me only a small percentage on the goods she bought, to the Misses Shah, who brought me books and company, was overwhelming. Ajit, harassed at the power house by the slowness and inefficiency of the men under him and by his own limited experience, never murmured about the lateness of his meals or the general discomfort of his home. Night after night he massaged my aching legs when he must have been exhausted himself from much standing in the summer heat, and as he rubbed he told me funny stories of the day's doings. I laughed to please him and to see the smile of relief in his eyes when he heard me chuckle.

So, through the cruel Indian summer, we clung to each other and wondered how long we could endure without breaking.

CHAPTER TWENTY-SEVEN

Just before the monsoon broke, when the weather had become intolerably humid, a peon in a white uniform and a scarlet sash presented himself at Ajit's office. He brought a letter from Chundabhai Patel, announcing his return to Shahpur from England and asking us to take dinner with him.

Ajit scribbled an acceptance, as I was a little better and he thought I would enjoy meeting an old friend. He suspected that Chundabhai would be more than glad to see us, as it was likely that he would be finding it difficult to readjust himself to Indian life, despite the ease which his father's wealth purchased for him.

Chundabhai was a Vaisya by caste and a Jain by religion; that is, he was of a lower caste than Ajit and his religious beliefs demanded that he should take no life and in consequence be a strict vegetarian. The last time we saw him in England was when he was sitting in a Manchester eating-house, famous for its steak and kidney pies, ordering a second helping of this delectable dish. On the table before him was a tankard of beer, and by his side sat his red-headed sweetheart, Sheila. In Shahpur there would be no beer, since prohibition reigned, and no Sheila, because he had been married since he was fifteen.

We were both excited at the prospect of visiting someone other than the families who lived in our isolated block of flats, and both of us longed to talk to an old friend.

'I will hire a tonga to take us,' Ajit said. 'Even if you were well, the heat at present is too great for walking.'

On the morning of the day of the dinner party Chundabhai's peon again presented himself and announced that Chundabhai would be sending a car for us, as he felt that the long journey to the other side of the city would be arduous, if we travelled by bus.

With trembling hands, I dressed myself carefully for the occasion, and Ajit declared that I looked like Sita herself. Make-up could not hide the drawn look of my face, but I did not oil my hair that day and instead let it curl softly round my face. I loathed the daily oil bath that the hot, dry climate made necessary, and was glad to abandon the practice for one day.

When Chundabhai's car arrived, the Misses Shah came out on to their veranda to wave us farewell; they were nearly as excited as we were and looked forward to enjoying our visit at second-hand, as soon as we could return and tell them about it.

We drove across the city through the narrow, busy streets and then out into a district where houses bigger than most dwellings in England were set apart from each other amid groves of trees. We were swept through high gates where a khaki-clad watchman sat staff in hand like a petty king, up a long drive lined with trees and eventually came to a stop before a wide flight of steps.

A peon opened the car door, and I looked out at a fairytale palace with pure white walls, marble verandas and teak doors. It was surrounded by shade trees through which the setting sun hardly penetrated. It was cool as I stepped out of the car, heavenly cool.

We followed a bearer through the porticoed frontage, through double doors flung wide open and into an immense circular hall, round the sides of which curved a staircase leading to a series of galleries above. In the centre of the hall a fountain played in a pool covered with water-lilies.

Ajit grinned at me slyly when he saw the wonderment on my face as we mounted the stairs, passing as we ascended a series of niches in the wall in which sat stone gods carved in meticulous detail. From above came the sound of a very loud voice shouting in Gujerati. It was not an angry voice – but certainly Chundabhai had not lost his vocal cords since we last saw him.

We entered a large, square room, where about a dozen ladies and gentlemen were seated on settees and drinking tomato-juice cocktails. In the middle of a pink Chinese carpet stood Chundabhai talking to four ladies of most sophisticated appearance. Chundabhai looked like a straining village ox amongst delicate ivory figurines; but there was nothing oxlike in the shrewd, hazel eyes glowing in the bullet head which crowned his mountain of a body. He was garbed in the handwoven cotton shirt and loincloth beloved of Congressmen, and his broad feet were slipped loosely into leather sandals.

At our entrance he stopped in the middle of a sentence, excused himself and strode across the floor to us.

'Welcome, welcome,' he boomed as he folded his hands together in salute. 'Singh, it is good to see you again – and Mrs Singh – how beautiful you look in a sari,' and he whispered impishly, 'Some men have all the luck. You must meet my wife.'

At the top of his voice he called his wife, and a voice at his elbow said: 'I am here.' A tiny, hard-faced woman came forward. She looked rather grim, but she was an accomplished hostess and carried me off to meet the other ladies present.

Ajit had told me that it was well known that Mrs Patel did not approve of her husband and, in fact, it was hard to find anything of which she did approve. There were no children of the marriage, and the story went that examination by specialists had showed that Chundabhai was at fault, which did not make his wife more tolerant of him; and they quarrelled frequently. Chundabhai had lingered abroad longer than he need, I knew, and I could see bitterness between his wife and him.

With frigid courtesy Mrs Patel conducted me round the room, which in its furnishings was a graceful mixture of Indian and English styles, and introduced me in a formal fashion to the other ladies.

Two young women dressed in the briefest of blouses and the most transparent of saris, having eyed me up and down rather insolently during Mrs Patel's introduction, made room for me on the red upholstered settee on which they were reclining. I sank down thankfully, still panting a little from the climb up the staircase.

The girls by whom I sat proved to be less sophisticated than their dress indicated. Their English was good and they were soon confiding to me that Chundabhai's dinners were always a bore, firstly, because his wife was such a spoilsport and, secondly, because no meat or alcohol were served. I was amused by their complaints and, having accepted a glass of tomato juice brought to me on a silver tray by a bearer, I sat back and prepared to enjoy myself.

The young ladies bent their flowerladen heads close to my ears and asked confidentially if I ate meat.

'No,' I said, having been previously primed on this point by Ajit, 'neither my husband nor I eat meat.'

Disappointed they drew back from me, only to lean forward again and whisper: 'Do you drink?'

To comfort them and gain their confidence, I said: 'I enjoy a glass of wine.'

Morbid interest sprang into their eyes.

'Do you drink whisky?' they asked in chorus.

'No. Not many English ladies do – and here you have

187

prohibition – so I am reduced to tomato juice.'

They sniggered. 'Aha, you do not know the secret,' exclaimed one, wagging her forefinger. 'Plenty of drinks are available – if you know where to look – but first you must go to the Civil Surgeon and be registered as an addict.'

'An addict?'

'Yes, then you can get a legal drink ration. After that you can buy on the black-market – and if you are found drunk you can always say that you drank all your ration in one day.' The lilting voice was full of laughter, and the speaker leaned closer to me to whisper into my ear a very improper story of the drunkenness of one of the ladies present. 'She employs two ayahs for the sole purpose of putting her to bed when she is drunk,' she finished up.

I was feeling very embarrassed at the malicious gossip poured into my ears, when a bearer announced to my relief that dinner was ready, and the guests rose and moved through an archway which had hitherto been curtained.

When I passed under the archway, I exclaimed with delight. I found myself on a large veranda round which the treetops swayed in the wind. A gold sovereign of a moon lit up the marble balustrade and floor. In the centre of the veranda, a dinner table had been set, and we ranged ourselves informally round it.

The servants under the direction of a bearer in a turban brought each guest a beaten silver tray on which lay the usual cups of curry and heaps of chutney, rice and puris. It looked most inviting and the guests ate with enjoyment, although one of my new acquaintances pulled a face at me across the table and mouthed the words: 'No meat.'

I was still clumsy at eating with my hands and I looked round my tray for a spoon but there was none. Cautiously I tore a puri, being careful to use only my right hand, and began to eat, but I dropped a morsel of curry on the cloth. Blushing with embarrassment, I tried to remember the Gujerati word for spoon so that I could ask a servant for one, but it evaded me. I could not remember it either in that language or in Hindi.

After a minute of quiet struggling on my part, a voice

rolled down the table: 'Mrs Singh, can I order anything that you would like to eat? Our curries are peculiar, I know.'

I jumped. I had forgotten the watchful eye of my host, beside whom Ajit was sitting.

Feeling my cheeks burning with blushes, I said: 'Patel Sahib, the curries are delicious but I am clumsy at eating with my hands. Would you kindly ask the bearer for a spoon.'

At this there was a burst of good-natured merriment from everybody, and the lady and gentleman sitting next to me both turned and said reproachfully: 'You should have told us. We would have asked for a spoon for you.'

The concern on their faces was almost ludicrous, and they spent the rest of the time at table making me feel at home, while Chundabhai kept sending the bearer to me with dishes that he thought I might like. Occasionally he shouted a cheerful query at me or teased the couple looking after me, who proved to be husband and wife. The husband was an astronomer and his wife, though not so well qualified, worked with him. The husband had educated his wife after marriage, and I was impressed with the earnestness with which she must have studied, just as I was daily impressed by the patient application of the Shah sisters.

I listened with interest to an account of the astronomer's work given by his wife. It was much interrupted, she said, by visits of important people, political leaders and Government officials.

'These people,' said the little wife with a laugh, 'they come expecting to see weird instruments making big noise. They are disappointed if my husband is not always looking through telescope – if he do the calculation or sit and think they imagine he not work. They think this man play with paper and pencil and waste good Government money. Jobs we must have and our student they must keep their scholarships, so we no disappoint our visitors. We make excellent assembly of noisy instruments with which visitors can play.' She waved her hands and shrugged her shoulders. 'Then we work at evening when no visitors come and it is quiet.'

I laughed heartily at this recital, although the husband

looked somewhat disapproving. I could well imagine Members of the Opposition in England bouncing out of their parliamentary seats to ask why Government funds were being wasted on astronomers who spent their time doodling, it seemed, or sitting in an easy chair doing nothing.

After dinner two servants brought a brass ewer filled with water, and a basin and towels. Each guest washed his hands by holding them over a bowl while a servant poured water over them.

It was while waiting to perform this ceremony that I found myself standing next to Chundabhai, a little apart from the other guests. He was staring through me, quite oblivious of his surroundings.

I said: 'It must seem strange to be catapulted back into India after so long in England.'

He jumped, looked at me gently and said: 'Indeed, Peggie, it is very strange – although this is my home and these are my people – and my true life is here.'

I thought of Sheila Ferguson and perhaps he did at the same time for he said quickly: 'I cannot expect to have everything in life – I have so much.'

I remembered Sheila's adorable roundness and her irrepressible laughter in comparison with Mrs Patel's frozen disappointment in life. If he had cared to invoke the old Hindu law, he could have replaced his wife by sending her elsewhere to live, and marrying Sheila as his second wife.

'Chundy, you are very good,' I said impulsively.

He grinned at me wickedly: 'My coat of virtue is thin,' he said. 'Go forward, Mrs Singh, and wash your hands – a brass bowl is at least a change from porcelain.'

Chundabhai moved over to a knot of male guests and began to tell one of his interminable funny stories. From the expressions on the faces of the guests it was obvious to me that they had heard the story before, but as a rich man's jokes are always funny they laughed uproariously, and Chundabhai beamed once more.

Mrs Patel came over to say a few words to me. She gave the impression of long since having lost all warmth of feeling for other people. When I considered her in conjunction with her husband I pitied her. Her marriage, I thought, would have been arranged by her father when she was about fourteen; it had been, I knew, the union of two great families of chemical manufacturers, and would have appeared a good match to an outsider. But even at fifteen Chundabhai must have been big and awkward; his tremendous desire to try everything, to explore, to take to himself all that life could give a rich man's son, must have frightened still more a terrified, purdah-bred fourteen-year-old. She must have feared his huge hands and the cold clarity of the brain that dictated their movements, and she must have shrunk away mentally and physically. And then to have no child would humiliate her in the eyes of her friends and complete her misery. Chundabhai needed someone tough and passionate like Sheila, not a shy young girl who had become a frigid, disillusioned woman.

The object of my reverie asked me how I liked India and whether my Hindi was sufficient to enable me to talk to my mother-in-law and sisters-in-law.

I said I was very happy in India, although I was having the normal difficulties of a newcomer. Absent-mindedly I added: 'As yet I have not met Ajit's family.'

Mrs Patel's eyebrows shot up and I realised my mistake too late. The implications of my remark were manifold.

'I came straight from Bombay to Shahpur, as Ajit had to take up a post here,' I said hastily.

'Doubtless one of your sisters-in-law came to help you start your new home?'

I could feel my face reddening. Damn Ajit's family, I thought.

'No,' I said sharply, 'my sister-in-law was not free to come.'

At that moment there was a stir as the guests prepared to leave, and I immediately got up from my chair. Mrs Patel realised that she had embarrassed me and said politely: 'Please call on me if I can be of help.'

I thanked her, and in the turmoil of farewells my face had a chance to recover its former whiteness; but a bitterness cankered in me as I thought of the indifference of Ajit's family. I had done them no harm but they were making me suffer a dozen steady pinpricks. A little help and advice from one of them would have saved me a lot of suffering.

In the car going home, Ajit mentioned that Chundabhai had asked him to have a look at the recording instruments in his works, and this might mean later a place as consultant and consequently more money for saris and blouses. I smiled and kissed him.

'As a Government servant, will you be allowed to be a consultant?'

'Probably not – but I am looking at this from a long-term point of view – I have a five-year contract with the Government at present – and after that possibly there will be other openings elsewhere. I do not want you to spend your life sweating in Shahpur. We shall see.'

'I like Shahpur,' I said. 'I like Pandipura – and the desert – and the wild animals – and the country people.'

Ajit looked down at me in astonishment. 'Do you really?'

'Yes,' I said.

'Well, I'm damned,' he said incredulously.

The next day, however, I was not interested in saris or Shahpur or anything else. The rich meal which I had foolishly eaten at Chundabhai's made me ill again, and after struggling to get Ajit's breakfast I crept back on to my bed.

Ajit promised to send the power-house peon for the doctor.

CHAPTER TWENTY-EIGHT

The last of the monsoon rain was dripping off the roofs of Delhi when a bored Bimla decided to call on Nulini. When she arrived at Ram Singh's house, however, she found that her friend had gone to a purdah party.

'Ma ji is at home,' Thakkur informed her, having explained about Nulini's absence.

'I will come in and see her for a few minutes.'

Thakkur escorted her through the house to the inner courtyard, her Ayah trotting behind them and noting that Khan was sitting with his hands folded in his lap, by the door leading to the courtyard. He scrambled to his feet and salaamed as Bimla passed.

Mrs Singh was sitting in a basket chair in the driest corner of the veranda. She held a letter in her hand and had just finished reading it; her generously curved mouth drooped and she was nodding her head disconsolately from side to side.

She greeted Bimla rather absent-mindedly, invited her to sit down on the chair beside her and then continued to stare silently at the letter.

She suddenly realised that she had a guest, and abruptly thanked Bimla for the invitation to her wedding, which, accompanied by a personal note from Bimla's father, had arrived that day; after which effort at conversation she again relapsed into silence.

Bimla made herself comfortable in her chair and wondered what bad news was contained in the letter. Mrs Singh was certainly far from being her usual gracious self. Although there was a great difference in age between the two women, there was an odd intimacy between them. After her hot-tempered mother, Bimla found Mrs Singh a sweet and loving confidante who listened to her childish woes as her mother never had the patience to do; and to Mrs Singh, Bimla had always been a prospective daughter-in-law whose beauty and honesty would one day grace her house. After a gloomy minute or two, therefore, Bimla ventured to ask if Mrs Singh had any news of Ajit – Bimla was now fully engrossed by her new fiancé and could think of Ajit with comfortable condescension.

Silently Mrs Singh handed the letter to Bimla.

Bimla glanced over it.

Ajit sent his best respects to his mother and father. His work was progressing satisfactorily. Peggie was still ill. A kind neighbour was helping to take care of her. And that was all.

Bimla returned the letter without comment, and for

some time they surveyed the garden glittering with raindrops.

'It is a hard family,' said Mrs Singh at last, 'that will not send a member to one who is sick. And these neighbours – who are they? The Gods only know what stupid things they will do – she might die.'

'You have been very patient . . .' Bimla began cautiously, but her remark was cut off as Shushila bounced up the steps, her sandals covered with mud and her hands full of wet, white flowers.

'Mummy, Mummy,' she cried, 'I want to go to the bazaar with Thakkur. He says in two days it is Ruksha Bandhan.' She dumped the flowers in her mother's lap, and went on importantly, 'I must prepare for it. All must be ready for Ajit and Bhim.'

Her mother smiled sadly. In their caste at this most important Festival all the young men renewed their vows to protect their womenfolk with their lives, and such protection could be claimed by any other woman if she placed a bracelet on the wrist of a young warrior.

'Hullo, Bimla,' said Shushila, her mind full of thoughts of the Festival, as she rubbed her cheek impatiently against her mother's shoulder, and then went on to announce that she must go immediately and buy two bright, tinsel bracelets to place on her brothers' arms. Would Mother also please give her some vermilion and could Maharaj give her some raw rice, so that she could make good caste marks for them? She would then have two mighty warriors to protect her. And would Maharaj make lots of sweetmeats, and please could they all go to the pictures together in the evening?

Finally, as her mother made no answer, she asked: 'Are you cross, Mummy?' and Thakkur, standing in the mud outside, eyed his mistress curiously.

'No, Shushi,' she said as she straightened the child's Turkish trousers and shirt. 'Unfortunately Ajit will not be able to come for Ruksha Bandhan this year.'

Shushila was shocked. 'But, Mummy,' she wailed, 'it's the first time I could play bracelets with him – he is naughty,' and she stamped her foot. The plump face crinkled up and tears threatened.

'Well – ' said her mother uncertainly, 'Bhim will certainly be here – and you could buy two bracelets, in case Ajit is able to come after all.' Her voice trailed away. She did not know what to tell Shushila. Although it was a choice titbit for gossip, the secret of Ajit's marriage had been well kept, both by the Singhs and the Chand Ranas. For once, Kasher Chand Rana had asserted himself in his own house, and had said grimly that his wife and daughter must be silent on the subject, otherwise Bimla would lose her second chance of a marriage. Ram Singh, Mrs Singh and Bhim had told no one, and though a faint rumour seemed to have gone round the neighbourhood it had apparently died.

Once she had recovered from the shock of the news of Ajit's marriage, Bimla had enjoyed herself, as Kasher Chand Rana, being wiser than his daughter realised, had allowed Ajit's handsome cousin to court his future wife. The boy really loved her and courted her with remarkable skill, with the result that Bimla had suddenly become quite dovelike.

Bimla's Ayah had presented a problem to Kasher, as her tongue was very likely to wag. He had, therefore, sent for her and with the air of a conspirator, had explained that for Bimla's sake nothing must at present be said about Ajit's affairs. Ayah could, however, be most helpful if she would let it be known in the course of casual gossip that, on meeting again, Bimla and Ajit had not felt suited to each other, and as the parents wished only for their children's happiness, a fresh suitor had been found. Delighted at being asked a favour by her master, the old Ayah had fulfilled the commission with an ability born of long practice in the art of gossip.

'Go with Thakkur,' said Mrs Singh to Shushila, 'and choose two pretty bracelets. I will also give you some annas to buy glass bracelets for yourself. Look,' she went on, trying to sound gay as she lifted up one fat wrist on which only two gold bracelets remained, 'look, you haven't a single glass bracelet left to match your dress.'

Shushila giggled. 'I broke the last one fighting with cousin Ranji,' she said.

Her mother opened her handbag and took out a rupee. Shushila joyfully snatched it away and ran down the steps to join Thakkur.

Bimla had been silent during Shushila's presence, except for acknowledging the child's greeting. Now she said: 'What a fine handbag that is.'

Mrs Singh nodded and clicked it shut. 'Yes, Ajit brought it from England.'

Ajit had told her that Peggie had helped to choose it. Now Mrs Singh looked at it again. Someone had really given consideration to her requirements. The bag was white and finished in such a way as to be washable and, although elegant in design, it had many pockets and sections, such as are loved by housewives.

Idly she opened the bag again and her slender fingers poked about in it. Bimla saw her expression change suddenly. She poked more purposefully and then drew out a small card. She turned it over slowly in her hand, and Bimla got up from her chair and came over to see what she had found.

The card had silver flowers embossed upon it and also something written in ink. Mrs Singh could not read the English words, so she handed the card to Bimla. 'What does it say?'

Bimla read out: 'To dearest Mother, with much love, Ajit and Peggie.' She translated it into Hindi.

'Hey, Ramji,' exclaimed Mrs Singh. It was not the kind of message which an Indian daughter-in-law would have penned, but the kindly meaning of it was undoubted.

'Dearest Mother,' repeated Mrs Singh thoughtfully and pursed her lips.

Bimla stared at the message which her rival had written without realising that she was to be ostracised by her dearest Mother. She thought of my lying sick in Shahpur, and she realised that if I had not come into Ajit's life, she would have had to marry him instead of the handsome, romantic boy who was soon to be her husband. She kept silent, however, and Mrs Singh began to speak slowly and reflectively as if talking to herself. 'I am a woman from a small village. When I first came to Delhi to be married my

196

ways were the ways of village people, and my mother-in-law taught me with great patience the ways of the city. We were in purdah and such confinement was new to me – but still we had to know how to make welcome the wives of the English and the wives of the powerful.' Mrs Singh laughed softly. 'I remember she had a special tea set for casteless visitors – it was kept in a special cupboard by itself, so that our vessels should not be polluted. So much she taught me – and I? Arree, what have I done for my daughter-in-law?'

'She is not of your caste,' said Bimla.

'Caste? What is that in these days? My son suffers because his wife suffers. Hey, Ram, what a mess!'

Khan, who had remained placidly seated out of earshot while he waited for his master, now rose and salaamed. Ram Singh swept on to the veranda, inclining his head in acknowledgement of the salaam. He saw his wife and Bimla and came forward to greet them.

Both women hastily covered their heads with their veils. Ram Singh motioned them to remain seated, put down the copy of the Upanishads which he had been carrying, and sat down in the basket chair. 'No tea yet?' he asked querulously.

'It will be coming soon,' Mrs Singh said, and at that moment Thakkur appeared from the direction of the kitchen bearing a tray. He set the tray on a table in front of Mrs Singh and departed, and Ram Singh leaned forward and took a pakaurhi which he stabbed irritably into the chutney.

'I shall have to go up to Simla,' he said. 'There is a land dispute on which I have been asked to give an opinion. Would you like to come too?'

Mrs Singh looked as if she had made up her mind suddenly.

'No. If you are agreeable to it, I should like to visit Jaipur sister while you are away. She has not been well for some time.'

'Sister ill? Is it serious?'

'Oh, no,' said Mrs Singh hastily. 'Just the hot weather has given her fever.'

'If it had not been for this dispute, I could have come with you . . .'

'Oh, no, no,' exclaimed Mrs Singh, 'there is no need for you to come with me. I will take Thakkur.'

'Well, I suggest that you go on the day after Ruksha Bandhan – I shall have to travel on the same day. The change will do you good – you are looking tired.' He took another pakaurhi and munched it more contentedly. 'By all means take Thakkur – have another pakaurhi, Bimla, they are good – how's Rana Sahib?' and he handed her the dish.

Bimla said: 'Quite well, thank you,' and took a pakaurhi. She had retired into the background upon the arrival of Ram Singh, her head covered and her eyes cast discreetly down while she laughed to herself. She had a suspicion that Mrs Singh's destination would not be Jaipur but Shahpur. Of course she would take Thakkur on such an expedition – Thakkur who would have died for her if need be. As a boy, he had come from Mrs Singh's own village and served three generations of Singhs. He loved them all, but his true loyalty was to Mrs Singh. He would certainly disapprove of such an adventure – but he would do as Mrs Singh bade him.

Ram Singh leaned back in his chair and twiddled his moustaches.

'Then it is settled. Nulini and Bhim will take care of Shushila – I do not wish that she should take a journey so soon after the monsoon – too much polluted water about – she might catch typhoid.'

Mrs Singh nodded.

'I will take Khan to Simla – after that he is to go home to be married.' He rambled on, teasing Bimla about her forthcoming marriage and saying that next hot season both families should make an expedition to Nan-y-Tal, since they had not been away this year. She answered shyly that her respected father would no doubt be delighted. She did not, however, hear Ram Singh's rejoinder – her attention had been caught by a movement behind Ram Singh.

Khan had again risen and salaamed. Nulini, returning from her purdah party, came through the house door and on to the veranda. Khan had kept his head down as he salaamed, so he did not see the expression that flashed across Nulini's face – but Bimla saw it.

As she looked down on the servant, her face had become unutterably sad, and then she smiled with a tenderness that Bimla had seen before only on the face of her own fiancé. When passing, her sari brushed Khan's salaaming hands, and when he squatted down again he put his hands against his lips.

The incident was over in a second, and Nulini was advancing towards her, hands together in salute, while the Singhs' Ayah made her appearance through the same door and grumbled that her sandals were soaked and it was too wet for any sensible soul to go visiting. Bimla pulled herself together and greeted her friend, although her heart was beating like a wedding drum. O Lord, so that was how Nulini knew about Ajit's marriage, she thought. A trusted servant could have overheard Ram Singh lecturing his son – and if the terrible suspicions which filled her mind were true, it was quite likely that Khan had told Nulini.

Bhim was going to pay dearly for his neglect of his scatterbrained wife, Bimla thought. Poor Nulini! She knew that her friend missed the club life which her father had permitted her to enjoy when single. She must have found the Singh household singularly dull, and this, added to Bhim's preoccupation with his work and her lack of a child, must have made her intensely lonely. Mrs Singh had the house to run, Shushila had her lessons and her games with her cousins, but Nulini had nothing to do all day except for a few simple tasks set her by her mother-in-law. She must have turned in despair, driven by the unsatisfied needs of body and mind, to the only love she could find – that of a servant. It was the age-old tragedy all over again – a wife cut off as usual from any other male society had sought a lover in the kitchen – although in this case it seemed more than lust. Bimla visualised again the tender smile and Khan kissing his hands – Ram have mercy on them – they really loved each other.

After exchanging a few politenesses, a very shaky Bimla took leave of the Singhs. She shivered although the weather was warm and sticky, and asked for her own Ayah to be brought from the kitchen. Ram Singh insisted that she should go home in the car and she had to wait a little while until it was brought round to the front door by Khan.

They climbed in, Khan shut the door, got in himself and drove them through the puddly streets. Bimla looked at the back of his proud head and straight shoulders. A warrior from the hills, she guessed, who had come down to the plains to earn some ready money to assist in a family crisis. No wonder Nulini had fallen in love.

But in the Name of God, what would they do to Nulini when her adultery was found out? And it would be found out. Some other eyes as sharp as Bimla's own would notice, and gradually a hasty whisper to someone else would become a crawling rumour, which would grow and grow until it strangled both Khan and Nulini.

Supposing Nulini was thrown out of her father-in-law's house – what then? Probably her father would not take back an adulterous woman, perhaps carrying a bastard child. There was no way, thought Bimla frantically, in which a middle-class woman without a degree could earn a living – except in a brothel. Bimla did not know much about prostitution other than that the women invariably died of revolting diseases; and she reeled as she thought of her friend, silly but not wicked, screaming out her death agony in some back alley.

And Khan? What of him? He would be beaten half to death – as he deserved, thought Bimla savagely – and then thrown into the street, to find his way back to his native mountains as best he could, since he would find it difficult to obtain another job without a reference. He could not help Nulini – supposing even that he was able to take her home, high into the Himalayas, she would die after a few weeks of harsh life as a mountain woman – would die as certainly as if she had remained in Delhi.

Bimla's sly old Ayah asked if she was well.

'Of course I am,' said Bimla testily, as the car drew up in her father's driveway.

Khan got down and opened the door for her. She cast a fleeting glance at him through her veil. He was a sturdy specimen of manhood, though small. The slightly

Mongolian cast of feature was not unpleasing and the expression was genial. Bimla wondered what it would be like to be kissed by such a man – and then hastily flung the thought from her as being most unmaidenly. She flinched, however, at the idea of such excellence being beaten into utter ugliness.

Ayah must have looked at him too, because she said as they walked up the front steps: 'If I were Singh Sahib, I would not employ a man such as that in a house where I had a young daughter-in-law. A man of more mature years would be a better choice.'

'What do you mean, Ayah?'

Ayah looked even more cunning than usual: 'Nothing, nothing,' she said. 'You are too young to understand such matters.'

'I am twenty-five and about to marry.'

'Tut, tut, my pretty. Do not be angered. I only made a remark.' And Ayah folded her lips virtuously, picked up the slippers which Bimla had kicked into two different corners of the hall, and went away, leaving Bimla full of dread that Nulini's secret was already out.

CHAPTER TWENTY-NINE

At lunchtime, two days after Ruksha Bandhan, as Ajit sat on my bed eating the thick village bread and lentil soup which had been prepared for him by our old sweeper woman, the postman handed him through the window an unusually bulky letter. There was also a letter for me from Mother.

As I had been largely confined to bed for over a fortnight Ajit had moved the bedstead into the living-room, and in this new position I had some hope of seeing, without getting up, what was going on in my neglected home.

Ajit had suspected that the doctor was deliberately not hurrying about curing me, since by his standards we were rich and well able to pay his bills. He had threatened to find another doctor unless I was cured within a fortnight, and whether it was the threat or a fortuitous combination of circumstances, I do not know, but I had become slowly better and for four days there had been no recurrence of the dysentery. I was very weak, however, and had no strength left with which to fight any other disease I might easily catch in such damp weather.

The monsoon had been unusually heavy for the district, and everywhere the earth steamed and gave birth to crops, insects and germs. I had been astonished to see the endless stretches of sand round our house become clothed in a few weeks with a closely patterned carpet of wild flowers and grass, and I longed to go out and walk and drink in the loveliness of it. But I was too weak and had to be content with the bunches of tiny flowers which Ajit stopped to gather for me on his way back from the power house.

Occasionally, I saw a snake slide silently along the path in front of the house, and Ajit warned me that if I found one in the house I was to leave it undisturbed, shut the door of the room in which it lay, and ask Kamala or the watchman to get someone to kill it; non-violence did not extend to snakes.

Typhoid and malaria were frequent visitors to the villages, and, according to Miss Shah, some cases of cholera in the city had made a harassed Director of Health order mass injections, to avoid a repetition of the epidemic of the previous year.

I dragged myself into a sitting position and pushed my damp hair away from my face. My head buzzed, but I asked as cheerfully as I could: 'What have you got there?'

Ajit gulped down the last piece of bread, picked up the letter again and turned it over and over in his hand. The address had been laboriously written in English. He tore open the envelope – and a glittering bundle fell out.

I could see that the bundle consisted of a piece of tinsel, to which was attached shiny red and green paper fringed with gold; a few grains of rice were clinging to the tinsel and there was also a folded paper stained pink and much finger marked. In addition, there was a letter.

'Ruksha Bandhan,' Ajit exclaimed immediately he saw

the collection from the envelope. His hands shook as he unfolded the letter.

'It's Shushila,' he said softly, and, after a pause to scan the letter, he added: 'Father did not even ask if I would be free to come home for Ruksha Bandhan.' His mouth quivered, as he reread the letter.

'Darling, what is it?' I asked, slipping my arms round him.

He dropped the letter on to the table and explained the ceremony to me, its importance to his caste and Shushila's disappointment at his absence. Normally, he would have gone home for the ceremony as a matter of course, but this year he knew he was not very welcome and he had hoped that his father would write and tell him to come. His father had not written.

I took the tinsel bracelet and, kneeling up on the bed, I tied the emblem round his wrist. 'Now,' I said gaily, hoping to divert his thoughts, 'you are my warrior and will protect me.'

He looked down at me and I must have seemed a helpless, tousled wretch to him. His eyes went moist.

'My dear,' he said, lifting me close to him, 'I have not been able to protect you from anything. You are so sick – and I dreamed of making you so happy.' He wept, his head resting against mine.

I stroked the smooth black head and tried not to cry myself. 'My love, don't cry. You have made me very happy – do you hear me – very happy. I would not change my present life for anybody else's. All I need is to get well – and I will get well, never fear.'

I crooned the words to him and because I spoke the truth he was convinced and a little comforted. In the depth of my being I was happy. I loved my husband and I was content in this strange, isolated flat, despite the crushing amount of work and the lack of any semblance of Western culture.

Since our misunderstanding on the morning after my arrival in Pandipura, Ajit had been careful to remember that I was a stranger to his customs and outlook, and we had spent many evening hours discussing religion, politics, love, domestic customs and so on, until gradually I began to understand at least a few of the complexities of Indian life and became less easily irritated by the slowness with which everything moved and the inefficiency with which even the smallest service was performed.

My heart went out to Ajit whose job it was to help to build a modern power house in a country where tomorrow is still a better day for working than today, where workmen's hands are more used to milking cows than fixing circuits and where persistent undernourishment and malaria make those hands soon tired. And yet the power house was going up. I had seen it myself, one day when I felt stronger and had sat on the back of Ajit's bicycle while he peddled me to it over the scrub land.

Occasionally some of his colleagues came to our flat for a game of bridge, which they played sitting on a mat spread on the veranda, and I heard their bitter complaints of the inefficiency here, the corruption there. Their complaints may have been well justified, but the fact remained that Mother India was building her children something better than they had ever seen before, and there was no doubt in my mind that very soon the water-drawing ox at the back of our flat would be replaced by an electric pump lifting water from a much deeper well, so that the villagers who owned it would be able to irrigate a larger area with less backbreaking work, and the food in the village would be that much increased.

There were plenty of men like Ajit, who, although their tongues were acid-dipped when talking about the shortcomings of their country, worked like demons, so that electric power might be provided and industry and agriculture might flourish in a district which otherwise was destined to become an unpeopled waste.

The man in my arms ceased to weep and lay rested. Usually buoyantly optimistic, he occasionally plunged into the depths of depression, and this seemed a particularly bad bout. I thought of all the small hardships he had had to endure, in addition to re-accustoming himself to his own country and teaching me how to live in it. I held him close.

'Darling,' I said, 'I think you forget the wonders you have performed since I came here. You have held down an important post although you are so young; you have struggled back and forth to work on that awful old bike in appalling heat; you have hardly known what it is to come home to a properly prepared meal; you have cooked and taught me how to cook when you must have been weak with hunger and weariness – and you have even had to wash and iron your own clothes. All this, from a man who has been waited upon all his life, is quite a wonderful achievement to me.'

I lifted his face and kissed him: 'Now the dysentery is gone, I'll soon get strong – you will see.'

He smiled. 'When you are stronger I will send you up to the hills.'

'Oh, no,' I said, appalled at the idea of going six hundred miles away to a hill station without him. 'No – I couldn't leave you – I just couldn't.'

'You are a strange girl. Most women would jump at the opportunity of a holiday in a fashionable hill station.'

'I would die of misery without you.'

He pinched my cheek, his eyes twinkled and he said: 'In that case, after I have been here six months I will take the ten days' leave which I shall have accumulated and we will go together to Bombay – it's at least a trifle cooler and the sea air may help you. We will have a honeymoon – yes? – and thus avoid a funeral pyre.'

'That would be wonderful.'

'I need a holiday myself.'

He did. I realised with some fear that his face was lined and thin. Poor food was having a deleterious effect on him too. Milk diluted to a blue thinness by the milkman, no butter, meat or fish, few eggs now I was too sick to fetch them, improperly cooked vegetables and bread – what chance had either of us on such a diet? I must get up, I thought, I must get up and I must learn to provide properly balanced meals. But from whom should I learn? The lecturers and teachers amongst whom we lived could not afford to eat very well, and most of them were undernourished, eating too much starch and too few proteins. Even the villagers looked better fed than they. I must ask Kamala how she prepared her father's food and find out what made her so strong. Unfortunately Mrs Patel was a very unapproachable person and had, in any case, gone to visit her parents in Kathiawar, so I could not get advice from her.

In the absence of his wife, Chundabhai had called on us several times and his visits were a delight. He always brought fruit and lettuces from his garden, and sat for an hour cracking jokes in his roaring voice, until his chauffeur came to remind him of his next engagement. Then he would depart in a cloud of sand, the big voice getting fainter and fainter as the car threaded its way through the narrow path.

'I must go back to work,' said Ajit, easing himself away from me. He seemed comforted, and kissed me lovingly before he left.

When he had gone, I lay staring at the dirty vessels on the table. The flies were already collecting on them. Suddenly I began to weep. To muffle the noise of the sobs that came from me I turned my face into the pillow.

'O Lord,' I prayed, 'if you really exist, help me to get well. If I can get strong, I can learn to do everything here. Help me, O God, to help my husband.'

But Lord Krishna looked down from his shelf near the kitchen door and smiled his same ivory smile and fingered his ivory flute with his ivory fingers; and from a print of one of Raphael's pictures which hung by my bed, the Holy Child smiled equally enigmatically. Ajit believed that they were two manifestations of the same great God, and I was prepared to believe him, but they were of little comfort to me.

I wept myself to sleep.

Now, although always warned by Ajit to keep the outside doors bolted, I never did so during daylight hours. Even the advent of the frightening stranger who had lit my fire had not been able to persuade me that there was anything outside that would harm me. The bleak land was always so quiet, and I loved to see the shifting light and shade on the sand. I used to take as much of my work as possible on to the veranda, and from there, as I cleaned grain or mended shirts, I could watch the crows and other birds go about their noisy business. A myriad of strange multicoloured insects, from locusts to tiny spiders like red velvet pin-cushions, lived in and around the veranda, and whenever I had time to spare I would squat on my heels and watch them work. With the coming of the monsoon their number had multiplied, and to keep out the larger and more dangerous ones, such as scorpions – and also snakes – Ajit had got a carpenter from the power-house site to screw a bar of wood across the threshold, so that when the door was shut nothing very big could crawl in. It was still necessary, however, to deter ants from entering. They were worthy adversaries and endless kettles of boiling water and sprays of insecticide stopped their coming only temporarily – they always returned to the attack.

There were plenty of animals to watch, too – baboons, wild ponies, jackals, wild cats and dogs, and, of course, cows, buffaloes, camels and goats which came to graze on the sparse herbage. With the domestic animals came the herdsmen and boys. I think it was knowing them that made me feel so safe. At first I was an intruder into their world, like the other people in the flats, but after a while they came to know that I would always give them water if they asked, and that I never made a cup of tea without sharing it with some small boy or girl. I was never angry if by chance a goat strayed into my living-room or a very small boy scrambled up my steps. My washing frequently blew off the veranda and when they brought it back to me they found I could speak their language a little, so they stayed to talk and thus they got to know me. The other flat dwellers swore that the village people would steal from me, but, although my open doors would have made it simple for them to do so and Kamala came and went freely, nothing was ever stolen.

Before I had become too weak to do so, I had wandered round the nearest villages, avoiding, however, the Criminal Tribe village about which Kamala had warned me repeatedly. This was a village started by the Government in an effort to transform a tribe that had lived for centuries by raiding into a peaceful farming community. The Government seemed to be having some success with their experiment, but the local inhabitants were still deeply distrustful of these ex-raiders. Most of the villages were a close huddle of huts, with an occasional small brick house. Narrow alleys filled with rubbish turned and twisted between the dwellings, and as I walked, stopping occasionally to stroke a baby goat tethered near a doorway, dogs barked and snapped at my heels.

People stared at me, but they soon found out from whence I came and almost invariably I was offered water or buttermilk to drink. Inside the huts, I saw, cleanliness and neatness reigned. The thalis and cooking pots were ranged neatly in niches in the wall, spare clothing was hung tidily over a clothes line across the hut and the floor was swept smooth. The thick mud walls gave some measure of protection in the heat of the day; but life went on mostly in the little space in front of the hut, where sometimes a rough wooden bed would be placed on which people could sit. During the monsoon, however, life in the villages must have been most miserable, as the water dripped through inadequate roofs and the cooking fires had to be brought indoors.

The village women heard from Kamala of the strange way of living of the Memsahib. They also heard that I was sick and although they were too shy to walk up the veranda steps to inquire after my health, they peeped through the window, smiled at me as I lay on my bed and wished me soon well.

I had other visitors – beggars and holy men, for whom I kept a pot of annas, and to each supplicant I gave two annas; a few of them came every week to collect this small dole but most of them travelled onward to unknown destinations. I kept also any food left over from the last meal and any old clothes we had, and these also I gave. Ours was the only well for several miles from the city and so I offered water to all who knocked at our door; this made the Brahmin lady who lived on the floor above point out that Ajit was a caste Hindu and his water pots should not be polluted by those of lower castes or by untouchables. When I told Ajit about her complaint, he just laughed and told me to scrub the vessels they touched very thoroughly as many beggars were diseased.

Although I hardly realised it at the time, I was slowly becoming part of India. Each friend I made, each custom I learned to understand and tolerate, was a thread which bound me closer to her and made me part of her multicoloured pattern. Just as in times past she had absorbed invader after invader, she was absorbing me, tolerating my idiosyncrasies and asking only toleration in return. The desperate mental loneliness which had afflicted me at first grew less as the good teachers living round me strove to understand me and meet me half-way in my struggles in a strange society. We did not always approve of each other, my neighbours and I, but we recognised each other's virtues and hesitated to condemn what appeared to be vices.

And so I slept with my door open to the hot desert wind, feeling perfectly safe amongst the people and animals who knew me. I slept so deeply that it was the eldest Miss Shah, and not I, who heard the taxi draw up. She immediately abandoned her vina practice and went outside to see who had been so extravagant as to hire a taxi, and it was she who directed a very fed-up Thakkur to Singh Sahib's flat.

Thakkur's disapproval of this journey was clearly observable in his long face and dragging step. At Jaipur, on the way to Shahpur, his mistress, his honoured Ma ji, had poured into his ear a confused story of how Ajit Sahib had married an English lady, about which his master was not pleased – and who would be pleased at such a marriage? Thakkur wanted to know. Anyway, Ma ji did not want her husband to be worried by anyone telling of this visit to her son. Thakkur was not, therefore, to write home about it. Ma ji and Thakkur would stay about two weeks in the house of the foreign lady.

Thakkur felt that he was the centre of some great intrigue when at Jaipur he posted a postcard to his master from his mistress. He read the card before putting it into the box, and discovered that he and his mistress were supposed to have arrived safely at the house of his mistress's sister at Jaipur, that sister was recovering from an illness and that they would stay about a fortnight. He was so glum for the remainder of the journey that although he remembered to buy a tray of food for Ma ji, he forgot to eat himself, and as he climbed the veranda steps in front of Mrs Singh, his feet were faltering.

The door was open and the house was very still. The lowering sun cast long rays straight through the entrance on to the bed. Thakkur gasped. As he told Ayah later, he saw stretched like a corpse on the bed the whitest lady imaginable. Even the hair spread on the pillow looked white in the sharp light.

He drew back for Mrs Singh to see.

She peered at her daughter-in-law and then glided over to the bed, signalling Thakkur to enter. Her keen eyes must have seen the traces of tears on my face, for she bent down and with one delicate finger brushed a tear away.

At the same moment Thakkur caught his foot on the ledge laid across the threshold to keep out snakes, and tumbled headlong into the room scattering luggage right and left.

I was up in a flash; the room seemed full of people made huge by the setting sun behind them.

'Ajit,' I shrieked in absolute terror, 'Ajit! Dacoits! Robbers!'

CHAPTER THIRTY

Mrs Singh drained her teacup, her chubby face still creased with laughter over the fright she had given me. I was laughing too. The mother-in-law whose goodwill I so much desired was much less fearsome than I had imagined. She sat on one of our bamboo chairs, her legs tucked up under her, while in the kitchen the sweeper crept about in awed silence and succeeded in cleaning the lunch trays without her usual efforts at orchestral percussion between floor and brassware.

I had myself crawled out of bed and made the tea, as it was certain that Mrs Singh would not drink tea made by an untouchable – I was agreeably surprised when she took it from me. I had also served Thakkur, who, after moving the luggage into the bedroom, was sitting on the veranda viewing, with great disfavour, the heatwaves dancing across the landscape.

Mrs Singh at first spoke rapidly to me; but I did not understand, so she made her subsequent sentences short and said them slowly.

'You have been ill?' she asked.

'I have had dysentery for some weeks,' I said, wondering at the same time how I was to gather enough strength to cook an evening meal for the visitors – mercifully Kamala had brought some fresh vegetables.

My mind fidgeted over domestic difficulties, as Mrs Singh subjected me to a long scrutiny. She could not really know how a white woman would look when sick, but the lines on my face must have told her of a rapid loss of weight because she nodded and said: 'You are thin.' She put down her cup, and added, 'I know how to treat dysentery.'

'The dysentery is gone – but my legs are weak.'

'Do you eat vegetarian food?'

'Yes,' I said, ignoring the eggs which I had consumed from time to time. 'Yes, I do – although I cannot yet cook such food very well.'

Mrs Singh laughed. 'Your servant will cook,' she said.

I gathered together my Hindi and tried to explain the acute servant shortage, but was finding my vocabulary hopelessly inadequate, when there was a soft tap at the open door. The eldest Miss Shah entered, making shy salutations to us.

'I came,' she said, 'to inquire how you are.'

I smiled within myself. The sisters' curiosity was insatiable; the crisp, unwrinkled sari in which the eldest sister was garbed proclaimed that she had hastily changed into a clean sari and had come to find out who my visitor was. So few happenings stirred the sisters' lives that my arrival had been a great event to them; and all my doings and my visitors were the subject, I was sure, of evening-long discussions between them and our other neighbours. They criticised the shortness of the summer frocks which I wore when doing housework, the frequent visits of

211

Chundabhai Patel and my friendships with the villagers. I had heard, however, that their comments were not at all unkind and that when a particularly fantastic rumour of my immorality – fantastic to an extent only possible in India – reached them, they came quickly to my defence and corrected the too-vivid imagination of the offending neighbour. As all the neighbours also gossiped to me, most stories reached me eventually, and I followed the old Yorkshire adage of 'hearing all, seeing all and saying nought'.

Miss Shah's eyes gleamed with interest when I introduced her to Mrs Singh and she was delighted to act as interpreter.

The sweeper fluttered by the kitchen door to indicate that she had finished her work, and although I was loath to let her go I knew that she must cook for her own family and I therefore dismissed her. She covered her face with her veil and went out the back door.

Ajit's bicycle wheels made a soft slurring sound through the sand and I usually heard his approach but that day he got a punture in one tyre and had to walk home. The first indication of his presence, therefore, was when a joyful voice suddenly shouted through the window: 'Mother!' He vanished; there was a cry of 'Thakkur, Namaste,' and Ajit was through the door in a bound and kneeling at his mother's feet, babbling incoherently to her.

In that moment I realised to the full what being estranged from his family meant to Ajit. I saw the ropes of affection which bound mother and son – and I felt very alone – but I vowed that never again should he suffer such alienation if it could be avoided.

Mrs Singh raised her son up.

'Arree, Ajit, have you been ill too?' she asked, anxiously surveying his face.

'No, Mother. It is Peggie who has been so ill.'

He looked round the room, and, seeing the teacups, he relaxed. Some hospitality had been offered. I slipped off the bed and found some tea still hot in a pan on the dying fire. I filled a cup and brought it to Ajit.

Miss Shah saw that it was time for her to go. As she

212

slipped on her sandals, which she had removed at the door before entering, I thanked her for translating for me.

'Don't mention it,' she said in her best English. 'It is a pleasure to me.'

The evening that followed was a turning point in my life. Mrs Singh was the first Indian lady I had met whose life had not been greatly affected by Western influence. My neighbours had all attended University and were widely read in English; Ajit and Chundabhai were more English than Indian in their habits; but Mrs Singh still kept most of the rules of her caste, although she was wise enough to waive them when she found it necessary. As she talked, I realised that many of her caste rules were only those of cleanliness and that if I adopted them I might avoid further illness. I listened to all that she had to say, and determined that I would discard her advice only if, after much consideration, I felt that it was founded on superstition alone.

She was full of the wisdom and fun of a country-bred woman, and as I studied the open, cheerful face and the small, gesticulating hands, I saw that she had the same trustworthiness as Ajit. When her face was in repose it had the calm of self-reliance, rather than the patient resignation I had seen on my neighbours' faces.

After sitting for a few minutes with mother and son, when Miss Shah had gone, I excused myself and went into the kitchen. I wanted to give them time to talk together, and also I had to prepare an evening meal. I leaned my head against the kitchen cupboard door to steady myself. Suddenly Mrs Singh's voice was raised: 'Where is my daughter-in-law?'

Ajit had watched me leave the room, anxiety clearly written on his face.

'She is in the kitchen,' he said.

'In the kitchen! She must not work – she must rest and eat to gain health again.' Turning to the door, she shouted: 'Thakkur.'

Thakkur, who was nodding quietly in the first gust of the cool evening wind, leaped up from the steps on which he had been sitting and found himself appointed cook, starting immediately.

Since he had expected to cook for his mistress during the visit, it was not such a blow as might be imagined, and he installed himself in the kitchen without comment, while I was borne protesting back to bed.

I whispered to Ajit that I felt very embarrassed that I was dressed only in a faded wrapper and, as his mother was present, I would like to make myself neat and put on a sari. He was delighted at the suggestion of my wearing a sari, and Mrs Singh clapped her hands when he told her; so I tottered to the bathroom, bathed myself as best I could and put on one of the saris which Mrs Singh had sent to me.

When I returned, she made me stand in the middle of the room while she pattered round me, straightening a fold here and there – and then she noticed that my wrists and neck were bare.

'What is this?' she cried, giving Ajit a disapproving look. 'No necklace – no ear-rings – no bracelets? What kind of a husband are you, to allow your wife to be seen without suitable jewellery?'

Ajit bowed his head and accepted the rebuke, omitting to say that he had not been earning for long, that the doctor's bills had been heavy and, moreover, I had not received the customary wedding presents.

Hot in defence of my husband, in an extraordinary mixture of Hindi and Gujerati, I said: 'I have a fine gold bracelet – and – and a loving husband is the finest jewel – I need no other.'

Ajit drew his breath apprehensively, feeling sure that my heated retort would offend his mother.

Mrs Singh, however, laughed. 'You speak the truth,' she said. 'It is good, though, to own jewellery – it is your insurance against hard times – it belongs to you without dispute. Ajit must buy you some as soon as possible – and add to it throughout your life.' She paused, then took a ruby ring off her finger. 'See,' she said, 'I will begin the collection,' and she took my hand and slipped the ring on to one finger.

I did not know what to say or even whether it was correct to accept such a present, which to my Western eyes was a valuable one; and I looked at Ajit for guidance.

He nodded his head slightly. I should accept.

There is no word in Hindi for 'thank you', so I did what I would have done in the case of an English mother-in-law: I bent and kissed her and said 'thank you' in English.

She looked quite stunned at such presumption. Ajit broke into explanations, to which she listened attentively. 'It is a charming custom,' she said firmly.

Tension slackened.

All this time Mrs Singh had been in her travelling clothes, although she had washed her hands and feet upon arrival, and I asked if she would like to take a bath before dinner.

She assented, so Ajit took her luggage into the bedroom and undid some of the locks for her, while I made another unsteady pilgrimage to get out clean towels and new soap.

While Mrs Singh made her toilet, I asked Ajit whether we should return the bed to the bedroom for Mrs Singh and ourselves sleep on mats on the floor in the living-room.

'She might like to sleep in the same room as us, but, of course, we will give her the bed.'

'Sleep in the same room!' I exclaimed.

Ajit grinned and pulled my ears teasingly.

'Oh, you English women with your stiff ideas of privacy! Family guests often share rooms with their hosts – they might feel lonely and lost in the middle of the night otherwise.'

I opened my mouth to protest, but before I could say anything, Ajit added: 'I expect Mother will like to have the bedroom to herself – so that she can make puja.'

'Say her prayers?'

'Yes,' said Ajit. 'Now she is getting old, she will take more trouble over her religious observances.'

'She can't be fifty years old yet,' I said.

'Fifty is old in this country.'

I made a face. 'I doubt if I shall be able to take to prayers and contemplation when I'm fifty,' I said. 'I shall probably want to play bridge, wear red saris and paint my face.'

Ajit looked serious and sat down by me on the bed. He put his arm round me – I was not much of an armful – and

215

said: 'And you will be able to do so, Rani. I shall always earn enough to indulge you in such simple pleasures; and if I die, I will leave enough money for you to make life as you please.' He rubbed his nose delicately against my cheek, savouring my perfume, as he went on: 'I ask only that you should say your prayers with me each day, so that we do not forget God, and that you give in charity either a little of your time or a little money.'

'You are never to die,' I said passionately, clutching one brown hand.

He promised dryly that he would not die just yet, and then sent me to see how his mother was managing.

I found her sitting cross-legged on the floor in front of a mirror on a stand, which Thakkur had evidently unpacked for her. She was rubbing oil into her freshly washed hair. I stood and admired the black, glossy waterfall of hair which touched the floor at the back, while I asked if I could help her.

She said promptly that I should rest and not walk about, but I lingered and she asked me to get a fresh sari for her out of the open tin trunk; when I had lifted out a neat bundle of pink cotton, she told me to go back to bed.

When she was dressed, she went into the kitchen, and I could hear her finding fault with everything that Thakkur had done. He was not cooking enough; he must cook lentil soup without spices for daughter-in-law; where had he put the lemon pickle which they had brought? – really, he was always mislaying things.

I heard her opening our grain bins and the shirr-shirr of the falling grain as she ran it through her fingers.

'The quality of the grain ration here is deplorable,' she said. 'Why does not my son buy good grain on the black-market?'

Thakkur murmured something about the Sahib always having been extremely honest.

'Am I not honest?' asked the lady tartly. 'Yet I always buy on the black.'

'Ji, hun, ji, hun, most honest,' assented Thakkur hastily.

Mrs Singh came within my line of vision as she crossed to the water pots. Standing on tiptoe, she took down the brass water-ladle from its hook, dipped it into one of the pots and filled a brass goblet.

She sipped.

'This water is not boiled,' she said. 'Paickie must have boiled water.'

My heart sank. I had daily asked the sweeper to boil water for drinking and daily she had said that she had done so; but apparently she had lied. Miss Shah had, in any case, assured me that although the water was very salt the well was new and its contents pure.

Before eating herself, Mrs Singh supervised the arrangement of my tray and watched me eat a bowl of tasteless lentils, some rice and curd.

As I ate, she lectured me on the necessity of boiling every ounce of water that I drank and washing all fruit with water containing permanganate of potash.

'Eat the fruit with a little salt sprinkled on it,' she advised. 'The salt kills little animals in it.'

She was vague about what kind of little animals, but I promised to do as she said.

'But, Mother,' protested Ajit, laughing at his mother's vehement tones, 'I have eaten and drunk the same things as Peggie and I am not ill.'

His mother sniffed. 'Foolish man, you were born here. All English people suffer when they come. They insist on living in their English style and then wonder why they become ill. They should adopt our ways, eating no flesh, taking curd daily and remembering our caste practices. Do you wash your mouth out after every meal?' she suddenly shot at me.

'No,' I said humbly.

'Then do so, child. Also take a bath and change your clothes on coming from the bazaar. Keep specially some clean clothes to wear when cooking. Do not allow sandalled feet in your kitchen.'

On she went, giving out laws of cleanliness that would have done credit to a London surgeon, while I ate and listened hard.

I could see from the trepidation in Ajit's expression that he feared I would be offended at his mother's peremptory

217

tones; he knew I was not used to submitting myself to the authority of an older woman.

He need not have feared; I guessed that Mrs Singh had not arranged her visit without opposition from the family, and that she had not, therefore, come from curiosity or to criticise. It was much more likely that she had come to help us and to heal the breach in the family.

I listened, therefore, and learned much. Ajit and I, I argued to myself, would spend most of our lives away from his family, and I could discard that part of the advice which seemed mere superstition and put to use the sensible part.

Thakkur brought trays of food for Ajit and Mrs Singh. It smelled delicious, and I said so hopefully – but Mrs Singh was adamant that rice, lentils and curd were all that I could have that night.

Ajit had previously asked after his family as a whole, but now he asked his mother cautiously if his father could not have spared time to visit us too.

Mrs Singh immediately looked so guilty and shifted about so uncomfortably, that Ajit guessed that she had somehow managed to come secretly, and he changed the subject; but there was a glint of amusement in his eyes.

To my relief, Mrs Singh elected to sleep alone in the bedroom, and Thakkur lifted our bed into it, opened her bedding roll and spread her own clean sheets and pillows.

We made ourselves comfortable on a couple of mats in the living-room. Thakkur also took a mat and curled up on the veranda. As no thief was likely to venture in while he lay there, we left the front door open so that we could have the benefit of the night breeze.

The floor was hard to one unaccustomed to lying on it, and I did not sleep much. Thakkur also had a bad night, because every time he went to sleep the pariah dogs crawled on their bellies up the veranda steps and sniffed at him from head to toe. One or two poked their noses through the door, but I quickly shooed them away.

Thakkur rose at five, cursing all dogs and uncivilised Gujerati builders who failed to build compound walls round houses. He was not up before Mrs Singh. She was already taking her bath preparatory to saying her prayers.

I fell asleep.

Awakened by the clank of the milkman's pail and the shouts of the drovers of a passing camel train, Ajit was surprised to find the visiting half of the household already busy. When he stirred I woke up; but all that Mrs Singh would allow me to do was to say my prayers and take a bath.

I was troubled that my visitors were having to work, but Ajit pacified me by saying that in any case Mrs Singh would not take food cooked by me, so Thakkur would have to cook for her, and it was not much more trouble for him to cook for us as well. To Thakkur the work of our little house would be nothing, he assured me. I was to rest and enjoy myself.

He moved my mat and pillow on to the veranda, and I lay down thankfully. Now was my chance to get well.

Ajit realised that on that day his home would be run like his father's house, so he took his bath leisurely and sat and talked with Mrs Singh and me, until at nine o'clock Thakkur presented us with a full meal of rice, lentils, vegetables, curd and bread – bread so light I said the fairies must have made it. Ajit promptly translated this remark for Thakkur's benefit and the old man's dismal face showed the faintest suggestion of a smile.

Again I had to be content with rice, lentils and curd, with the addition of one piece of bread.

Ajit explained that this meal was meant to last him until evening; there would be no lunch, although something good would probably arrive for nibbling with my tea, and there would be a good evening meal, to all of which Mrs Singh nodded agreement as she sat cross-legged on a chair like a jolly, feminine Buddha.

As the day progressed, I learned just how much work a good Indian servant could do. The sweeper came and washed the dishes and swept the floor; but Thakkur, without fuss or hurry, cooked, cleaned grain and had it ground, and went to the city to buy vegetables. He returned with finer vegetables than I had ever been able to buy, and as he spread them out on the newly scrubbed storeroom floor I was amazed at their succulence. When I admired them, he gave me the first real grin he had been able to muster since he arrived.

Mrs Singh spent hours talking to me, and it was remarkable what we managed to say to each other with the aid of a dictionary. Once or twice, I drew pictures on my writing pad to illustrate clearly what I meant; and Mrs Singh laughed at the little drawings until her ear-rings rattled.

The youngest Miss Shah, a bundle of agonised shyness, came to inquire after my health, and at the same time the Brahmin lady from upstairs slipped in through the back door, keeping her face closely covered until Thakkur had moved away. She kept purdah from preference, her husband being quite willing that she should go out if she wished. From the demeanour of the two women in front of my mother-in-law, I realised that I had omitted many forms of outward respect to Mrs Singh. After they had gone and she had expressed her approbation of such well-behaved acquaintances, I asked her forgiveness if my Western ways seemed very disrespectful to her.

She smiled affectionately upon me and said that she had been surprised how much I had learned of Indian ways; I asked her if she would teach me the usual forms of behaviour before certain people and she readily agreed. 'There is no strict etiquette, as the English have,' she said.

I was feeling better. When Ajit saw me that evening, he was pleased and his own spirits went up. As I reclined on my mat in the moonlight like some Indian Cleopatra and Mrs Singh sat cross-legged on a cushion, he regaled us with funny stories, all of which seemed to begin: 'There was once a Sikh . . .'

Mrs Singh stayed with us for a fortnight and during the whole time she never made me feel jealous or left out of proceedings. There was no doubt that she loved Ajit deeply, but her thoughts always seemed to be for us as a pair. She made me feel that I was part of Ajit and, therefore, to be cared for equally with him. No word of criticism ever passed her lips and yet she managed to teach me how to put my house in order. I begged that Thakkur should give me some cooking lessons, which the old man happily did, and before they left I could at last make good bread.

When Thakkur found that I could not sit cross-legged without pain, he suggested to Mrs Singh that he should buy from the bazaar a cheap table and a 'piece of the cloth that does not burn', so that the stoves could be put on the table and I could cook standing up.

Ajit reproached himself for not having thought of this before, and Thakkur was despatched to the carpenters' bazaar with instructions to buy a strong table and a piece of asbestos.

I also had a private conference with Thakkur, with the result that he came back with a proper, long-handled English broom and a similar mop, things which I had not been able to find in the bazaar. At Mrs Singh's suggestion, he also bought a big water boiler. Thakkur carried none of these purchases himself, but engaged no less than three coolies for the purpose. The table and boiler were, of course, too heavy to be carried in any way except on the head, and it was beneath the dignity of a member of the warrior caste, such as Thakkur, to be seen carrying brooms.

Apart from teaching me the simplest method of running a house, Mrs Singh taught me to make puja, that is, to say my prayers while accompanying them with small offerings of spice and oil thrown on to the first fire of the day. The ivory Lord Krishna had incense sticks burned in front of him, and Mrs Singh, when she heard that the Raphael print was a picture of the Lord Jesus, asked me if I would like to place incense sticks in front of that as well; to please her I placed them there also. God is God, no matter what his manifestation, and this was one way of acknowledging his existence.

The preoccupation of Indians with matters of the spirit was strange to me after the lukewarm interest of my fellow countrymen. The fact, however, that death sits grinning on the shoulder of every man in a country of famines and huge natural disasters, makes an interest in the next world imperative if one is to avoid being always afraid. An Indian peasant's burden of suffering is so terrible that he tends to draw away from the agony of the present and to dream of a rebirth into a higher, more privileged caste or of his return to his Maker.

Various political parties were trying to convince people that their current lives could be made much more bearable, by their own efforts; but it was a slow and difficult task, and to most men life was still something to be borne patiently until death gave release from it.

New ideas were, however, stirring among the young; I occasionally saw newspaper reports of local leaders of dynamic personality who had succeeded in obtaining co-operative action, and practical results had followed, such as a village road built or a new type of well bored.

As I lit the incense sticks and said my muntras, I vowed that when I was well and had a reliable servant, I would help in one of these new movements.

'Do not meddle with customs you do not understand,' my conscience warned me.

'I will first learn to understand,' I muttered to myself. 'I will be humble; first learn and then teach.'

CHAPTER THIRTY-ONE

At last Mrs Singh's bedding roll had to be buckled up and farewells said. A tonga was ordered to come from the city to take us to the station.

Before they left, Ajit managed to extract from Thakkur the details of Mrs Singh's arrangements for her visit. Thakkur venutred to say that the Big Sahib should have come too; he would have enjoyed the visit. The little Memsahib was not at all like the Memsahibs he had met before Independence; she was like an Indian lady but more peaceable.

Ajit laughed when he told me this. At least I had gained one adherent in his father's house, he teased. He did not tip Thakkur in the ordinary way, but bought him some good, white-papered cigarettes and slipped a ten-rupee note into the tin.

I was sufficiently recovered to drive into the city with Ajit to see the visitors off. At the station, I placed round my mother-in-law's neck a farewell garland of flowers, and it was with real sorrow that I waved goodbye.

'I will send a servant to you soon,' shouted Mrs Singh, as she leaned out of the purdah compartment in which she had elected to travel for safety's sake.

'Namaste, namaste, Sahib, Memsahib,' called Thakkur from the servants' compartment, his face contorted into a smile. 'Come soon to Delhi – come soon.'

Come soon! How could we visit until Ajit's father gave permission? Though we did not know it, at that moment he was in no mood to even look at his foreign daughter-in-law.

We took a tonga home, since my legs were still not too strong; and against the jingling of its bells we did not at first hear the shouts of the Misses Shah, who, when we arrived, were all standing on our veranda instead of on their own.

In front of our flat was a coolie cart in which reposed a very large wooden box; two coolies, one woman and one man, were squatting on their heels nearby smoking bilis, while in a tiny hammock made by a piece of veiling attached to the shaft of the cart, a baby lay whimpering.

'What can it be?' I asked. 'Have you ordered something?'

'I haven't ordered anything. I would not do so, without consulting you first,' said Ajit, a trace of indignation in his voice.

As we descended from the tonga and paid the tongawallah, a man who had presumably been knocking on our door fluttered down the steps. He peered at us through silver-rimmed spectacles and his nail-brush moustache quivered like a rabbit's nose. In one hand he held a fountain pen and in the other a piece of paper.

'Singh Sahib?' he queried.

'Yes.'

'Sign here, please,' and the pen was pushed into Ajit's hand.

'Wait a minute,' said Ajit. 'Who are you and what is this?'

The little man drew himself up and thrust out his chin. 'Shahpur Electrical Supply Company associated with the Bombay Marine Electric Company one refrigerator Class A ex our Bombay associates,' he recited without taking breath.

'Ramji,' exclaimed Ajit, appalled. 'I have not ordered a refrigerator.'

'I forgot,' said the representative of the Shahpur Electrical etcetera. 'I have a letter to deliver to you also.' He drew out a crumpled envelope from his shirt pocket and handed it to Ajit, while the eyes of the Misses Shah nearly popped out of their heads as they murmured: 'A refrigerator? A letter?'

Ajit ripped open the envelope and, holding the letter close to his eyes in order to see in the waning light, he read it.

I fidgeted with impatience.

A slow grin spread over his face and became a great laugh.

'Well, I am surprised,' he said, a very sweet expression on his face.

'Tell me, tell me,' I implored like a child.

'It's a wedding present,' said Ajit, 'from Chundabhai. Take the letter and read it.'

'A wedding present?' chorused the Misses Shah, as I read. 'Whoever heard of a refrigerator for a wedding present? Most extraordinary! Quite unorthodox!'

I read: 'Dear Ajit Sahib, I am sorry that this fridge has been so long in coming to you, but it took some time to get it shipped from Bombay. Nevertheless, it comes to you and to Peggie with all good wishes for a long and happy married life from my wife and me. I feel that it will probably give Peggie more pleasure than a pile of saris – and somebody has to make ice cream soufflés for me! Kindest regards and good wishes, Yours, Chundabhai.'

Feeling dazed, I slowly folded the letter up. I had forgotten that such things as refrigerators existed.

'It's a tremendous present,' I said. 'Should we really accept it?'

'Of course we are going to accept it,' Ajit said. 'Chundy is my oldest college friend, and he is simply rolling in money – if he had sent saris or silver it would have been quite expensive. He is so good-natured that he probably spent weeks cogitating over what to give us – and by Heaven, he could not have thought of anything more helpful than this.'

'Fresh milk,' I said, a sob in my throat, 'no more rancid butter – meals prepared ahead of time – only one journey a week to buy vegetables. Oh, darling, what a present!'

Ajit put his arm round me and hugged me. The Misses Shah giggled and the coolies stirred out of their lethargy. He dropped me as if I was a newly-made piece of bread red-hot from the tava, and took the delivery note and signed it. The coolies got up reluctantly and with much puffing, blowing and complaining, heaved the box up the steps and into the living-room. They then opened the wooden packing case under the direction of the representative.

The refrigerator was large, with a commodious freezing section. Its white, polished glory looked incongruous in the stone-floored, colour-washed Indian room; but to me it was a marvellous release from labour.

'How could he guess what it would mean to us?' I asked, as I ran my fingers tremulously along the immaculate metal shelves and the enamelled boxes.

'He was in England for six years,' said Ajit, as he tipped the coolies.

I hastily fetched water for both the coolies and the representative and they departed. It is doubtful if the coolies knew what they had unpacked.

The Misses Shah, although they knew the purpose of a refrigerator, had never had the opportunity before of examining one closely, and they stole round it as if it was an unexploded time bomb.

'Will it really keep food from rotting?' asked the eldest lady.

'Not yet,' said Ajit. 'An electric power line is being run out here soon, and when the refrigerator is plugged in, food will keep for days in it.'

'Wonderful,' they chorused.

'It has no lock,' remarked the second Miss Shah. 'How will you avoid a servant's stealing from it?'

I was nonplussed, and looked at Ajit.

'We shall keep it in this room,' he said firmly. 'We can lock the room when we go out.'

My first reaction was that I could not have a refrigerator in the living-room, but on consideration I realised that it was the only place in which to put it, to avoid pilferage when a servant occupied the kitchen.

The Misses Shah declined tea, being quite unable to refrain from speeding up the stairs to our other neighbours to tell them of the extraordinary arrival.

The younger neighbours, being educated, had few taboos, and merely called in a body next day to inspect the wonderful machine; but a few old parents wagged their heads in horror at the thought of eating food which had been kept for days. It was against the laws of nature and of caste.

We did not care what anybody thought. We were blissfully happy as together we cooked our dinner, after Ajit and the watchman had managed to ease Chundabhai's magnificent present into a corner. When we had eaten, Ajit dragged the bed to the front door and we sat on it together, enjoying the coolness and the songs of the insects.

I saw that from Ajit's shirt pocket a letter protruded, and I asked him from whom it was. He immediately drew it out.

'I'm sorry,' he said. 'I picked it up from under the door as we came in this evening. It is for you.'

I straightened myself, took the letter, saw it was from Mother and opened it. It was a long and garbled letter, full of bits of local news. Towards the end she wrote: 'You will be pleased to know, dear, that James's practice has grown so much that he is taking an additional partner in – his mother is very proud of him. Naturally your dear father and I hope that he will marry Angela – though they do not see as much of each other as they used to do.

'Angela is very quiet these days. She does not go out much – not like her usual self at all – I get quite worried about the amount of work the child is doing. Sometimes she goes on far into the night – says she is writing another paper. Dr Wu has called several times, and talks to her about her work – far above my poor head, I fear. Such a nicely behaved young man, but Father gets furious about his visits. I can't imagine why – he does not stand a chance with Angela now that James is doing so well – Angela has such a matter-of-fact outlook on life and would not prefer a penniless oriental student to the most successful solicitor in town . . .'

There were several paragraphs more, but my mind did not absorb their contents. How little Mother and Father knew about their daughters. I could imagine Father's fears of another oriental son-in-law, and yet I sensed that Wu could give Angela all that she needed most to make her flower into a warm-hearted, contented woman. James might have been able to help her, but his chances had been spoiled by his brother.

'Bad news?'

'No.' My voice was hesitant.

'What is it, Rani?'

I snuggled my face into his neck.

'It is nothing.'

'Something is.'

'It's Wu.'

'Wu?'

'Yes. He is courting Angela and my parents don't like it.'

Ajit's laughter was deep and rich. 'Good old Wu,' he said.

'I want him to marry her,' I said.

'Well, why not? He is my good friend.'

'My parents don't realise how excellent a man he is; they would like her to marry James.'

'Ah, yes. I remember James – he would not be good for Angela.'

I looked up at him. 'You realise also what Angela needs?'

'I know, my dear. She is very like you.'

'Like me?'

'Yes – only you are afraid of the world and of people and shrink away from them – you need always to have a little protection to which to retire, while Angela plunges into life, and nearly drowns.'

'How do you know she nearly drowns?'

'Her trials are written on her forehead.'

Then he smiled at me. 'I think Wu will win her,' he said.

'I hope so.'

'This James looked very cold fish to me,' remarked Ajit, as he flicked a moth off my pillow.

'He is a kindly man,' I said, 'and he might understand Angela quite well – but I want her to start afresh with Wu. James is thinking only of his career at present.'

'I will pray that he continues to succeed in it, so that Wu has time to acquire a beautiful wife,' said Ajit mischievously.

'And what will Lord Krishna say about such a weird prayer?'

'He will know what to do – he is an expert on affairs of the heart – did he not have sixteen thousand wives and thus found the Indian race?'

CHAPTER THIRTY-TWO

Late one evening, a few days before his wife's return from Shahpur, Ram Singh came home from Simla. He found that his house had been kept in good order under Nulini's guidance and that Shushila was her usual bouncing self.

'Papa,' she shouted joyfully, 'Nulini has shown me how to play caron properly – I will beat you next time we play.'

Her father pulled her ears lovingly. 'We will play tomorrow,' he promised.

When he sat down to eat, he remembered to praise the pickles that Nulini had made earlier in the year, and he told Bhim that his wife was learning to keep house very well. Bhim smiled absent-mindedly at the compliment and asked about the result of his father's investigation into the land dispute at Simla.

They sat and chatted for some time after the meal was finished, relishing the legal intricacies of the dispute. Bhim asked if he might examine Ram Singh's notes on the subject and the elder man agreed. He took out from his brief case a large, untidy file, which he handed to his son, after which he went away to take his bath, say his prayers and go to bed. He asked Khan to find his Gita for him, which the servant did, and then he dismissed him for the night.

The cooking fires in the servants' quarters flickered out, Khan turned restlessly on his cot outside his master's room, Shushila slept and the house was still for the night.

Hours later, Dr Singh awoke feeling ravenously hungry. He called Khan, but the man did not answer.

Ram Singh reluctantly got out of bed, gave his dhoti a characteristic hitch and again shouted for Khan. There was no reply. He wrapped a shawl round himself and went to the door of his room. Khan was not in his cot, so he went in search of Ayah, who slept at the door of his wife's room.

Ayah slept the light sleep of the old, and at the sound of his footfall she sat up and screamed, clutching her sari tightly round her.

'Noisy one,' said Ram Singh petulantly. 'I don't know where Khan has gone, and I'm hungry. Find me something to eat.'

'Ji, hun,' said Ayah, delighted to be singled out for a special service, and she leaned over the edge of her cot and scrabbled beneath it with one gnarled hand, feeling for her spectacles.

'Here,' said Ram Singh, lifting them off the window sill.

She hastily relieved him of their weight and with fumbling hands hooked them round her ears, after which, like a pair of pariah dogs, she and Ram Singh slunk silently along the inner veranda to the kitchen. The kitchen, however, was as barren of food as the desert itself. Nulini had locked up everything before Cook Maharaj had departed to the servants' quarters. Not so much as a humble rôti was to be seen.

Ram Singh looked dismally round him. Each cupboard exhibited a neat padlock on its door. Each cooking pot sat on its shelf emptily upside down. He turned and looked at the storeroom doors. The room in which most foodstuffs were kept was locked up. The grain storeroom padlock, however, hung loosely down from its chain. He shivered – the kitchen was quite chilly.

'Ayah.'

'Ji.' She saw that Ram Singh was shivering. 'Sahib, why do you come to the kitchen? I will bring food to you in your room.'

'I don't know why I came,' said Ram Singh, like a cross, small boy. 'The grain storeroom is open. See if there is any parched flour – that will do.'

'Sahib,' protested Ayah, 'that is only for beggars or for pilgrims.'

'I am hungry – where does Maharaj keep the cashew nuts, I wonder,' growled Ram Singh, and Ayah scuttled across the kitchen while her master followed her with greater dignity.

Ayah pulled the heavy door open and peered into the dark store.

'Sahib,' she shrieked suddenly, pushing her spectacles up the bridge of her nose. 'Sahib.'

Ram Singh covered the kitchen in a couple of strides. 'Hey, Ram,' he exclaimed in horror, and then shouted in a paroxysm of rage. 'Come out!'

On a pile of sacks in a corner of the storeroom and just visible in the moonlight from the window, lay a man dressed only in a loincloth. Although apparently paralysed by fear, he had raised himself on his elbow and half lay over a woman, as if to protect her from view; but her bare legs were clearly visible, the sari pulled up from them, and the sharp, terrified gasps of her breath could be heard in the silence which followed Ram Singh's command.

'Come out,' repeated Ram Singh, ice beginning to overlay the rage in his voice.

The man swung himself carefully off the sacks, still keeping his body between the woman and Ram Singh. The woman's legs vanished, as she drew them up under her sari.

'Khan!' exclaimed Ram Singh.

The hill man hung his head and said nothing.

'I will not have women brought into my house,' shouted his enraged master. 'In a month you are to be married – and yet you have to bring some beggar off the streets.' He stopped abruptly. His eyes had got used to the gloom of the storeroom, and he saw for the first time part of the sari which the woman was wearing. It was no beggar's sari. It was red – red silk.

'Ramji,' he gasped and pointed at it.

Ayah looked where the finger pointed. 'Arree,' she wailed at the top of her voice.

Ram Singh covered the distance between the door and his delinquent servant in a second, pushed the man aside and grabbed the trembling heap that was the woman. Roughly he pulled her off the sacking and by the power of his grip on her shoulder kept her from sinking to her knees.

'Nulini,' he said in a horrified whisper.

She stood with her eyes cast down, her sari fallen to her waist. She was blouseless – the tiny scrap of red silk still lay on the sacking – and the large, exquisitely formed breasts were naked. In the soft hollow between the breasts lay the gold necklace that Ram Singh had himself given her at her wedding time. He lifted his free hand as if to snatch it off her, but something held him back and he flung her down on to the sacking, where she lay motionless.

Khan fell on to his knees. 'Sahib,' he beseeched. 'The fault is mine. The little lady is but a weak woman and I tempted her. She is unharmed, Sahib, quite unharmed, I swear it.'

He caught at Ram Singh's feet and kissed them; for the first time in his life Ram Singh kicked a servant, but Khan seemed hardly to feel it. He lay prostrate before his master, the muscular back awaiting further blows.

'Sahibji,' he said. 'Punish me as you will, but do not tell Bhim Sahib. Let your respected daughter go back to him – she is untouched. I swear it, I swear it. She is most innocent, Sahib – the fault is all mine.'

In speechless rage, Ram Singh bent and struck his defenceless servant again and again with his clenched fists, while Ayah moaned in the background.

'The fault is mine,' said a calm voice behind them.

Ram Singh straightened up and turned round sharply. Bhim stood in the doorway. He had presumably been wakened by Ayah's shriek and had followed the sound of voices echoing through the house. His hair was rumpled and his garments creased from sleep, but his step was firm and he held himself in a dignified manner as he crossed the storeroom to his wife, who lay still on the sacking, her face hidden and her shoulders heaving as she wept silently.

'Nulini,' he said stiffly, 'cover yourself and come with me.'

There was no reply. Khan raised himself to his knees and hid his face in his hands.

'Nulini.'

Nulini shrank closer to the sacking.

'Come, child,' said Bhim, his voice soft as if he were really coaxing a child, 'I will not beat you.'

'Don't bother with her,' said her father-in-law angrily. 'Tomorrow she leaves this house. She can go back to her parents, if she dare face them, or she can join those whose profession she has already emulated.'

Bhim did not answer immediately. He put his arm round his wife and raised her to her feet. She stood passively, her eyes shadowed by their lashes, while he carefully draped the sari over her shuddering form and over her head, so that she was shielded from Ayah's fascinated gaze.

'Father,' he said slowly, 'Nulini has done wrong and I am sure she realises it. Yet I know that it is in part my fault. I have not always remembered my responsibilities to her.'

'You have been a good husband,' said Ram Singh tartly as he arranged his shawl round himself. 'Tomorrow she goes.'

Bhim drew himself up. 'She is my wife. If she goes, I go.'

'Don't be ridiculous,' said Ram Singh.

'Does not the scripture say that if a wife errs the husband must be punished for it?'

'It does,' said his father coldly. He looked Nulini up and down as if she was something unclean. 'Do with her as you will.' His anger boiled up uncontrollably. 'Father a bastard if you wish.'

'And as for you,' he said, glaring at the supplicating Khan. 'Get out of this house and out of this province. Never let me see your face again. Get out!'

There was a loud hammering on the kitchen door. The watchman, attracted by the sound of voices, shouted: 'Kon heh? Kon heh?'

'It is I,' bawled the exasperated Ram Singh. 'Go away.'

'Sahibji,' said the watchman obsequiously, and padded away.

'Ayah, open the door and let this untouchable out,' said Ram Singh, his voice trembling.

Ayah had been watching the proceedings with rapt attention. 'Miss Nulini has the key, Sahib,' she said.

Nulini did not move, so Bhim bent down and unhooked the key ring from the waist of her petticoat. He flung it at Ayah's feet, and, mumbling that the present generation was not fit to live, she picked up the keys and moved to the door.

Silently Khan rose to his feet. Ram Singh caught him a staggering blow across the face with the flat of his hand, and the man stumbled. He made no sign that he had felt the blow, but straightened himself and walked with head erect past his master. He did not even glance at Ayah as he glided lightly on his bare feet out of the door, his dhoti gleaming white in the moonlight and his sacred thread making a dark line across his chest.

Ayah shut and locked the door, and then hooked the key ring into her sari.

Ram Singh saw the last movement, and resented that Ayah had put herself in the place of a deposited member of the family.

'Give me the keys,' he said, his moustache bristling. 'Say no word to anybody of what has happened tonight or by Ram himself I will make you suffer.' He glared at Ayah, whose heart gave a little leap of fright as she handed him the keys.

Bhim put his arm round Nulini and began to propel her across the floor towards the inner veranda, when suddenly there was a sound of running feet and a heavy pounding on the door.

'Sahib, Sahib,' yelled the panic-stricken voice of the watchman, 'Sahib, come quickly.'

'What is it? What is it?' shouted Ram Singh as he

233

fumbled for the key and put it into the lock.

'Arree, Sahib, Khan has fallen down the well. I tried to save him but he slipped from my fingers.'

Ram Singh flung open the door and ran outside; from the servants' quarters Cook Maharaj was already racing for the well, while frightened, sleepy voices behind him asked if it was a Muslim raid or was there a thief in the compound?

Nulini moaned and then fainted. Bhim laid her back on to the sacking and said to Ayah: 'Take care of her – good care.' He then ran out of the house towards the well.

In the light of the moon people ran about confusedly, shouting for a rope, for someone who could swim.

'Maharaj! Pratap!' called Bhim. 'Let me down with the water-skin – I can swim.' He snatched a torch from the gardener's hand.

'My son,' cried Ram Singh, fear for his eldest boy obliterating every other feeling.

'I shall be safe, Father,' said Bhim, and seized the flaccid water-skin. Maharaj and Pratap let it down slowly, muttering that they hoped the rope would stand the weight. Ayah, not being able to bear being left out of the excitement, had deserted Nulini who lay in a faint in the storeroom, and was now peering down the well.

There was no sound of splashing; only the creak of the wheel broke the tense silence.

Just above the water line Bhim yelled to those above to stop letting him down. He flashed the torch around the dank, green walls and across the still water. He could see nothing of Khan. He clung to the rope for another minute, swaying perilously, but nothing stirred, and he called to be pulled up.

'Only a man who wanted to drown could have drowned so quickly,' he said to his father, as, aided by Pratap, he eased himself over the lip of the well. Cook Maharaj dropped the rope and assisted him to his feet while the rest of the servants and their families stood in stupefied silence.

'It appears that Khan has drowned,' Ram Singh told them. 'There is nothing that we can do tonight. In the morning we will get the body out and Pratap shall go and fetch the Thanedar from the police station. Chowkidar, continue on your rounds and the rest of you go back to bed.'

'Arree-ee,' a little sigh went through the knot of people, and one or two women began to weep softly. Khan had been popular in the compound, and it was with sad faces that his fellow servants reluctantly turned and went back to their homes, the womenfolk keeping close to their men in fear of the nearness of death.

Bhim spotted Ayah amongst the crowd. 'Get back to my wife,' he yelled at her furiously. Ayah fled.

Father and son walked slowly back into the house, both heavy with thought. They went through the kitchen, Ram Singh locking the back door, saw that Ayah had apparently moved Nulini from the storeroom, and walked along the veranda together.

Was Ram Singh remembering Khan's patient service through many months? Did he feel that he had driven the man to his death? Nobody knows. But the next day Ram Singh obtained from his clerk the name of Khan's father and of his village so that he could send news of the man's death – and with the letter he enclosed his wages for six months to come – the clerk showed to Ayah the note of the amount written in the housekeeping book.

And of what was Bhim thinking? His was a difficult position in which to be; and because he was a conscientious man he probably reproached himself bitterly for not taking more care of his wife; but that he was prepared to stand by her was made abundantly clear just as he and his father were passing Shushila's and Nulini's sleeping-room.

The silence of the house was broken by a muffled cry. 'Give it to me,' panted Ayah's voice, as if she spoke with difficulty. There was a sound of scuffling and of laboured breath, as if two people were fighting.

'What now?' exclaimed Ram Singh, and leaped towards the apartment with an agility surprising for a man of his years. He was, however, not quicker than Bhim, who tore apart the curtains of the doorway and stood for a second paralysed by what he saw.

'Nulini!' he exclaimed in a hoarse whisper, fearing to wake his little sister, who still slumbered on her cot at the far side of the room.

'Ayah,' cried Ram Singh.

Locked together like wrestlers, Nulini and Ayah fought for possession of a small dagger. The younger woman held the weapon in her right hand and was attempting to drive it down upon herself, but Ayah had caught her wrist with one hand and forced it back, while she held the girl's body in a bony grip close to her own, so that Nulini could not strike without first killing or wounding the old nurse.

Bhim shot forward and snatched the dagger from his half-naked wife. Nulini wrenched herself away from Ayah and stood swaying unseeingly in the middle of the room, her hair loose down her back with a few withered flowers still tangled in it. Naked to the waist, she looked like the ill-used captive of some ancient Muslim conqueror.

'She was about to stab herself,' panted Ayah quite unnecessarily, while she tucked her sari into the waistband of her petticoat and readjusted her spectacles which were hanging from one ear.

'Hey, Ram!' exclaimed the harassed father, nodding his head helplessly from side to side.

Bhim tucked the dagger into the waist of his dhoti and then silently supported his fainting, unprotesting wife out on to the veranda. Ram Singh and Ayah followed him, while Shushila still slept on.

Nulini looked ghastly in the moonlight, blood oozing down her face from a scratch.

'Father,' said Bhim urgently. 'Let me deal with this matter. There will be no scandal, I promise you – if you can shut the mouth of Ayah.'

Ram Singh's anger had evaporated, and he looked old and sad. 'Do what you will,' he said shortly, and turned on his heel, and with trembling steps sought the seclusion of his own room

Bhim picked up his wife and carried her to his room – a strange room to her, which she had hardly entered since her marriage. Impelled by curiosity, more than a desire to help, Ayah trailed along after her swiftly-moving young master.

Bhim sat down upon his cot, his wife upon his knee, took

his shawl from amongst the rumpled sheets and wrapped it round Nulini, who had maintained a dazed silence seeming hardly aware of what was happening to her. He rocked her back and forth as if she was a baby, whispering encouragement to her, while Ayah, uncertain what to do, fluttered nervously in the doorway.

'Bring a glass of water, Ayah,' said Bhim.

She went and fetched the water from the kitchen, handing the glass to him with silent disapproval. She was full of indignation that Bhim thought it necessary that she should be instructed to keep her mouth shut. Keep her mouth shut, indeed – as if she was going to betray the honour of the family. It was Nulini who had done the betraying, and what the girl needed in Ayah's opinion was to be thrown out on the street, not nursed and soothed by her husband.

Bhim forced a little water through Nulini's lips. It ran partly down her face, but it brought her back to her senses, and she moved as if to jump off her husband's lap. Bhim held her firmly, however, continuing to rock her and whisper in her ear. She turned her face into his shoulder and suddenly great sobs shook her; she clenched one hand and beat a tattoo on Bhim's shoulder.

'You don't care – you don't care – not about me – not about Khan.' Her voice rose. 'Why did you drive him to his death? you and Father-in-law.' She wailed in mourning, and continued to reproach her patient husband in between sobs.

Bhim went a sickly grey. 'You may go,' he said frigidly to Ayah, and very reluctantly Ayah went. She remembered that Ram Singh was hungry and trotted along to his room, calling quietly at the open door: 'Sahib, Sahib.' There was no reply, so she entered, tentatively ready to retreat: 'Sahib, shall I bring you something to eat?'

Ram Singh was sitting on his divan and staring into space, his shawl wrapped round his shoulders and head. He seemed at first hardly aware of his old questioner, but when she repeated the query, he said coldly without looking at her: 'No.'

Ayah turned to go back to her bed, only to be brought

to a halt by Ram Singh's saying in the same frigid tone: 'Woman, if you speak a word of this night's happenings to anyone, I will beat you to death – to death.'

Ayah shrank away. Small as Ram Singh was, he had a terrifying presence.

'Ji, hun,' she said, 'I shall say nothing.'

And she kept her promise for years, until time had made the events of little interest to any but the family.

CHAPTER THIRTY-THREE

Ram Singh's clerk drove his master and Shushila to the railway station to meet Mrs Singh. The clerk had silently shouldered a lot of extra work during the previous few days. It was he who directed the operation of recovering Khan's body and he who kept the police constables from wandering all over the house and making themselves a nuisance in the kitchen, while Ram Singh dealt courteously with the Police Inspector. The Inspector had come to make routine inquiries and was made so comfortable that he remained for the day, taking meals with Ram Singh. He was quite satisfied that in a house such as Ram Singh's nothing untoward could have occurred – the lip of the well was low and easily stumbled over in the darkness. He suggested that Ram Singh should have the wall built higher and keep the well covered at all times, and he was flattered when Ram Singh said that he welcomed such ingenious suggestions.

It was the clerk who arranged the funeral, buying a stretcher for the body, cloth in which to wind it and ghee and wood for the funeral pyre. He did not himself touch the body; some strange old women, like witches, came from the nearest village and wound the faithful lover and arranged him on the stretcher.

Khan did not lack mourners at his funeral. The servants went, and many of the people he knew in the village followed in straggling procession down to the burning ghat where his body was consigned to the flames.

Bhim did his best to keep from Nulini the sounds of the disturbance caused by the police and the rescuers; but it was impossible, even with the windows shut, not to be able to follow the whole operation from the shouts outside. She lay on his bed, staring wide-eyed at the ceiling, while he sat and chafed her limp hands. When a half-triumphant wail announced the bringing of the body out of the well, she was suddenly sick, retching helplessly on an empty stomach, while Bhim held her and Ayah ran to and fro with bowls and cloths. When the sickness eased, Bhim, who had not slept during the night while he sat with his tossing wife, went to his father and asked permission to send for a doctor.

Ram Singh refused flatly. He evidently feared what a doctor might be told of the night's happenings, and he assured Bhim that Nulini would get over her hysterics in a day or two. She ought to be grateful, he said, that she had such a forgiving husband.

In the early evening when the funeral procession had gone its noisy way under the window, Nulini became feverish, muttering and turning restlessly on the bed. Bhim sent Ayah to his mother's storeroom for blankets, and when they came he packed them over Nulini. In the absence of Cook Maharaj at the funeral, he himself went to the kitchen and cracked ice from the big block which was delivered daily, filled an ice bag and placed it on Nulini's forehead, but she writhed so much that it was hard to keep it there.

'I wish Mother was here,' he said to Ayah.

'She comes tomorrow,' said Ayah, pity for the boy making her gentle-voiced for once.

Shushila, on her way to the station with her father, knew nothing of Khan's death, her father himself having taken her over to her uncles' house immediately she had eaten her breakfast on the morning after the tragedy, on the excuse that sister Nulini was not very well and it would be dull for a little girl if she had no one with whom to play.

Shushila, therefore, gave her mother a tremendous welcome, complete with a garland which she had chosen herself in the bazaar on the way to the station.

Thakkur sat with the clerk in the front of the returning car and, of course, asked where Khan was, and the clerk told him in an undertone of the accidental drowning, while Shushila babbled happily to Mrs Singh.

'Nulini has fever,' Thakkur heard her say. 'It is a pity because she has given me her badminton racket and was going to teach me how to play.'

'Nulini ill?' exclaimed Mrs Singh, full of concern.

'She is not well,' said Ram Singh, 'I shall tell you more about it at home.'

'When she is better, Bhim is going to take her to Simla for a holiday,' said Shushila. 'I asked if I could go too – he says I can go next time – not this time.

'He's going to learn to play badminton too, so that we can all play together,' she added. 'Can I buy some shuttlecocks, Mummy?'

'Of course, dear.'

Ram Singh asked how Mrs Singh's sister was progressing and Thakkur held his breath while Mrs Singh said calmly that she was now quite well and sent her namastes to her brother-in-law.

As soon as they arrived home, Ram Singh drew his wife into his study and shut the door behind them. 'Before even giving her a glass of water,' remarked Ayah indignantly.

He must have told her about Khan and Nulini, because without even waiting to wash her feet and hands, she hurried to Shushila's room, while Ram Singh stumped up the stairs to his prayer room, looking like a small thundercloud.

'Sahib and Ma ji must have disagreed,' thought Ayah, as she hurried after her mistress. 'Nulini Bahu is in Chota Sahib's room,' she informed Mrs Singh, a little breathlessly.

'Is she very sick?' Mrs Singh asked, as she changed direction and headed for Bhim's room, her sari end wafted out behind her in the breeze of her passing.

'Temperature is down, Ma ji.'

They reached Bhim's room.

'Wait here, Ayah,' said Mrs Singh, pointing to a spot out

of earshot, and disconsolately Ayah sat down on the stone floor and waited. Mrs Singh lifted the door curtain, and Ayah could see Bhim sitting at work at his desk, while Nulini lay quietly on his cot, which he had moved close to the desk. The boy rose, and the curtain dropped.

Nobody ever knew what passed between Mrs Singh and the young couple, but having nursed one daughter-in-law back to health, she silently nursed the other one, and about ten days later she saw Nulini and Bhim off to Simla.

Ram Singh did not speak to his elder son before he left. Apparently Bhim's quiet acceptance of his wife's infidelity was too much for the old man, and the thought that his first grandchild was likely to be a servant's bastard must have burned in him.

Both parents looked old and tired. The beautiful, big house which had been built to hold lots of grandchildren was silent and empty. Even Shushila, robbed of her playmate, was quieter and spent more time at her uncles' house playing with her cousins.

The warm, damp days of the monsoon went slowly by like monotonous drips from a tap, and the first cool breath of autumn rippled softly along the verandas.

'Soon it will be Diwali,' shouted Shushila, 'lovely, lovely Diwali.'

Thakkur was serving his master with lemon water when the sound of her cheerful shouting to Pratap echoed through the garden. He saw Ram Singh's moustache twitch as if the mouth beneath was trembling, and Mrs Singh cleared her throat nervously. He might well look dismal, thought Thakkur, with one son under a cloud at Shahpur and the other sent to Simla out of season as if he was also in disgrace. Thakkur did not know why Bhim should be in disgrace, but he had marked the unusual lack of communication between father and son and the departure to a hill station at the wrong time of year. What was the use of Diwali, Festival of Light, ruminated Thakkur, a time of family reunion, when there was no family to reunite?

He pottered off to the kitchen and when, later, he returned to clear away the glasses, Mrs Singh was saying rather diffidently: 'Father, can we not have a real family party here for Diwali?'

'Who is there to ask?' asked Ram Singh sulkily, not having noticed Thakkur's approach.

'You have sons,' said Mrs Singh reproachfully.

'They have brought me nothing but sorrow and worry,' said Ram Singh, full of self-pity.

Thakkur mopped up imaginary spots of lemon from the side table; it always amused him how Mrs Singh managed her husband, and he did not wish to miss any more of the conversation than he had to. The couple were sitting on a sheet-covered mattress enjoying the mild late afternoon sun, and Mrs Singh moved closer to her husband. She patted his hand just as if she was a young wife, as Thakkur remarked later, and said: 'Is it not our duty to guide our children lovingly and not to leave them to struggle alone in the world? This is surely our duty and should be our pleasure while we are here.'

Ram Singh said nothing but did not withdraw his hand. She smiled impishly at him, and Thakkur found some more imaginary spots to mop up.

'I have a story to tell you,' she said. 'Before I tell you, however, you must promise me something.' Her voice had a gay inflection.

Ram Singh showed faint interest.

'Yes. The promise I ask . . .' and she looked at him with her fine eyes in such a way that he had to smile at her. 'The promise that I ask is that if I make you happier with my story, you will buy me a present, and if I make you unhappy you will not upbraid me.'

'Humph,' said Ram Singh grumpily. 'There might as well be one happy person in the house – I will buy you a wrist watch.'

'Oh, how lovely,' breathed Mrs Singh.

Her husband bridled a little, rather enjoying the impression he had made. In fact, Mrs Singh looked so hugely satisfied at his offer that in the end he laughed.

'Well,' said Mrs Singh, taking a big breath. 'There was once a young man of great ability, whose father desired that he should enter the family silk business. The boy was unfortunately not very obedient and swore that he would never be any use as a merchant; instead he wanted to be a lawyer. His father was furious and said that the young man would come to a bad end . . .'

Reluctantly Thakkur drifted unnoticed back to the kitchen. Ma ji had more courage than ten men. He would never, if he were a woman, be brave enough to tell the Burra Sahib that he himself had been an unfilial son of great strength of character, and that his sons had merely inherited their father's propensity for independent thought. Thakkur could remember being told, when he first came to the Singh household, about the fierce family row that had occurred when Singh Sahib had demanded further education so that he could become a lawyer. He had won his point, the second and third brothers had entered the silk trade, and the old father had lived to see all his sons flourishing.

Ma ji was a woman of strength, too. No wonder her sons demanded to go their own way. He hoped very much that Ma ji would prevail upon the Burra Sahib to bring the family together. Thakkur had served the family for so many years that he felt a part of it, and it distressed him very much to see the courtyard empty and the dining-room next to the kitchen barely used.

It was queer how Bhim Sahib had suddenly taken his wife away to Simla. He never would understand how they had suddenly become such a loving couple. They never seemed to bother much about each other before, although he had to admit that Miss Nulini was quick to serve her husband whenever he asked anything of her. Now it was just as if they were newly married and could not be enough in each other's company. Bhim Sahib had hardly left his wife throughout her illness, and even Cook Maharaj had noticed his solicitude for her when they set out on their journey. Ayah knew something, Thakkur was sure – she looked so secretive. Well, there was only one kind of secret women ever kept and that was when a new baby was expected, and they were always so cheerfully secretive about it, that it was never a secret for long. He grinned to himself as he thought he had reached the core of the mystery; no doubt the tailor would soon be called in to stitch small garments.

But it was eleven months before the sewing machines whirred on the back veranda, so Thakkur never found out what caused Bhim Sahib's sudden interest in his wife.

Thakkur sat in the shade of the house and smoked a bili while Cook Maharaj prepared dinner – such a small dinner. The house was, indeed, far too empty. He wondered if Khan haunted it – and shivered at the thought. Strange how he fell down the well – as if he did not know where it was, after being so many months in the house. There were rumours about him. Chowkidar said that on the night of his death Burra Sahib had found the hill man stealing and had turned him out. Thakkur could not imagine Khan stealing – he would have trusted him with his life. He had been a very quiet man but in Thakkur's opinion he was no thief. Anyway, if he had stolen, no doubt in his next life he would be born a sweeper as punishment.

Thakkur watched Mrs Singh's wrist for several days. Would there be a suitable Diwali celebration? Would the boys be coming home? He had nearly given up hope, when one day Ayah told him that Burrah Sahib had bought Ma ji a fine, new watch, the best she had seen for a long time.

Thakkur was ironing a sari for Mrs Singh, and slowly he put down his charcoal-heated iron, looked up from his position on the floor of the kitchen and began to smile, his face nearly cracking with the unaccustomed effort. He gathered up the sari and made Ayah help him fold it, while the grin gradually expanded across his face. He picked the ironing cloth up off the floor, giving a peculiar snort as he did; then he suddenly threw back his head and laughed aloud, the cackles echoing round the kitchen and making Cook Maharaj and the little kitchen boy look up from their work in astonishment.

'I don't see what there is to laugh at,' said Ayah testily. 'Come to think of it,' she added sourly, 'it's the first time I've seen you do anything but moan for years past.'

'Be patient, my old fox – here, take the sari for Ma ji – this is going to be the best Diwali for years.'

'I don't know what you mean – and I am not an old fox – and I will not be spoken to like that.' Her voice rose shrilly. 'And why Ma ji always gets you to iron her saris instead of me, I can't understand,' she added, full of suppressed resentment at Thakkur's privileged place in Ma ji's affections.

'Now, now, Ayah,' said Cook Maharaj. 'He meant no harm. We could all do with a bit of a celebration – although I don't know what it has to do with watches. There hasn't been a really good do since Ajit Sahib's sacred thread ceremony – and how many years ago is that?'

'Hmm,' sniffed Ayah. 'Some people seem to enjoy extra work – and right busy you'll be if there's a big Diwali party.'

'It'll be big all right,' said Thakkur, his face relapsing into its usual mournful lines.

'Good,' said Cook Maharaj. 'I shall make carrot hulwa for Ajit Sahib and suji hulwa for Bhim Sahib – it's his favourite – and something special for our Shushila.' His kind, round face beamed, as he kneaded the dough in the pannikin before him. 'And I must ask Ma ji about savouries for Burra Sahib.'

CHAPTER THIRTY-FOUR

Our flat seemed very empty after Mrs Singh had returned home. I had enjoyed her visit more than I could have believed possible; her calmness had soothed my harassed nerves and her advice had smoothed away many of my physical woes. Ajit also took heart from his mother's visit and he often talked about her and about his childhood spent in his grandfather's house – the same house in which his uncles now lived. His grandfather had been a terrifying domestic despot, who, for business reasons, had cultivated the goodwill of the English civil servants in the district, with the result that his patient, orthodox wife and her daughter-in-law had found the comfortable untidiness of their purdah apartments invaded at times by casteless, staring white women. His grandmother, Ajit told me with a chuckle, plied the strange ladies with sweetmeats and tea, but refused to eat a crumb in their presence or touch the special tea set kept for such visitors. I was, therefore, not the first English woman that Mrs Singh had observed at close quarters, although I was the first wife with whom she had carried on much conversation – she had been far too shy to speak in the presence of her mother-in-law's visitors. She was, however, relieved to find that I was not very much like these visitors – I was much less formal.

In between my household tasks, I often stopped to talk to Kamala as she squatted in the shade at the back of the flat and made cow dung cakes for her cooking fires, from the dung which she collected in a basket beforehand. Kamala was full of excitement, as in the following spring she was to be married to a man from another village, with whom she had fallen in love when he came to her own village with a marriage party. The fathers had been prevailed upon by the young people to open marriage negotiations and, as they were of the same sub-caste, the arrangements had been concluded most amicably.

'Supposing he had been of the wrong caste, Kamala?'

'Then Father would have found somebody else,' said Kamala with calm acceptance, as she slapped her cow dung cakes between her slender, aristocratic-looking hands.

I was sitting on the back step one day, talking to her and at the same time feeding a kid with cactus leaves from a nearby bush – to the amusement of the goatherd – when the postman cycled up.

'So many letters, Memsahib,' he said as he handed me three. I smiled. He was reminding me that he worked hard for us, so that his Diwali tip would be generous.

Only one letter was addressed to me personally. It was from Father, who hoped I was well, informed me that he was having some success with his chrysanthemums, had been made Chairman of a Red Cross Committee, and that the country was going to the dogs. I felt a tug of homesickness and for a moment the tangy smell of chrysanthemums obliterated the odour of the desert.

The other letters were for Ajit, one from Delhi addressed in a firm Italian hand of slender up strokes and heavy down ones, and one from Simla in the crabbed, hasty writing of a note maker. I propped them against a silver candlestick in the living-room and returned to the kitchen to cook the dinner.

'Letters for you, love,' I called, when I heard Ajit's step on the veranda, and, wiping my hands on my pinafore, I went to kiss him.

He was looking at the letter in the Italian hand. 'Father,' he said softly, and quickly slit the envelope.

I felt as awed as if he had said God had written, and sat down on the edge of a basket chair to hear what had caused such an event.

Ajit sat down by the table and read in silence, and when he came to the end he put his head down upon the table and burst into tears.

Horrified, I ran to him and put my arm round his shoulders, begging him at the same time to tell me what had happened.

He buried his damp face in my pinafore, sobbed a moment or two and then with a beaming smile looked up at me and said: 'It is joy. I cry for joy.'

'Your father has written kindly?'

Ajit hugged me round the waist. 'He has written that we are both to come home for Diwali. He has announced our marriage, and desires to make the acquaintance of his new daughter.'

'My darling,' I exclaimed, 'I am so happy – so very happy, for your sake.'

'Life is kind,' said Ajit, hugging me tighter. 'You are well – the house blossoms under your feet – and now we have again a family.'

'What about the other letter?' I asked, laughing at his poetic flights.

'Oh, yes. It's from Bhim. What's he doing in Simla at this time of year?' he queried as he examined the postmark.

'Open it and see.'

He opened the letter. There was only one sheet of paper, closely covered with Hindi characters. Ajit translated it as he read: 'Dear Brother, Nulini and I have come here for a rest, as she has had fever – Bannerji is looking after my practice during my absence. Mother writes that you are coming home for Diwali, and Nulini and I expect to return in time to welcome Peggie and you. Father announced your marriage. Mother says Uncles were amazed and she has been inundated with visitors who have come to ask about Peggie. There is great interest, although I believe no animosity.

'Nulini is becoming strong again, and she is teaching me to dance. I did not know that she liked to dance. On our return to Delhi we shall join a small club, so that we can dance and play a game of bridge occasionally.

'When you come to Delhi, I shall consult you about buying a radio and a pickup. I have never really listened to Western music – Nulini says I am missing much enjoyment.

'We both send namastes to Peggie and you.'

Ajit looked at me out of the corner of his eye and grinned. 'There is more to this letter than meets the eyes,' he said. 'What on earth has driven Bhim to learn to dance?'

'Ha,' I said wickedly, 'what about your learning to dance – I didn't know that one could dance in India.'

He looked at me appalled. 'No!'

'Yes,' I said ruthlessly. 'You could dance a little when you were in England. We'll start again tonight – and you can take me to a dance when we go to Delhi.'

'Oh, no,' he wailed in mock misery.

We had a most entertaining evening while he renewed his knowledge of the waltz.

Ajit was dizzy with excitement during the days that followed. He nearly burst with happiness. So obvious was it, that the eldest Miss Shah inquired if I was going to have a baby.

'Not just yet,' I said.

When I lay ill, she had asked me if my parents-in-law had accepted me, because it was strange that no one had come to my aid from the family. I had asked her not to talk about the matter to anybody else and had then told her what had happened. Knowing the situation, she had rejoiced with me at Mrs Singh's visit, and now I expected that she would share my pleasure again; but instead she looked very troubled. At last she said: 'Are you not afraid of being poisoned?'

'Poisoned? Good heavens, why should I be?'

Miss Shah said uneasily: 'It is not an unknown way of getting rid of an unwanted daughter-in-law.'

'Ridiculous,' I said.

But as the train to Delhi carried us through the bleak country of Rajasthan, the clattering wheels chanted: 'Poison, poison, poison,' until I wanted to scream. As it slowed down to enter Delhi junction, it said: 'Could be poisoned and burned in a night, burned in a night, burned in a night.'

At the station before Delhi junction there was a general exodus from our carriage and nobody else got in; Ajit and I were left in possession. I sat quietly as the train jerked forward again. We had long since rolled up our bedding and packed away the books we had bought to while away the thirty-hour journey, and nothing remained to be done, except listen to the chant of the wheels.

My face must have shown something of my sickening doubts, for Ajit looked at me and asked: 'Are you all right, Rani?'

I could not answer. Unreasonable fear clamped my throat shut.

Ajit looked alarmed: 'Dearest, what is it?'

I found my voice. 'Ajit, I'm so frightened.'

'Why should you be frightened?' He put his arm round me comfortingly.

'It's something Miss Shah said,' I said hesitatingly. I felt I must lay this terrifying ghost. Common sense told me I was being ridiculous – and yet I did not really know how bitter were the feelings of my father-in-law. Dreadful crimes had been committed at the time of the partitioning of the country, and how could I be sure that an equal anger might not descend on me?

'Well, and what did Miss Gossip say?'

I told him.

'Women!' he exclaimed, 'and some in particular.'

The typically Lancashire exclamation which he had picked up made me giggle, in spite of my fears.

'Do you honestly believe that my father would murder my wife?'

'I don't know,' I said defensively. 'How can I know what people will do – anything could happen in such a strange country.'

'You deserve to be spanked,' said Ajit grimly. 'To begin with, if Father really wished to get rid of you, there are a thousand more easy and less incriminating ways than poisoning you in his own house.' He shook me playfully, and went on: 'Secondly, although I know this is to you a queer, rickety old country, we do not as a rule spend our time poisoning people, even if we dislike them. There are probably not many more murders per head of population here than there are in England – and not even Father could escape official inquiry into the sudden death in his home of a perfectly healthy young woman.'

I felt ashamed.

He continued: 'Miss Shah is romancing. Perhaps such things did happen long ago – I cannot say – but she has no right to fill your head with such rubbish. Why did you not ask me about it before?'

'I did not know how you would take it.'

He was hurt. 'Rani,' he said very gently. 'I have told you before that you must never be afraid to confide in me. I love you and you could not do anything which would break that love.' He bent his head and kissed me; the kiss became a deep and long one. 'Love you, love you, love you,' recited the wheels.

'Porter, Sahib?' asked a very intrigued man, as he put his head through the carriage window.

We laughed and jumped apart. Ajit looked out of the window nearest to him. 'I can see them,' he shouted. I straightened my travel-stained sari, took up my handbag and shawl and picked my way after Ajit through the luggage strewn on the floor. The porter wrenched open the door, we gave him hasty instructions, took his number and stepped down on to the platform. Then we were running hand in hand towards the little couple, who looked so fragile and lonely in the milling crowd.

I let go of Ajit's hand and allowed him to approach first.

He took dust from their feet, while Shushila, whom I had not noticed previously, danced up to me. 'Are you my new sister?' she asked.

I smiled. 'If you are Shushila, I am.'

'Mummy, Mummy,' she shouted, 'I have found sister – see.'

Ajit had drilled me well for this meeting. My sari veiled my head and most of my face. I kept my eyes a little down and made my best namaste to my parents. I was a foot taller than Ram Singh, but he had an awe-inspiring dignity as he looked at me coldly for a moment. Then the big moustache twitched and he smiled, as he said in perfect English: 'You are welcome, daughter.'

'Thank you,' I said.

'Allow me to take your shawl,' he said, just as Father would have done. The quiet, Western courtesy, remembered presumably specially for my benefit, to make me feel more at ease, touched my heart, and I handed the shawl to him with a frank smile, looking shyly into his eyes as I might well have done if he had been an elderly Englishman. He seemed to like it and straightened himself, smoothed his whiskers and called Shushila. Meanwhile, Mrs Singh turned from Ajit to ask me if I was now quite well and not too tired. I assured her that I was now comparatively strong and whispered that it was due to her great kindness. She giggled like a girl, but did not reply; possibly she had not yet told her husband of her visit to Shahpur, and I resolved not to betray her by an idle word.

We went through the vast halls of the station to the world outside, where I pulled up short. I had forgotten that it was Diwali.

The city was bathed in light. It burst upon my senses as if the sparkle of a huge catherine wheel had enveloped me. Lights were everywhere, outlining every building; arc lamps added grace to new buildings, tiny separate lights outlined the older establishments and left their ugliness in darkness, lights in the gutters and on the pavements kindled from carefully collected scraps of paper, by beggars and refugees; but best of all, thousands of tiny oil lamps outlining Ajit's home, as we drove up to it.

251

Every balustrade, every window sill, had its row of lamps; intricate patterns in the brightest colours had been painted on the wide entrance steps; several small children were chasing each other backwards and forwards across the veranda, and through the windows came a buzz of conversation from their elders. Somewhere someone was plucking at a stringed instrument and the plaintive notes reverberated through my head, as I descended from the car after Mrs Singh, and stood hesitating at the foot of the steps looking up at the family before me. I hesitated only a moment, but it was sufficient to photograph upon my memory a picture which would stay with me always; long after the family had scattered I would remember them as I saw them then.

At the top of the steps stood a tall, glittering woman and by her side an equally tall, handsome man. It was my first glimpse of Bimla, who was to give me an intimate friendship; the man by her side was her new husband. Behind her stood Ayah and Thakkur, whose affection I was to enjoy through many years; they were craning their necks to catch a glimpse of the new daughter-in-law. Bimla had her arm round the shoulders of a slender, veiled woman – Nulini, I guessed correctly. Half-way down the steps was a big, shy-looking man, bending down to catch Shushila, who ran up to him. 'Bhim,' she cried. 'Brother Bhim, we have brought sister.'

Finally, at the foot of the steps was the father, who, once having made up his mind to accept me into his family, was to enrich Ajit's and my life by his learning and wisdom, and a few steps further up was the mother, to whom I would turn in times of stress as automatically as if she was my own mother.

The moment came and went. The photograph remained.

The group broke into movement. Bhim rushed down the steps, Shushila tucked under one arm and protesting loudly.

'Ajit!'

'Bhim! – How well you look – and how happy, you old scoundrel.'

'I am happy,' he replied simply. He smiled at me, but I

was not introduced – I was a member of the family and needed no introduction. Nulini and Bimla started down the steps towards me, as Ajit, talking gaily to his mother and his brother, ascended towards Bimla's husband and a bevy of aunts, uncles and cousins, who came pouring out of the house. I prepared to follow Ajit, but Ram Singh stepped back until he was level with me. He viewed his house with approbation, and gesturing towards it, he asked: 'Do you know why we light up our houses like this?'

'No, Sir,' I said respectfully.

'We believe that Lakshmi, the Goddess of Fortune, will come to the house which is most brightly lit up.'

'May she enter your house,' I said.

Ram Singh looked round at his family chattering on the steps; he saw the children of his brothers playing on his verandas; he heard the merry voices of his kinsmen enjoying his hospitality; and he looked up at his wife, who had turned round on the top step, to see why we were not following her in.

She smiled down at her husband and I saw him look up at her with the same sweet expression that Ajit had for me. He turned and looked at me, making a gay little gesture towards Mrs Singh. 'I think Lakshmi has been in my house for many years,' he said roguishly, his moustaches twitching and his heavy eyebrows curving upwards over the eyes which were narrowed in merriment.

I laughed. 'I feel sure she has,' I said.

Ajit ran down the steps again, and I put my hand into his. 'Come and meet your family,' he said.

Helen Forrester

Twopence to Cross the Mersey
Liverpool Miss
By the Waters of Liverpool

– the three volumes of her autobiography –

Helen Forrester tells the sad but never sentimental story of her childhood years, during which her family fell from genteel poverty to total destitution. In the depth of the Depression, mistakenly believing that work would be easier to find, they moved from the South of England to the slums of Liverpool. The family slowly win their fight for survival, but Helen's personal battle was to persuade her parents to allow her to earn her own living, and to lead her own life after the years of neglect and inadequate schooling while she cared for her six younger brothers and sisters. Illness, caused by severe malnutrition, dirt, and above all the selfish demands of her parents, make this a story of courage and perseverance. She writes without self-pity but rather with a rich sense of humour which makes her account of these grim days before the Welfare State funny as well as painful.

'Records of hardship during the Thirties are not rare; but this has features that make it stand apart' *Observer*

FONTANA PAPERBACKS

Fontana Paperbacks: Fiction

Fontana is a leading paperback publisher of both non-fiction, popular and academic, and fiction. Below are some recent fiction titles.

- [ ] COMING TO TERMS Imogen Winn £2.25
- [ ] TAPPING THE SOURCE Kem Nunn £1.95
- [ ] METZGER'S DOG Thomas Perry £2.50
- [ ] THE SKYLARK'S SONG Audrey Howard £1.95
- [ ] THE MYSTERY OF THE BLUE TRAIN Agatha Christie £1.75
- [ ] A SPLENDID DEFIANCE Stella Riley £1.95
- [ ] ALMOST PARADISE Susan Isaacs £2.95
- [ ] NIGHT OF ERROR Desmond Bagley £1.95
- [ ] SABRA Nigel Slater £1.75
- [ ] THE FALLEN ANGELS Susannah Kells £2.50
- [ ] THE RAGING OF THE SEA Charles Gidley £2.95
- [ ] CRESCENT CITY Belva Plain £2.75
- [ ] THE KILLING ANNIVERSARY Ian St James £2.95
- [ ] LEMONADE SPRINGS Denise Jefferies £1.95
- [ ] THE BONE COLLECTORS Brian Callison £1.95

You can buy Fontana paperbacks at your local bookshop or newsagent. Or you can order them from Fontana Paperbacks, Cash Sales Department, Box 29, Douglas, Isle of Man. Please send a cheque, postal or money order (not currency) worth the purchase price plus 15p per book for postage (maximum postage is £3.00 for orders within the UK).

NAME (Block letters) _____

ADDRESS _____